MURDER
at the
VILLAGE
FAIR

BOOKS BY HELENA DIXON

HELENA DIXON

MURDER
at the
VILLAGE
FAIR

bookouture

Published by Bookouture in 2023

An imprint of Storyfire Ltd.
Carmelite House
50 Victoria Embankment
London EC4Y 0DZ

www.bookouture.com

ISBN: 978-1-83790-066-4
eBook ISBN: 978-1-83790-065-7

Murder at the Village Fair is dedicated with love to my family.

PROLOGUE

TORBAY HERALD

JUNE 1935

ADVERTISEMENT

> *Are you looking for a healthful and relaxing holiday amidst breathtaking scenery? Why not visit Yorkshire? Easily accessible by rail or by road for the modern motorist. Visit the spa town of Harrogate and take the waters or try a variety of treatments to restore your health and leave you feeling refreshed. Take a trip to the coast for bracing air on our beautiful beaches or travel the Dales for unsurpassed scenic beauty.*
>
> *Send away now for your free guide to Yorkshire.*

THE YORKSHIRE DAILY
JUNE 1935

This Saturday will see the return of the annual village fair held in the grounds of Quixshotte Hall, hosted by Colonel and Mrs Brothers in aid of Quixshotte Church tower restoration fund. This year's Indian theme has added interest with performers from the Big Top Circus making appearances. Expect to see monkeys, snakes and Bluebelle the elephant, amongst many other extraordinary delights. The fair opens at 2 p.m., entrance fee one shilling for adults, sixpence for children at the gate.

CHAPTER ONE

Postcard to The Dolphin Hotel, The Embankment, Dart-mouth, Devon.

Darling Grams,

We have arrived safely at Matt's aunt's house. Only one punc-ture on the way! The village looks very pretty, and the weather is set to remain fair. I think the holiday is doing us the world of good. I hope Rascal is behaving and has not climbed the curtains again!

Yours affectionately, Kitty xx

Kitty set down her pen and applied a postage stamp to the corner of the postcard. She hoped her kitten was behaving and not clawing her grandmother's furniture. She was seated on the patio of Matt's aunt Euphemia's house in Yorkshire. The summer sun was high in the sky, and she was glad of the shade from the umbrella that his aunt's elderly gardener had set up over the table.

Matt lay relaxing on one of the ancient and rather rickety rattan steamer chairs with his cream Panama hat shading his face. Bertie, the roan cocker spaniel, lay snoring contentedly in a shady patch at his side. Pink summer roses spilled petals and perfume over the weathered stone balustrade surrounding the small, grey stone-flagged area. Bees buzzed industriously amongst the blooms and a pair of white butterflies danced their way along the terrace, before disappearing into the kitchen garden beyond the stone wall.

Their original intention had been to travel overseas on a belated honeymoon. Their last case had triggered Matt's old problems with his injuries from the Great War. Smoke had affected his lungs after they had been caught in a house fire causing the terrible nightmares that had plagued him in the past as a result of his experiences to resurface.

Instead, they had succumbed to the lure of a newspaper advertisement and decided on a motoring tour of Yorkshire. They had spent a pleasant few days with Kitty's cousin Lucy and her husband and a less pleasant few days with Matt's parents. Matt's parents did not approve of Kitty. Now they were to stay at Matt's aunt Euphemia's near Harrogate for two weeks or so before making their way back to Devon.

Matt's elderly aunt had terrified Kitty when she had first met her at Lucy and Rupert's wedding the previous summer. However, since then she had come to enjoy that lady's forth-right company and had been instructed to call her Effie like the rest of the family and other acquaintances.

The cold damp spring weather had given way to warmer, sunnier days as they had journeyed north. Kitty was relieved to see that the harsh, racking cough which had been plaguing Matt had diminished. The night terrors that led to him destroying his room or trying to get outside as he relived the war in his dreams also seemed to be settling.

She leaned back in her chair and gazed contentedly about

the garden. Matt's aunt occupied what had once been the Dower House on the edge of the Quixshotte estate. A pretty little Queen Anne style house, it was surrounded by green fields with views across the parkland. The curious name came from the Old English name of the stream which meandered through the grounds and went on to join the river several miles away.

The only passing traffic was the occasional wagon or motor going to and from Quixshotte Hall, a much grander building which stood inside the iron railings of the park. According to Matt's aunt, the Hall was now occupied by a Colonel Brothers and his wife. There had been an increase in the traffic over the last few days as the estate was to host its annual village fair.

'Of course, the dear colonel has insisted on giving it an eastern theme this year. He says it reminds him of his days in India,' Matt's aunt had explained over breakfast that morning. 'He has this moth-eaten stuffed tiger that he drags out and charges visitors' sixpence to have a photograph taken with it.' She had rolled her eyes at this before helping herself to kippers.

'What else goes on at this fair?' Matt had asked as he topped up his and Kitty's teacups.

'All sorts of things one would expect to see at an English country fair: various stalls, bowling for a pig, raffles, a tombola. This year, however, he has really gone to town. There is to be a snake charmer and an elephant, would you believe?' Aunt Effie had shaken her head in mild bemusement.

'An elephant? How on earth has he managed to acquire an elephant?' Kitty had asked in astonishment.

'The Big Top Circus is performing in the next village, and he has persuaded the ringmaster to send an elephant and the snake charmer to the fair. Really, I don't know how poor dear Hilda puts up with all of his nonsense.' After saying this, Aunt Effie had attacked her kippers with relish.

Kitty had assumed that Hilda must be the colonel's wife. 'And this fair is to raise money for the church?'

'Oh yes, my dear, you know what churches are like, always got their hands out for something or other. Apparently, the tower needs strengthening. Something to do with the bells,' Aunt Effie had replied carelessly after swallowing her breakfast.

'What does the vicar think of having an elephant at the fair?' Matt had asked with a smile.

'Oh, Reverend Drummond lives in a world of his own. I'm surprised he even remembers that we have a village fair. A very scholarly man, always got his nose in a book.' Aunt Effie had finished her kippers and pushed the floral-painted plate to one side.

'It sounds as if the colonel is firmly in charge of it all, then.' Kitty sipped her tea.

'Oh yes, my dear, well, aided by Miss Crowther, of course. She is quite indispensable when it comes to organising matters in the village. The vicar's wife has very little interest in what goes on, so she is of no practical use. Lilith is his second wife you see, much younger than him. I think he had hoped she would be a good stepmother to the twins, Ruth and Frank, when they first married some years ago, but, well, they are grown up now.'

Kitty had gathered from Aunt Effie's tone that this wish of the vicar's had not been met by the mysterious Lilith. 'It all sounds terribly interesting. We shall have to go to this fair, if only to see the elephant.'

Matt had laughed. 'Indeed, although I don't think we shall require a souvenir photograph with the tiger.'

Kitty had suppressed a shudder. 'Dear me, no. I can't say that I am over keen to see the snake charmer either, but it does sound fun, and I suppose restoring the church tower is a good cause.'

Breakfast had ended with an agreement that they would all attend the fair.

. . .

The rumble of another large wagon going over the pretty stone bridge near the entrance to the park brought Kitty back to the present. The heat haze shimmering over the terrace convinced her to remain seated in the shade. She decided to walk down to the village later in the afternoon when it was a little cooler so Bertie could stretch his legs. She could post her card for Grams in the scarlet pillar box on the village green, along with another one she had written for Alice.

Alice was a maid at the Dolphin Hotel in Dartmouth and Kitty's dearest friend. She wondered if Alice had ever seen an elephant, other than at the picture house. Her friend was very fond of movies.

Her peaceful contemplation was further disturbed by the tapping of Aunt Effie's ebony cane on the parquet floor and the sound of female voices approaching from the direction of the house.

'Kitty, Matthew!'

Bertie lifted his head to sound a short bark as Aunt Effie strolled out of the house onto the terrace, accompanied by another lady.

'Bertie,' Matt reproved their dog as he struggled into a more upright position ready to rise and greet the visitor.

'Miss Crowther, may I present my nephew, Matthew, and his wife, Kitty, from Devon. They are staying with me this week. Miss Crowther is Chair of the Lady's Guild, she assists the colonel with organising the fair.' Aunt Effie dropped down onto a vacant seat at the table and indicated to Miss Crowther and Matt to join them.

Matt and Kitty shook hands with the guest. Miss Crowther was a tall, thin, middle-aged woman with untidy brown curly hair and a prominent nose.

'I'm delighted to meet you both, I'm sure. Effie told us all about your wedding at Christmas.' She sank down onto the other empty chair. 'I was just on my way home from the Hall and thought I would stop in to thank you, Effie, for your generous contributions to the various stalls.'

'It was my pleasure, my dear, I assure you. Cook will send our contribution to the cake stall on Saturday morning. I think she has made several cakes and will do a couple of dozen scones. Now, since it's such a warm day, will you take some refreshments? I've asked Parker to bring out some lemonade.' Aunt Effie smiled congenially at Miss Crowther who did appear to be rather pink cheeked and hot.

'That's very kind, very kind indeed. I have been running around all day. One doesn't like to complain you know, but if only Lilith would take just the slightest bit of interest in village affairs. Still, you know how she is.' Miss Crowther fanned herself with a tiny, folded paper fan that she produced from inside a capacious white leather handbag.

'I know, my dear, but the vicar's twins, Ruth and Frank, are helping, are they not?' Aunt Effie said as the maid appeared bearing a tray containing a jug of lemonade, iced fancy biscuits and some glasses.

'Ruth does her best, but that nephew of the colonel's, Jamie Martin, is proving quite the distraction this year. And as for Frank, well, you know what young men are like. It's very trying and the colonel's wife Hilda is only interested in the plant stall.' Miss Crowther perked up at the sight of the tray.

'Hilda did say something about Jamie having been a bit wild in the past, but he seems to have settled in well now. He seems very fond of Hilda and the colonel.' Aunt Effie smiled at Kitty as she poured lemonade for them all.

'Now that he has his feet under the table, you mean, with expectations. And that wretched car of his, my dear Effie, tearing about the lanes like a man possessed.' Miss Crowther gave Aunt Effie what Kitty's grandmother would have termed *a speaking look*.

'I believe he is the only relative left on both the colonel and

Hilda's side of the family. The war, you know, and the colonel and Hilda were not blessed with children. I think it only natural that he should be expected to inherit the estate in due course.' Aunt Effie passed the plate of biscuits to Miss Crowther.

'I still feel he is rather disreputable, why the reverend allows him to call at the vicarage so often I can't imagine. Well, anyway, the marquees for the fair are all up now and this good weather is set to continue for a few more days. That's one worry off my plate at least. It's always so difficult if it rains. The last time we had to move everything inside the Hall at the last minute. Hilda said it took the servants ages to get the parquet flooring back to anything decent in the ballroom.' Miss Crowther selected a biscuit and nibbled decorously at the edge.

'Kitty is keen to see the elephant,' Matt said, the corners of his mouth lifting in a mischievous smile as he caught Kitty's eye.

Miss Crowther's skinny shoulders grew rigid with disapproval. 'An elephant, I ask you. Bluebelle, it's called, apparently. I supported the idea of an Indian theme as it reminded me of my own dear brother, but an elephant, really.'

'I must admit I've only ever seen one in a book before. Grams disapproves of circuses, so I never went to one when I was a child,' Kitty said.

Her grandmother had been busy raising Kitty and running the Dolphin Hotel in Dartmouth for years since Kitty's mother had vanished when she was a child. There had been few opportunities for outings to things like zoological gardens or circuses.

'Well, there will be the elephant and a snake charmer, and I think the colonel said something about a man with a monkey. The idea of an Indian theme for the day sounded delightful when it was proposed but it is quite out of hand now,' Miss Crowther explained gloomily. 'I rather wish he would focus on the things that actually make money like the cake stall and the plant sale.'

'That reminds me, I have some plants to bring along as well.

My gardener tells me we have some quite nice cuttings that have rooted,' Aunt Effie said.

Kitty thought the village fair sounded fascinating. It was clearly a much bigger event than any she had attended in Dartmouth.

'Thank you, Effie dear, you are always so generous.' Miss Crowther picked up her lemonade and drained the glass. 'I really must get off as there is so much still to do. I trust we shall see you all there on Saturday then?' She looked around the table.

'It sounds marvellous,' Matt assured her as he rose to say goodbye. 'We wouldn't miss it for the world, would we, Kitty?'

'Absolutely not. How often does one get to see a real elephant, and in Yorkshire too?' Kitty smiled as she spoke.

Aunt Effie struggled to her feet and collected her silver-topped ebony walking cane to see her visitor out.

'I'll be sure to let you have the plants early on the day,' Aunt Effie's voice faded as she and Miss Crowther disappeared back inside the house.

'It all sounds jolly exciting.' Kitty snapped the last biscuit in half and gave some to the waiting Bertie who had been looking hopefully at the plate.

'It certainly does. It doesn't sound like one of your average run-of-the-mill village fundraisers, does it?' Matt grinned at her, his blue eyes sparkling.

Kitty raised her lemonade glass. 'No indeed not. To Blue-belle the elephant.'

CHAPTER TWO

The day of the village fair dawned clear and bright. Kitty offered to drive Aunt Effie up to Quixshotte Hall where the fair was being held. The mile-long path was too far for the elderly woman to manage with her walking cane and it was still very hot.

'Park your motor car around the side of the house in the shade, Kitty dear,' Aunt Effie directed her from the passenger seat, as she motioned with her stick in the direction of the large, grey, square stone building. A large wisteria ran along the front and side of the house and the large windows promised good views over the gardens and the estate. The estate appeared well kept and prosperous.

The Hall was set in several acres of rolling parkland, which included a lake, fed by the meandering river. The fair had been set up on the meadow land below the formal gardens and there was already a buzz of excitement in the air. In the far distance Kitty noticed a herd of deer grazing peacefully under the trees away from the hubbub.

Kitty drove her small red car to the area Aunt Effie had indicated and parked beside some other motor vehicles and a few horses and carts. Matt got himself and Bertie out of the car and assisted his aunt to disembark from the front passenger seat.

'Effie! Yoohoo!' A plump woman in her late fifties wearing a wide-brimmed beige hat that gave her the resemblance of a mobile mushroom hailed Matt's aunt as she got out of the car.

'Hilda, my dear.' Aunt Effie turned to embrace the woman before introducing her to Kitty and Matt.

'Matthew, Kitty, may I introduce Mrs Hilda Brothers, Colonel Brothers' wife and our host for today's events. Hilda, my nephew, Matthew, and his wife, Kitty.' Aunt Effie leaned on her stick as they shook hands with Mrs Brothers. Bertie sniffed interestedly at her ankles.

'I think we should have a good turnout today. The weather is simply marvellous, isn't it?' Hilda beamed at them as they made their way towards the entrance to the lawned area in front of the house.

Two Boy Scouts stood at a makeshift gate collecting the entrance fees for the fair under the watchful eye of their leader.

'I must admit, we are quite excited,' Kitty said as Matt handed over their ticket money to enter the fair.

'I'm sure you'll enjoy it. My husband has been working very hard with Miss Crowther to get everything set up. I believe a lot of people are coming to see Bluebelle the elephant.' Hilda Brothers led them along the gravel path towards the collection of large white marquees and stalls set on the emerald turf.

'Now then, you two young people run along and enjoy yourselves. I intend to visit the plant stall and then take my ease at the refreshment stand.' Aunt Effie dismissed Kitty and Matt with a wave of her white-gloved hand.

'There are some wonderful cuttings and a couple of pear trees you might like, I noticed,' Hilda said to Aunt Effie as they linked arms and walked away.

'I suppose that leaves us free to go and find Bluebelle the

elephant.' Matt tucked Kitty's free hand into the crook of his arm and smiled at her.

'I expect it should be easy to find an elephant.' Kitty beamed back at him, and they continued to where the largest crowd seemed to be forming.

Bluebelle was standing in the shade under a couple of pine trees with a low wooden fence making a temporary enclosure. A vast tub of water and a large bale of hay stood next to her, and her keeper was in attendance to prevent the crowd from getting too close. Bertie was unimpressed by both the elephant and the amount of people, tugging at his leash in an attempt to go and explore the more interesting smells emanating from the hog roast stand.

Kitty stood for a few minutes, mesmerised by the fascinating creature. She was much larger than Kitty had expected. A great iron chain was around the elephant's front foot, securing her to a large oak tree. A red cap trimmed with gold fringing adorned Bluebelle's head and the keeper was dressed in red with braid to match. He was busy answering questions from the excitable crowd of small children gawping over the fence.

'I shall have to send another postcard to Alice. She will never believe this. Look how lovely her eyes are, such long lashes.' Kitty's hand tightened on the linen sleeve of Matt's jacket in her excitement.

The dimple in Matt's cheek deepened at her obvious delight. 'I must admit it's not something you expect to see in such a small, quiet village.'

After a few minutes more they gave in to Bertie's wish to leave. Kitty had a delightful time wandering around the various stalls, buying tickets and admiring the different events. Matt had a turn on the Hook-a-Duck and the coconut shy, before winning a large, bright-green teddy bear at the shooting range which he presented to Kitty.

'Um, thank you, I think.' She laughed. The bear was almost

as large as Bertie, who eyed it suspiciously as they walked back towards the refreshment stall in need of a sit down and a cup of tea.

'There is still so much to see,' Kitty exclaimed as they took a seat at a recently vacated table. She sat the giant green bear carefully on the other vacant seat.

'I notice you have avoided the snake charmer,' Matt said as he secured a bowl of water for Bertie.

Kitty wrinkled her nose. 'I'm not sure how I feel about snakes, or, to be honest, this bear.'

'You wound me deeply.' Matt clasped his hands to his chest in an exaggerated manner. 'Although, it does look a bit cross-eyed,' he admitted, before laughing at the teddy and Kitty's expression.

A pretty young woman aged about seventeen with her dark hair in a long braid approached their table. 'Good afternoon, may I take your order?'

'Tea and strawberries and cream for two, please,' Matt ordered their refreshments, and the girl headed back to the stall.

Kitty looked around at the throngs of people surrounding them. 'We were fortunate to get a table. I can't see your aunt anywhere.'

'She is probably loading your car with plants. I expect Bertie and I will have to walk back to her house later; there'll be no room for us if she has acquired two pear trees,' Matt replied with a chuckle.

The girl returned with their teas and two glass dishes containing fresh strawberries sprinkled with sugar and topped with a large blob of whipped cream. Matt pulled his wallet from his pocket to pay.

'Ruth, have you seen Jamie anywhere? The colonel is looking for him.' A young man appeared at the girl's side as Matt paid the bill. He had the same facial features as the girl and the same dark hair, only his was cropped short in the latest style.

'Sorry, no. I think he was supposed to be looking after the tiger.' The girl gave Matt his change.

'Bother, we could do with him helping here. Lilith is so slow at serving,' the boy grumbled and hurried off.

The girl shrugged her shoulders and moved away to clear some of the tables.

'I wonder if they are the vicar's twins?' Kitty said. 'Miss Crowther mentioned them the other day.'

'Probably. They did look like brother and sister. I wonder where Miss Crowther is? She's done so much to organise all of this, according to Aunt Effie. I thought she would have been on one of the stalls.' Matt looped Bertie's lead around the leg of his chair.

Kitty agreed it was a little odd but gave herself up to enjoying her treat. It was so nice to have Matt back laughing and joking with her again after the last dreadful few weeks. This holiday really did seem to be doing them both the power of good. Matt's night terrors had stopped, and she felt lighter in spirits than she had for some weeks.

The strawberries and cream were delicious, and Kitty was glad of the respite from the heat of the sun under the shade of the gaily painted parasol above their table. She had dressed for the day in a pale-pink linen frock with a pretty straw hat trimmed to match but despite her light clothing, it still felt hot.

'Which stall shall we try next?' Matt asked.

'Not the snakes,' Kitty said and laughed.

A chubby little boy, aged about two, dressed in a blue-and-white sailor suit was seated in his perambulator at the table next to them. He was staring avidly at the stuffed toy sitting on the vacant seat.

'Bear.' He lifted his hand to point at Kitty's prize.

'Hush, Tommy, that's the lady's bear.' His mother

attempted to divert his attention.

'Bear!' The child's lower lip wobbled into a mutinous pout.

Kitty looked at Matt. 'May I?' She smiled at her husband knowing that neither of them really cared about the rather ugly toy.

'It would save us carrying it around and I don't think Bertie likes it,' Matt replied with a grin.

'Indeed, I wouldn't be surprised if he thinks it's competition,' Kitty said and offered the bear to the small boy who received it with rapturous delight, hugging it close and beaming at them.

'That's very kind of you. Say thank you to the lady, Tommy.' The child's mother looked at her son who was clearly thrilled with his new toy.

'Fank you.'

Kitty collected up her bag and stood ready to continue her exploration of the fair. Matt stooped to untie Bertie from the chair leg, but before he could collect the lead, the dog spotted something interesting and darted off into the crowd.

'Oh no! Quickly, Matt, catch him.' Kitty dived after Matt as they headed off as quickly as possible after the errant Bertie.

'Wretched dog,' Matt grumbled as Kitty caught up to him and they gazed about looking for Bertie. They had arrived at the edge of the fair where the crowds were thinner. A smaller white tent stood nearby with a hand-painted sign outside reading *Madame ZaZa knows all and sees all. Fortunes told, 1 shilling.*

A smaller notice which said *back in ten minutes* was pinned on the entrance of the tent. Kitty was just in time to see Bertie's plumed tail disappearing inside the fortune teller's booth.

'Hurry, Matt, he's gone into the fortune teller's tent.' Kitty rushed ahead and unfastened the flap of the tent.

'Bertie, you naughty boy, where are you?' Kitty peered into the gloomy interior of the small space. Her eyes took a minute to adjust from the bright sunshine outside to the shadowy interior.

A circular table draped with a dark-purple glittery cloth stood in the centre of the tent with a large glass ball on a wooden stand on top of it. Two wooden folding chairs were also there.

One chair was empty. The other one was occupied by someone clad in a flowing eastern dress, a large dark-purple turban covered their head, and the figure was slumped forward onto the tabletop, a floral-patterned china cup and saucer at their elbow.

The errant Bertie sat next to the table happily wagging his tail. Matt arrived at Kitty's side.

'Hello?' he said.

The figure at the table didn't move and the sick feeling that had started in the pit of Kitty's stomach when she had entered the tent increased.

Matt strode forward and took secure hold of Bertie's leash before approaching the figure at the table. Kitty followed him, realising the prone person had to be Madame ZaZa. Matt's gaze met Kitty's and he reached out his hand to touch the lady on her shoulder. As he did so she slid sideways and collapsed onto the grass floor of the marquee.

Kitty let out a small scream and skipped backwards as the very obviously dead Madame ZaZa fell across her feet.

'Take Bertie for a moment, Kitty.' Matt handed her the dog's lead and knelt down beside the prone female figure.

Her heart pounded as Matt felt for a pulse in Madame ZaZa's neck, dislodging the lady's turban to reveal a mop of untidy mouse-brown curls.

'It's Miss Crowther,' Kitty said, suddenly realising who was disguised inside the costume.

'And she's dead.' Matt straightened back up, his face sombre.

Outside the tent marching music had started up and Kitty realised the local brass band had commenced their concert.

'We need to get the police.' Matt's gaze locked with Kitty's.

'I'll go to the plant stall. I think Hilda Brothers was staffing it. She will be able to telephone from the Hall, I expect. What do you think, natural causes or foul play?' She knew where her instincts lay. She thought she had caught the faint scent of bitter almonds when Miss Crowther had landed at her feet.

Matt took a cautious sniff of the air and looked at the empty cup standing on the table, taking care not to touch it. 'At a guess I would say poison.'

Kitty nodded. 'I agree. I'll be back in a moment.' She turned to leave the tent to fetch help. As she lifted the flap to go back out onto the field a glint of something silver in the longer grass near the door caught her eye. A small silver button lay on the turf half-hidden by a clump of daisies just inside the tent.

'Matt, look at this.'

Matt joined her immediately.

'Interesting. It has quite a distinctive design, with that oak-leaf pattern. I wonder when it was dropped and by who,' Matt said.

'Indeed. I'll be back as quickly as I can. Come, Bertie.' Kitty tugged at Bertie's lead to hurry him along and she made her way through the crowds to the plant stall, leaving Matt with Miss Crowther's body. Luckily the plant stall was almost empty having sold most of its goods and Hilda was seated at the table counting her takings.

'Mrs Brothers, I'm afraid I need to use your telephone.' Kitty halted and tried to catch her breath.

'Of course, my dear, whatever is wrong?' Hilda peered up at her from under the brim of her mushroomy hat. A puzzled frown on her plump, pleasant face.

'I'm afraid something dreadful has happened to Miss Crowther. I need to call the police.' Kitty was about to say more but a couple of ladies were approaching, and she suddenly realised that Hilda was missing a silver button patterned with oak leaves from the sleeve of her dress.

CHAPTER THREE

Matt waited patiently inside the tent for Kitty to return. Outside the canvas walls of the booth he could hear the strains of the brass band and the murmured conversations of people walking past. Hopefully the *back in ten minutes* sign would prevent anyone from trying to enter the tent before the police could arrive.

He examined the distinctive silver button Kitty had discovered closely, taking care not to touch it. Another look around the interior of the tent revealed no further clues. All the pegs were securely in place and the only way to enter or exit the booth was via the front flap.

The cash box that Miss Crowther had been using was open at her feet, partly obscured by the tablecloth. It was full of money, and it seemed Madame ZaZa had been doing a brisk trade. Miss Crowther was also still wearing her silver rings and bracelet so it appeared that robbery was not a motive.

If his and Kitty's suspicions were correct about poison, he wondered who could have wanted Miss Crowther dead. Whatever had killed her must have been in her drink as he could see no empty phials or bottles inside the tent. Someone must have brought her a cup of tea whilst she took a break. Or had she fetched it herself? Had the young girl who was serving refreshments, Ruth, brought it to her? Or Lilith, the vicar's wife?

The flap of the tent rustled, and he hurried back over to it to see who was trying to enter.

'It's me, the police are on their way down. I've managed to persuade Hilda not to come, she's gone to find the colonel, but the local doctor will be here in a moment. A Doctor Masters.' Kitty stepped inside the tent. 'I've left Bertie with your aunt. She's feeding him titbits at the refreshment stall.'

'Good idea,' replied Matt, but before he could say anything more someone else appeared.

'Hello, may I come in? Mrs Brothers asked me to attend. Is Miss Crowther ill?' A tall, good-looking man slightly older than Matt walked inside. He carried a brown leather bag similar to the one their friend Doctor Carter used when out on calls.

'I'm afraid, Doctor, that Miss Crowther is beyond medical assistance. We are waiting for the police,' Matt said as Kitty stood aside to allow the doctor to enter the tent.

'Oh, I say.' Doctor Masters looked quite taken aback when he took in the scene. He went to Miss Crowther's side and checked her vital signs in the same way that Matt himself had done already.

'We had better not move her until the police arrive,' Matt said.

He could see from the doctor's expression as he stood back up that he too had detected the signs of foul play.

The doctor's gaze fell on the teacup and saucer standing on the table. 'I assume that was here when you found her?' he asked.

Matt nodded. 'I'm guessing you noticed the faint scent of bitter almonds?'

There was a noise outside the tent and the flap opened once more to admit a large, older man in a crumpled pale-grey suit. He gazed at the scene with a mild, almost bovine countenance.

'Good afternoon, I'm Inspector Woolley, I received a telephone call from a Mrs Bryant to say there had been a sudden death.' He looked at Kitty.

'That was me, sir,' Kitty said. She introduced herself and Matt. Doctor Masters appeared to know the inspector already.

Kitty moved closer to Matt as Doctor Masters quickly explained his thoughts about how Miss Crowther had died.

The inspector turned to Matt. 'You and your wife seem to have acted with remarkable presence of mind to notice the anomaly in this unfortunate lady's demise?'

Matt drew his silver card case from his jacket pocket and presented the policeman with his card. The inspector's silver eyebrows rose slightly as he read it. 'Private Investigative Services. Torquay, Devon, eh?'

'Yes, sir,' Matt said.

The inspector took out a small, black leather-bound notebook from his pocket and tucked the business card inside it, before taking the address of Aunt Effie's house.

'Right then, I would appreciate you saying nothing of what has happened here, beyond Miss Crowther being taken fatally ill. My constable will secure this area. I assume this teacup is from the refreshment stall?' Inspector Woolley looked at Kitty for confirmation.

'Yes, sir, it's the same pattern as the ones Matt and I drank our tea from earlier when we stopped there for refreshments,' Kitty agreed.

The inspector nodded and turned to Matt. 'Then I suggest, Captain Bryant, that you and your good lady return to the fair. I shall be in touch to take further details from you about how you came to discover Miss Crowther.'

Matt placed his hand on Kitty's waist as they prepared to leave the tent.

'We noticed something else in the grass, sir, by the entrance of the tent. We haven't touched it in case it might prove important,' Matt said, and indicated Kitty's find on the grass.

The inspector grunted and bent to peer at the silver button.

'Mrs Brothers has an identical button missing from the sleeve of her dress,' Kitty added, taking Matt by surprise. 'I noticed it when I went to use the telephone to call you.'

The inspector's brows rose another notch at this information, and he made another note in his book. 'All right, thank you. That's all I need for now.'

Matt ducked under the tent flap and steered Kitty back out into the afternoon sunshine.

'Are you all right, old thing?' he asked as they passed the constable who had taken up his post outside the tent.

Kitty nodded. 'Yes, I think so. It was rather a shock though. Poor Miss Crowther, what a thing to happen.'

'You say that button came from Hilda Brothers' sleeve?' Matt asked.

'Yes, when I went to ask her if I could telephone the police from the Hall, I noticed it. I told her that Miss Crowther was dead and as it was unexpected the police had to be called. She seemed terribly shocked. She took me to the house to telephone and asked her butler to find Doctor Masters and send him along.' A shudder ran through Kitty's slim frame.

'That looks like Mrs Brothers now, and I assume the chap with her must be the colonel,' Matt said.

Hilda was trotting along the path towards them, accompanied by a tall, elderly man with straight, military bearing. He was dressed in a nautical outfit with a jaunty sailor-style cap on his head and a bright-blue neckerchief at his throat.

'Mrs Bryant, Kitty!' Hilda spotted them and flapped her hand in the air to draw their attention, before she and her husband arrived at a breathless halt. 'I see the police have arrived,' Hilda gasped as she looked at the constable standing outside the entrance to the tent.

'I'd better go and have a word. I can't believe Miss Crowther is dead. What is the world coming too?' The colonel marched off towards the marquee.

'I'm so sorry it took us a few minutes to get here. My husband is in charge of the duck race, and it's only just finished,' Hilda explained breathlessly as she peered around Kitty, clearly wishing to follow the colonel inside the tent. Matt assumed the race explained the colonel's nautical clothing. He noticed the loose thread dangling from Hilda's sleeve just above her elbow where she had lost her button.

The tent flap opened again, and the colonel re-emerged and marched briskly back towards them. Matt could see that the older man appeared annoyed. His cheeks were flushed, and his mouth was set in a grim line beneath his salt and pepper military moustache.

'Dashed impertinence of the fellow. Threw me out without so much as a "by your leave", and on my own property too.'

'These new-fangled police methods, sir. I'm sure the inspector will wish to come and see you personally once he has surveyed the scene,' Matt said soothingly, picking up on the warning in Kitty's gaze before he responded.

'The grounds are still so busy. I'm sure he thought that someone as important to the event as you, sir, would draw unwanted attention to the scene. Perhaps we should all go and get a cup of tea?' Kitty suggested.

Matt knew that she was playing to the colonel's ego, but he thought the idea a good one. Especially if it provided an opportunity to snoop around the refreshment stall.

'Yes, oh yes, of course, my dear. Where are my manners?

You must have had the most frightful shock discovering poor Miss Crowther. Please allow me to escort you to the tea stall. Colonel Brothers, at your service.' He bestowed a charming and solicitous smile on Kitty and shook hands with Matt, before leading them back towards the refreshments.

The stall was much quieter than when Matt and Kitty had been there earlier. It seemed that many people had drifted off to listen to the brass band or had begun to make their way out of the park.

'Do sit down, Mrs Bryant. I'll order tea.' The colonel saw that they were all seated around an empty table before heading over to the stall.

Matt could see no sign of Ruth, the vicar's daughter, who had served them earlier. In her place was a very beautiful and glamorous woman in her early thirties who looked rather bored.

'I could use something stronger than tea,' Hilda Brothers said, her gaze flicking momentarily to the capacious cream leather handbag hanging from the arm of her chair. 'I'm sure you feel the same, Mrs Bryant. Such a terrible shock. Was it her heart? She was always dashing about the place. She did far too much, you know. I was always telling her to slow down.' She raised her voice to call to the colonel as he approached the table bearing a tea tray. 'Wasn't I, dear? Always telling Miss Crowther to slow down?'

The colonel plonked the tray down on the wooden picnic table. 'Quite so, my dear. A very busy woman, Miss Crowther. I don't know how the village will function without her.' He took his seat beside his wife.

'Did you tell Lilith what has happened?' Hilda inclined her head in the direction of the woman running the stall.

'What? Lilith? Oh no, not yet. She wouldn't be interested, I don't suppose, or she would make a terrible fuss. We'll need to tell the vicar though. Miss Crowther was his right-hand woman.' The colonel started ladling sugar into Kitty's cup before she could protest.

'Sugar is good for shock,' Hilda informed her when Kitty tried to place her hand over her cup.

Matt bit the inside of his cheek to stop himself laughing at the horrified expression on his wife's face when confronted with the sickly sweet tea.

'Have you both known Miss Crowther long?' Kitty asked as she picked up her teacup.

'We bought the Hall in '22. It was a fresh start for us after we returned from India. Miss Crowther came with the estate really, we always say. She's lived in the village all her life, knows everyone and everything.' The colonel looked troubled. 'She'll be much missed. I say, I hope this won't cause a problem with Bluebelle. The keeper is staying with her tonight in the grounds.'

His wife reached across the table and patted his hand. 'I'm sure the police will understand about the elephant, dear. Such a dreadful thing to happen and today of all days. Poor Miss Crowther. She always did the fortune telling, you know. She used to claim that she had the sight and that was why her fortunes were so accurate and popular. No one ever recognised her in her robes with her make-up on.'

'Were her predictions accurate?' Kitty asked. Matt could see her trying not to grimace at the taste of the tea.

Hilda exchanged glances with the colonel. 'Oh yes, but, of course, Miss Crowther knew everyone's business you see, nothing to do with being able to predict the future.'

'Did you see her at all this afternoon? After the fair opened?' Kitty asked as she lowered her cup.

'I popped in as she was setting up, before I went to the river to set up for the duck race. Wanted to make sure she had enough change in her box.' The colonel tugged at his moustache. 'She looked perfectly all right then. No sign of illness.'

'I don't think I saw her. Not since this morning when we were finishing putting the plants out on the stall,' Hilda said. 'I've been run off my feet.'

Matt glanced at Kitty. If that was true then how did Hilda's button end up in Madame ZaZa's tent?

CHAPTER FOUR

'We should go and find your aunt,' Kitty said to Matt. 'I left her looking after Bertie, and you know what he's like when he gets restless.' She set her barely touched cup of tea back on its saucer, unable to finish the overly sweetened drink that had been pressed upon her.

A handsome blond man in his mid-twenties approached the table just as she began to gather her things together ready to leave. 'I say, Aunt Hilda, Uncle Stanley, whatever is going on at the fortune telling tent? There are policemen roaming about all over the place.'

'Do keep your voice down, Jamie. Miss Crowther has passed away. The police have been called as obviously none of us knew she was ill.' Hilda glanced around her as if to ensure that no one nearby was listening to their conversation.

Kitty guessed that this must be Jamie Martin, the nephew that Miss Crowther had spoken so disparagingly about a few days earlier.

Jamie grabbed a vacant chair and pulled it up beside his aunt. Turning it around, he sat down and rested his arms on the back to stare interestedly at his relatives.

'Creepy Crowther is dead?'

'Jamie, please! A little respect.' The colonel glared at his nephew.

'Sorry, Uncle.' Jamie didn't sound particularly apologetic. 'What happened to her? She seemed perfectly chipper a couple of hours ago when she made me change one of the chairs in her booth.'

'What time was that?' Kitty asked. She wondered if Jamie might have been one of the last people to see Miss Crowther alive.

'A little bit before the band started, about half past two, I think. She flagged me down and said her seat had a wobbly back. Got me to swap it for one of the chairs on the book stall.' He looked at Kitty. 'Jamie Martin, by the way.' He offered his hand to her.

'Kitty Bryant, and this is my husband, Matt, we're here on holiday staying at the Dower House. We found Miss Crowther.' She and Matt shook hands with Jamie.

'Crikey, not a good start to your holiday, tripping over a body,' Jamie said.

His uncle glowered at him.

'It's not ideal, I must say. Did you know Miss Crowther well?' Kitty asked.

Jamie shrugged. 'Not especially. I mean we were on "*Good morning, isn't it nice today,*" type terms. Miss Crowther was always terribly busy, and I don't think she liked me very much. I've only lived here for a few months, but she always seemed to have something cutting to say whenever I saw her. She hated my motor car.'

'Jamie came to us when he finished his education, not long after my sister Gertie, his mother, passed away,' Hilda explained.

'Oh, I'm so sorry.' Kitty saw that Hilda had suddenly become teary at the mention of her sister.

Hilda blinked and fished in her bag for a handkerchief. 'Poor Gertie had been ill for quite a while.' She dabbed at her eyes and blew her nose on the plain cotton square.

Jamie placed his arm awkwardly about his aunt's shoulders to give her a clumsy hug. 'There, there, Aunt Hilda.'

'Well, we had better go and relieve my aunt Effie of our dog. Bertie can be quite a handful and I daresay she will want to get her plant purchases back to the Dower House. I'm sure Miss Crowther's death will have come as a great shock to her too.' Matt rose ready to assist Kitty.

'Thank you for the tea. It was very kind of you, and it was nice to meet you all, even under such tragic circumstances,' Kitty said. She still felt surprisingly wobbly after the discovery of Miss Crowther's body and was quite glad of Matt's support.

'Not at all, my dear, it's been a most horrid shock for all of us. I'll telephone Effie later. You must all come to supper one evening while you're here,' Hilda said.

'That sounds most delightful, thank you.' Kitty leaned on Matt as they made their way across the lawn towards the now empty plant stall near the entrance.

The crowds had thinned considerably now and most of the stalls were packing up for the day. The heat had subsided a little and a gentle breeze wafted across the grounds.

'There's Aunt Effie, but I can't see Bertie.' Matt indicated towards the terrace where Aunt Effie was making her way towards them leaning heavily on her cane.

'Oh, Kitty, Matthew, thank goodness. I just heard about Miss Crowther. One of the helpers saw the police outside the fortune telling booth. They said a young couple of visitors with a dog had found her. I knew it had to be you two, especially after the way you dashed off, Kitty dear. Everywhere you two go a body seems to turn up.' Aunt Effie's eyes were bright with curiosity.

'Speaking of dogs, where is Bertie?' Kitty asked anxiously. She hoped he hadn't slipped his lead again.

'I asked young Frank Drummond to take him to a cooler spot and get him some water. They should be back in a minute.' Aunt Effie fell into step beside them as they walked slowly towards the now almost dismantled plant stall. 'Anyway, whatever has happened to Miss Crowther? The woman never even complained of so much as a headache. Fit as a flea she was with all the running around that she did.'

'We're not entirely certain,' Matt said.

'Ha ha, foul play, eh?' Aunt Effie gave him a sharp look.

'The police are investigating as it's a sudden death.' Kitty was aware of Inspector Woolley's instructions so chose her words carefully.

Aunt Effie tapped the side of her nose with a gloved forefinger. 'Don't worry, my dear, I shan't breathe a word.'

The dark-haired young man they had seen at the tea stall was being towed towards them by an enthusiastic Bertie.

'Thank you, Frank,' Aunt Effie said as Matt accepted the lead back from the lad. Kitty bent to fuss her dog who was busy trying to tie them all up with his leash by winding his way around their legs.

'It was no problem, Miss Effie.' The boy patted Bertie's head. 'The last of the plants are in your car, by the way. I'm afraid the back seat is full.'

Kitty heard Matt groan quietly. 'I had better start to walk back to the Dower House with Bertie.'

His aunt looked unrepentant. 'The exercise will do you good. The air will aid your lungs. Thank you for your help, Frank. I expect we shall see you and Ruth in church tomorrow?'

'Yes, Miss Effie.' The lad smiled and slipped away to go and assist a lady struggling to fold up her table.

'Nice boy, young Frank. His sister, too, although she is a bit spikier than her brother. I like her, she has a bit of gumption about her,' twinkled Aunt Effie as they walked towards Kitty's car.

Kitty's cheeks heated, aware that Matt's aunt had described her to Matt's parents using very similar terms. They reached Kitty's car and Kitty could see the back seat was full of greenery. If she hadn't left the roof down, the two potted trees would never have fitted into the small car.

'Drive slowly going back, my dear. I'll get my gardener to unload when we arrive. He'll be expecting these.' Aunt Effie slipped into the passenger seat and waited for Kitty to get behind the wheel to start the car.

Kitty smiled to herself and turned her car around to head back down the long gravel driveway. She wondered if Inspector Woolley would call to see them later, or if he would turn up the following day. He had said he needed to take their statement.

They passed Matt, Bertie, and various other people all walking back towards the large, black wrought-iron gates at the entrance of the park. Kitty spotted the woman with the perambulator balancing the large green teddy bear.

'Had you known Miss Crowther long, Aunt Effie?' Kitty asked as she turned off the main drive and into the little lane leading to the Dower House.

'Oh yes, my dear, Emily Crowther has, or rather had, lived here all of her life as have I. My parents bought the Dower House years ago when the family that originally owned the estate started to feel the pinch financially. Matt's father lived here as a boy. He will be quite upset when he hears Emily is dead. She was a regular bridge partner whenever he and Matt's mother came to stay.' Aunt Effie gathered her cane and bag as Kitty drew to a halt outside the house.

'What was Miss Crowther like?' Kitty asked curiously as she jumped out and ran around the bonnet of the car to open Aunt Effie's door for her. 'I mean, I know she played a big part in village life, but did she have many friends or any family?'

Aunt Effie accepted Kitty's hand to get out of the car. 'She had a younger brother who she doted upon, but he was killed a long time ago. A military accident out in the east, India, I believe. She never liked to speak of it. Her back room was practically a shrine to him. Photographs and things everywhere. Kenneth, his name was. I don't think she had any other family, oh except her cousin Margery. She lives nearby in Barnsover, they didn't get on.' Aunt Effie inspected her plants by peering into the back of Kitty's car. 'I don't think she had close friends as such. She was very sociable and was invited out to dinners and bridge, all that malarkey, but she wasn't popular.'

'Why do you think that was?' Kitty asked.

Aunt Effie snorted. 'Too nosy, my dear, and too fond of offering her opinion. That's the truth of it.'

The gardener was coming around the corner of the house pushing a large wooden barrow.

'Shall I take these round for thee, Miss Effie?' He nodded towards the plants.

'Yes, please, set them up in the walled garden in the shade and we can decide where they are to go on Monday.' Aunt Effie set off towards the house with Kitty at her side. They had scarcely passed over the threshold when Matt and Bertie joined them.

'I rather think we need something stronger than that dreadful tea,' Matt announced cheerfully as he headed towards his aunt's cocktail cabinet. 'What do you say, Aunt Effie? The sun must be over the yard arm somewhere by now.'

His aunt raised an eyebrow. 'I doubt you've ever worried about that, Matthew dear, but, yes, a drink does seem to be in order. I must admit I do feel rather shaken about Miss Crowther.'

Matt poured his aunt a glass of her favourite Madeira and handed it to her. 'Kitty?'

'A gin would be rather marvellous,' Kitty replied.

Matt duly poured himself and Kitty a generous measure in his aunt's cut-crystal glasses and added orange juice.

'Thank you.' Kitty smiled at her husband as he passed her a glass before taking his seat beside her. Bertie settled at their feet and promptly went to sleep.

'Had Miss Crowther fallen out with anyone lately?' Matt asked his aunt, before taking an appreciative sip of his drink.

'She was always falling out with someone or other. She couldn't help it.' Aunt Effie settled herself comfortably in her armchair, clearly enjoying speculating on who might have wished to murder Miss Crowther.

'Anyone in particular who may have held a grudge against her?' Kitty asked as she leaned her head on Matt's shoulder.

Aunt Effie sipped her Madeira. 'Well, she was always arguing with Lilith, the vicar's wife. They were like chalk and cheese those two.'

Kitty recalled the attractive woman who had clearly not wished to be assisting on the tea stall. 'What kind of things did they argue about?' Surely it would have to be something serious if Lilith turned out to be the one who had added poison to Miss Crowther's cup of tea.

Aunt Effie snorted. 'Miss Crowther disapproved of Lilith being the vicar's wife. She is uninterested in the work of the parish and has handed the rearing of the twins to a succession of nannies. And, also, Miss Crowther considered her to be too low class to marry a clergyman. Personally, I always thought that Miss Crowther had hoped at one time that she might have married Reverend Drummond. But then he met Lilith and, well, he was swept off his feet.'

'Did Lilith argue back with Miss Crowther?' Kitty asked. She had noticed from her brief meeting with Miss Crowther when she had called at the Dower House that the deceased woman had been sharp-tongued.

'Lilith never really bothered most of the time, far too indolent. She would just ignore Miss Crowther's remarks as much as possible. Although, they did have a huge argument a week or so ago. I don't know what started it. There was a meeting about the fair, organised by Miss Crowther. The usual thing, who was to be on what stall and so on. After it had ended everyone else had gone but I couldn't find my walking stick, so I was late leaving the church hall. As I walked around the corner to find my driver, I came across them. Lilith looked furious and I heard Miss Crowther say that something had to stop or it would create a scandal.' Aunt Effie took another sip of her drink looking pleased at her recollection.

'A scandal, eh, wonder what she meant by that,' Matt mused.

Aunt Effie shrugged. 'I have no idea, but whatever Miss Crowther said clearly hit a nerve with Lilith. If looks could have killed, then Emily Crowther's card was marked.'

CHAPTER FIVE

The good weather continued to hold and the short drive to the village church the following morning was bright and sunny. Kitty parked her car near the wooden lychgate and waited as Matt assisted his aunt from the passenger seat. They had opted to leave Bertie back at the Dower House in the company of the gardener.

After everything that had happened at the fair the previous day, Kitty had to admit that she was somewhat curious to meet Reverend Drummond. She had heard enough about Lilith's apparent unsuitability to be a vicar's wife that she now wanted to meet the man himself. She was intrigued by the idea that a romantic story lay behind their marriage.

There was a steady procession of villagers walking through the churchyard into the small stone church. The melodic clang of the bell rang out from the tower, calling people into worship and disturbing the birdsong.

Aunt Effie nodded and greeted various friends and acquaintances as they walked along the narrow stone path between the ancient, moss-covered stones. Kitty recognised Colonel Brothers and his wife just ahead of them talking to the doctor they had met yesterday.

'Effie!' Hilda Brothers wearing a navy version of yesterday's mushroom-shaped hat waved them over.

Before any of them even had chance to exchange pleasantries about the weather or anything else, Hilda had hold of Aunt Effie's arm. 'Doctor Masters says Miss Crowther was murdered! What do you think of that? Inspector Woolley called at the Hall early this morning asking lots of questions. We were almost late setting off for church, I thought then that it was rather peculiar.'

'Most peculiar indeed,' Aunt Effie agreed.

'And you found her, didn't you?' Hilda continued in the same low excited tone as she looked at Matt and Kitty.

'Effie said you were a private investigator?' The colonel looked at Matt. 'That's right, isn't it, Effie?'

'Yes, sir, that's right, but I'm sure Inspector Woolley will have the case well in hand.' Matt glanced at Kitty.

She knew that they both had a few reservations about being thrown into another murder investigation. The last one had not gone as well as they would have wished, and Kitty privately felt that they needed this holiday with the chance to recover before taking on another serious case. If they had to keep finding crimes, why couldn't they have just stumbled into a robbery or a blackmail case rather than finding another corpse?

'If you'll excuse me for a moment, I must just speak to Lilith.' The doctor slipped away and headed to where Lilith, dressed in a rose-printed frock and straw hat, was about to enter the church with the twins.

'We really should go inside too,' Kitty said.

The path was almost empty now with just the last few stragglers hurrying in from the lane, and the sound of the bells had stopped.

'Oh yes, better not be late.' Hilda and the colonel moved

away into the church. Kitty and Matt followed Aunt Effie to take their places in the pews for the start of the service.

Kitty had scarcely taken her seat when she realised the large, bovine figure of Inspector Woolley was seated at the rear of the church, partly obscured by a stone pillar. As they stood for the first hymn, she noticed Lilith and the twins were at the front, along with Doctor Masters and Colonel and Mrs Brothers. She couldn't see the colonel's nephew, Jamie anywhere.

Reverend Drummond took the service. He appeared to be a tall bespectacled man with stooped shoulders and thinning hair. The sermon he gave seemed to Kitty to be rather dull and scholarly. She considered him an unlikely partner for his much younger and more glamorous wife. It was small wonder their union had caused so much gossip in Quixshotte.

Towards the end of the service, at the time for notices, Reverend Drummond asked the congregation to pray for the late Miss Emily Crowther, paying tribute to all of her good works for the community. The formal announcement of her death from the pulpit sent a ripple around the congregation. It appeared that the news had not yet fully circulated around the village. This surprised Kitty given the village was small and Miss Crowther so well known.

The vicar closed the service, and everyone rose in a rustle of hushed conversation as they left the church. Kitty gathered her cotton gloves and large cream-leather handbag, ready to shake hands with Reverend Drummond where he was bidding his parishioners farewell near the front door.

Inspector Woolley, she noticed, had discreetly positioned himself a few feet away from the vicar, seemingly admiring the historic stonework of the church. Lilith and the twins appeared to have already left for the vicarage, which she assumed was the large, handsome stone house just along the road from the church.

'Thank you for coming, Effie, such a tragic loss yesterday.' Reverend Drummond shook hands with Aunt Effie.

'Indeed. Reverend, may I present my nephew, Matthew, and his wife, Kitty. They are staying with me at the moment. They found poor dear Miss Crowther, you know,' Aunt Effie said as she moved aside to allow the vicar to greet Kitty and Matt.

'Oh dear, how very shocking.' The vicar's pale-blue eyes blinked behind his wire-framed spectacles.

'The colonel says Miss Crowther was murdered,' Aunt Effie added.

Kitty saw the Adam's apple bob in the vicar's throat as he digested this piece of information. 'Surely not, my dear Miss Bryant. Who could possibly have done such a thing?' Reverend Drummond asked as he attempted to collect himself to continue saying farewell to the remainder of his parishioners.

'Who indeed?' Doctor Masters joined them. 'Such a hard-working, respectable member of our little community.'

'Quite so,' Reverend Drummond agreed mildly.

Kitty thought there seemed little real warmth in the doctor's words. In fact, they almost held a hint of something less flattering. She wondered if he too had argued with Miss Crowther over something.

Doctor Masters tipped his hat to them and hurried past on the path. Aunt Effie made to move off towards the gate, leaning on her cane as she walked. Kitty and Matt walked behind her.

'Captain Bryant, Mrs Bryant, may I call on you after lunch?' Inspector Woolley had caught them up, moving surprisingly swiftly and quietly for a man of his size. 'I should like to complete your statements about what happened yesterday when you discovered Miss Crowther.'

'Of course, Inspector,' Matt agreed.

Kitty had been wondering when the policeman would call

to see them. Perhaps they might learn more about what had happened to Miss Crowther when he called.

The inspector nodded and tipped the brim of his hat to Kitty and Aunt Effie, before going back to speak to the reverend.

* * *

After a generous lunch of roast lamb, followed by a rich and creamy rice pudding for dessert, Aunt Effie announced she intended to retire to her room to rest her eyes. Matt was well aware of his aunt's habit of retiring on Sunday afternoons with the newspaper from the servants' quarters that her butler always thoughtfully placed on her bedside table. She had a secret fondness for the more lurid scandals and news items but would never admit to reading anything lowbrow.

Kitty joined her husband outside on the terrace under the shade of the umbrella. Bertie flopped down with a contented sigh in a pool of deep shade, his furry grey tummy full of scraps from the lamb they had all just enjoyed.

A slight breeze ruffled the frilly edge of the blue and white striped canvas above their heads and stirred the cotton table-cloth covering the ancient rattan table. Kitty sat down and glanced out over the garden, shading her eyes with her hand.

'Such a glorious day, I can hardly believe that we have stumbled into something so awful in such a gorgeous setting.' Kitty sounded troubled.

'It is rather hard to believe.' Matt knew what she meant. The view from the terrace at the Dower House across the park-lands of Quixshotte Hall was quite beautiful.

He had wondered if Kitty regretted joining him as a partner in the investigation business. Ever since their last case when they had almost been killed in a fire, she had seemed withdrawn and pensive.

At first he had thought it was due to the length of time it

had taken him to recover from the effects of the smoke and the memories that had been stirred up of his time in the Great War. The smoke had also affected Kitty, leaving her pale and with a sharp cough. Thankfully the cough at least had now gone, and the sun had removed the pallor from her cheeks.

'Darling, we don't have to be involved in this case if you would rather remain on holiday. We could just pack up and start for home, take in a few more places along the way. Aunt Effie would understand.' Matt looked at her.

Kitty turned her head to smile at him. 'We both know my insatiable nosiness will never be satisfied with that solution. You are right though, we can just continue with our holiday here and let the police handle this one.'

Matt was not convinced. He knew his wife all too well. If they continued their stay with his aunt as they had planned, he had no doubt that Kitty would be poking around asking questions.

'I'm sure they'll catch the culprit quickly. I mean, it's a small community,' Matt replied blandly. He hoped the case would be solved quickly and that Inspector Woolley would be more competent than the inspector involved in the last murder case they had been embroiled with in Yorkshire.

That particular policeman, Inspector Lewis, had since transferred forces to Torquay, and they were now lumbered with him back in Devon. A foxy, rude man, he had made it clear that he disliked private investigators and, much to Kitty's annoyance, especially female investigators.

Chief Inspector Greville had been promoted from the inspector's role and was now above Inspector Lewis. It was fortunate that they had always enjoyed a good relationship with him. This had helped considerably to mitigate the difficulties they had encountered with Inspector Lewis.

His unfortunate arrival had also upset Kitty. Since stepping back from a lot of the day-to-day management of the hotel she had seemed unsettled. She'd even allowed her grandmother's friend, Mrs Craven, a woman Kitty had no fondness for, to draw her into assisting with her charity work.

'Begging your pardon, sir, ma'am, there is an Inspector Woolley here to see you.' One of his aunt's maids ushered the now familiar figure of the inspector onto the terrace. The inspector looked hot in his crumpled linen suit and his broad forehead was beaded with sweat beneath the brim of his Panama hat.

'Thank you, could you bring us out a jug of lemonade, please?' Matt asked.

The maid bobbed an acquiescence and disappeared back inside the house.

'Do come and sit in the shade, Inspector. It's dreadfully hot today and there is at least a tiny bit of breeze here,' Kitty suggested.

The inspector lowered himself into one of the vacant rattan chairs with a sigh. 'Thank you, Mrs Bryant, that's most kind of you.'

The maid reappeared a moment or two later bearing a wooden tray containing a large glass jug of lemonade and several crystal glasses. She set her load down on the table and returned to her duties.

Kitty busied herself pouring drinks. 'Lemonade, Inspector? Aunt Effie's cook makes it beautifully and it's most refreshing.'

'Thank you, Mrs Bryant.' The inspector accepted her offer and gulped down half a glass quite quickly.

'I presume you have had quite a busy morning, Inspector?' Matt accepted his own drink from Kitty.

The policeman nodded. 'Yes. There were quite a few people that I needed to speak to. Obviously, some of those I had already interviewed yesterday evening.' He stopped to take another large swallow of lemonade.

Kitty topped up his glass. 'It seemed from the reaction in

church this morning that there were many in the congregation who hadn't heard that poor Miss Crowther had died.'

'No, a lot of folk had already gone home from the fair by the time we arrived and we asked those that were in the know, so to speak, to keep it quiet, at least until we had a chance to examine the scene.' Inspector Woolley met Kitty's interested gaze with a bland, brown stare.

'I take it that foul play is confirmed, sir?' Matt asked. He knew from what he, Kitty and Doctor Masters had observed at the scene that there could be little doubt in the matter. Still, he was interested to hear what the inspector might say.

The inspector switched his gaze fully to Matt. 'Yes, sir, as you no doubt suspected, Miss Crowther was poisoned.'

'And it was administered in the cup of tea that was on the table?' Kitty asked as the inspector drew his notebook from the inner breast pocket of his jacket.

'It would seem so, Mrs Bryant, although the laboratory tests have yet to confirm everything.' The policeman fumbled about his coat pockets for a moment before producing a pen.

The inspector asked for their home address and telephone number, making careful notes in his book as he listened to their replies. He fingered the corner of the crisp white business card that Matt had given him the day before.

'One of our inspectors has moved to your neck of the woods. An Inspector Lewis, might you have run across him?' Inspector Woolley looked first at Matt and then at Kitty.

'Yes, sir. We met him originally here in Yorkshire. You may recall the murders at Thurscombe Castle last June, my cousin, Lady Woodcombe's, estate?' Kitty said, her voice level.

Inspector Woolley's thick silver eyebrows rose fractionally in reply.

'And, of course, he was involved in our last case. The murder of a young woman who had taken part in the jubilee beauty pageant at Dartmouth. You probably saw it in the national press,' Matt finished the explanation.

He couldn't determine from Inspector Woolley's expression what his feelings were towards his former colleague. If Inspector Woolley held Inspector Lewis in any kind of regard Matt knew that both he and Kitty would be very wary of the Yorkshireman.

'Aye, happen I did.' Inspector Woolley made no further comment and Matt assumed that the man's curiosity about them and their business had been satisfied.

'Where do you think the poison came from that killed Miss Crowther?' Kitty asked, steering the conversation deftly back onto the purpose of the inspector's visit.

'An unsecured garden shed in the grounds of the Hall. Apparently there has been a lot of problems with wasps since this nice weather started.' Inspector Woolley sighed gently before continuing. 'I had a word with the colonel on the inadvisability of leaving dangerous and toxic materials unsecured. Especially when a public event is being held. However, it's all rather too late now, I'm afraid.'

Matt could see that Kitty was itching to ask more questions but felt it prudent to at least provide the inspector with their statements first. They gave him a detailed description of what they had seen and how they had come to enter the fortune telling booth.

'And, of course, there was Hilda Brothers' button from her dress, lying inside the tent near the door.' Kitty turned her bright eyes to the inspector.

'Yes, Mrs Brothers' button.' The inspector spoke softly, almost as if talking to himself.

'What has she said about it? Has she admitted visiting the tent?' Kitty asked eagerly.

The inspector looked up from his notes. 'Mrs Brothers says

she was there earlier in the day when it was being set up. She thinks she must have lost it at that point.'

Matt saw Kitty's shoulder's droop a little at this.

'Do we know who made the tea and took it to the tent?' Matt asked.

'Mrs Lilith Drummond, the vicar's wife, was mostly in charge of pouring the tea. No one seems certain if anyone took the cup to Miss Crowther as the cups for the stallholders had been placed on a special tray at the back of the stand. The colonel's nephew, Mr Jamie Martin, was assisting as was Master Frank Drummond. The stall was very busy at that time and the cup may have been unattended for a minute or so while Miss Ruth Drummond served another customer.' Inspector Woolley read from his notes.

'Was anyone else on the stall? We saw Lilith Drummond, Frank and Ruth when we were there just before we found Miss Crowther dead,' Kitty said.

The inspector replaced the cap on his pen and put both notebook and writing instrument away in his jacket pocket.

'I think the doctor may have been there too at some point assisting Mrs Drummond. There are a number of people that may have had the opportunity to administer a noxious substance to Miss Crowther,' the inspector said.

'I wonder who took her the tea?' Kitty mused.

'The biggest question, I think, is why she was killed. I'm certain that once we have the motive then, no doubt, we shall find the person responsible for her death.' He picked up his glass from the table and finished his drink. 'Thank you very much for your hospitality, Mrs Bryant, Captain Bryant. If you come across anything that may help the investigation you can find me at the Quixshotte Arms in the village. The landlord has set aside a room for us to use during the investigation.'

'Of course, sir.' Matt rose from his seat at the same time as the inspector so he could show him out of the house.

The inspector raised his hat once more to Kitty and left the terrace with Matt.

Matt had no sooner set foot back on the terrace after seeing the policeman off when Kitty pounced. 'Well, what do you think? Did he say anything more as he left?'

CHAPTER SIX

Kitty leaned forward on the edge of her seat. Her earlier lethargy caused by the large lunch and the afternoon heat had been usurped by her interest in the murder.

Matt lowered himself back onto the lounger. 'Not really. I tried asking if he knew of anyone who had cause to dislike Miss Crowther and he was very noncommittal on the matter.'

Kitty shuffled back in her chair feeling quite deflated. She had hoped the inspector might at least have given them a hint. Still, at least he had been polite, and they had learned quite a lot from his visit.

'I wonder what his feelings are towards our chum Inspector Lewis?' Matt smiled as he posed the question.

Kitty returned his grin. 'Yes, he was very silent on that particular matter, wasn't he?'

'Let us hope that he is not one of Inspector Lewis' admirers,' Matt said.

Kitty giggled. 'Does he have any admirers? Mrs Craven is definitely not a fan.' She couldn't think of anyone so far in Dartmouth who had been impressed by Inspector Lewis. She suspected that Chief Inspector Greville would have had him transferred back to the Yorkshire force if possible.

'We shall have to see how the investigation progresses under Inspector Woolley's direction I suppose, but he does seem to be on top of things at the moment.' Matt looked thoughtful.

Kitty agreed. The policeman certainly appeared to be quite thorough so far.

A loud rumble came from the road, and she caught a glimpse of the large, brightly painted circus wagon going over the stone bridge leading to the Hall.

'I expect they have come to take Bluebelle back to the circus,' Kitty said.

'Yes, I believe they are to move on tomorrow. The colonel said her keeper had spent the night sleeping outdoors with her,' Matt agreed.

'He did seem to be taking good care of her.' Kitty had noticed the elephant keeper had kept a close watch on his animal when they had been at the fair.

Kitty decided she would write a letter to Alice later rather than just send her another postcard. There was so much to tell her. Who could have predicted that her desire to see an elephant would have led to them becoming involved in another murder? It definitely was not the kind of message to send on the back of a pretty view of Quixshotte village.

Aunt Effie joined them for a high tea of salads and cold ham and cheese. Most of the servants were given time off after three o'clock on Sundays so they could attend evening service or visit family.

'What did the inspector have to say?' she asked as she took her place at the head of the dining table.

'Miss Crowther was poisoned as we suspected, and it seems the poison was from the gardeners' shed at Quixshotte Hall.'

Matt helped himself to a slice of pork pie and ignored Bertie's begging eyes.

'Oh my dear, that's not good. I always thought the colonel was very on the ball about making sure things were secure. Even more so with the fair taking place.' Aunt Effie frowned as she filled her plate with cheese and pickles.

'The inspector said the shed was unlocked so I suppose anyone could have gone in. They were using the poison to deal with a wasps' nest.' Kitty frowned at Bertie who had now placed his nose on Aunt Effie's knee.

'Hilda did say they had been having a problem with wasps. They had settled in the wisteria by the front door, and she was concerned that any visitors might get stung. It's rather early in the year for wasps, but I suppose this spell of fine weather has brought them out.' A slice of ham mysteriously found its way from Aunt Effie's plate into Bertie's waiting mouth. 'Are you intending to investigate Miss Crowther's death, Matthew dear?'

Matt choked on a crumb of pastry. 'Um, Kitty and I had rather thought that we should stand back and let the police get on with this one, Auntie.'

Kitty's mind flew back to the conversation they had held earlier in the day before the inspector's visit. It had all seemed quite simple then, to agree to leave things in the hands of the police. Now though, she had to admit she really did want to ask a few questions and poke around a bit to see what they could find.

Aunt Effie snorted. 'When did that ever stop you from looking into things? You and Kitty have a good track record of solving these matters.'

Matt caught Kitty's gaze and she gave her husband an almost imperceptible nod.

'Well, I expect if the case isn't wrapped up quickly, then we may be able to help Inspector Woolley, if, and only if, he is amenable to our help.' Matt gave his aunt a warning look.

'Marvellous.' Aunt Effie beamed happily at them and gave Bertie another slice of ham.

After tea, they settled back into the drawing room. Aunt Effie switched on the radio, while Matt applied himself to the crossword. Kitty opened her latest book. A new detective fiction by Mrs Christie that she was particularly looking forward to reading. A knock on the glass of the French doors took them all by surprise, sending Bertie into a round of barks.

'What ho! Hope I'm not disturbing you all?' Colonel Brothers appeared in the open doorway.

'Not at all, do come in.' Aunt Effie turned off the wireless and Kitty popped the crocheted bookmark that Alice's sister Dolly had given her for Christmas back inside her book.

'Hush, Bertie.' Kitty called the dog to her and settled him back at her feet.

'Drink, Colonel?' Matt set aside his newspaper and went to the polished cherry wood cocktail cabinet.

'Thank you, don't mind if I do. A whisky and soda would be capital.' The colonel took off his white Panama hat and took a seat on the leather armchair nearest to the open French door. 'I say, it's still quite warm out there.'

Matt fixed the older man his drink and one for himself. Aunt Effie requested a sherry and Kitty opted for a lime and soda. Like the colonel she found the heat still quite oppressive, and she wanted something refreshing.

'Out for your evening walk, Colonel?' Aunt Effie asked.

Kitty gathered from the question that it must not be uncommon for the colonel to drop in on one of his postprandial excursions around the estate.

'Yes, Doctor Masters says I should take more exercise. A gentle stroll he suggests to aid my circulation. Poppycock, a good cigar and a large brandy would probably benefit me more,' the colonel grumbled good-naturedly. 'We had the police around again after church. That wasn't good for my blood pressure.'

'Oh dear, sir, how so?' Matt asked as he settled back in his seat, whisky glass in hand.

'He reckons Miss Crowther was killed with poison from my shed. The stuff we got for the gardeners to deal with the wasps. I always insist the outbuildings are kept locked. My head gardener says the shed was open and someone had gone in and taken the tin with the poison. They found it discarded in a bush near the tea stall after everyone had gone.' The colonel's complexion had turned an unhealthy shade of plum with indignation as he recounted the story.

'That's terrible, sir,' Kitty soothed. 'Who was responsible for locking the shed?'

'The head gardener, been on the estate all his life, man and boy. He says it was locked up every day.' The colonel took a sip of his whisky.

'And you believe him, sir? Could someone have taken the key and unlocked it to get to the poison if they knew it was there?' Kitty asked.

The colonel frowned. 'That's what the inspector chappie asked. My head gardener has always been a most conscientious kind of fella, so I find it hard to believe he would have forgotten. Especially with the fair being on. He lives on the estate in a cottage near the other gatehouse on the far side. I suppose someone could have taken his key from the hooks. He keeps them on a rack inside the back door.' The colonel sounded bewildered. 'But that would mean someone had planned this in some detail in order to murder Miss Crowther.'

Kitty thought that if someone had taken the trouble to add poison to the woman's tea, then the end result was definitely planned. The theft of the key to access the shed would simply be another step.

'Do you know if the key to the shed is missing?' she asked.

Colonel Brothers took another large swallow of whisky before answering. 'The inspector asked that as well. Turns out it wasn't on the hook when they sent a constable down to check.'

'So, the key has gone,' Matt mused thoughtfully.

'Yes, and then there's the business over the button. You know they found a button off Hilda's dress in Miss Crowther's booth? Well, it's quite upset Hilda. All the questions, when did she lose it? When was she in the tent? Had she fallen out with Miss Crowther?' The colonel slumped back in his chair pressing his free hand to his forehead.

'Poor Hilda, it must be terribly trying for you both, especially with all the work that goes into the village fair,' Aunt Effie responded in a sympathetic tone.

'Exactly, and you know Hilda is not good with stress.' Colonel Brothers raised his head and looked at his hostess.

'I think your wife said she lost the button from her dress in the morning, when the booths were being set up, sir?' Kitty asked.

Colonel Brothers switched his gaze to Kitty. 'Quite, my dear, quite. At least she thinks that's what may have happened. She can't recall visiting Miss Crowther's booth after lunch.'

'And she hadn't argued with Miss Crowther, had she?' Matt asked.

The colonel looked a little uncomfortable at this question. 'You know what women can be like.' He suddenly appeared to recollect that there were two women in the room. 'Present company excepted, of course. You know small arguments over trivial matters. Hilda would bend my ear about Miss Crowther being too nosy and minding everybody's business. She disliked Jamie and, obviously, Hilda would defend the boy.' The colonel sighed. 'Hardly the stuff to commit murder over.'

Kitty sipped her lime and soda. She wondered if any of these supposedly petty quarrels had run deeper than the colonel was willing to admit. What had Miss Crowther discovered about Mrs Brothers that had led that lady to say the dead woman was nosy and in everybody's business? And Miss Crowther had disliked Jamie Martin, there was something significant there, Kitty was prepared to bet her last shilling on it.

'No, you're right, of course, people fall out all the time, don't they?' Aunt Effie drained her sherry glass and looked at Matt. 'Matthew dear, would you oblige? Colonel, have you time for another?'

'Thank you, most kind.' The colonel handed his glass across, and Matt duly refilled both glasses, before topping his own back up. Kitty declined as she still had half a glass left.

The colonel nursed the crystal whisky glass between his hands, seemingly lost in his own thoughts for a moment. Kitty's gaze flickered wistfully to the closed cover of her novel. She had been looking forward to a peaceful evening with a good yarn.

When the colonel spoke, his words took her by surprise.

'This investigation service of yours, Captain Bryant, I know you are here on holiday, but I wondered, well, will you be looking into Miss Crowther's death?'

Matt cleared his throat. 'As you said, sir, we are here to holiday, and we wouldn't wish to impede the local force, or annoy them.'

The colonel sighed. 'It's just, well, it feels as if whoever did this has done so to try and point the finger at Hilda and me. To murder the woman on the biggest day of the year for the village, on my grounds, with poison from my shed. Then for a button from Hilda's frock to be at the scene. I don't know what it's like where you live, Captain Bryant, but this is a small community. No smoke without fire, that's what they'll say if the police don't catch whoever did this.'

Kitty frowned. 'You think it's personal towards you and your wife?'

'We came here in '22, so while we've been here for some time we are still outsiders to an extent, Mrs Bryant. In order to escape detection, I think the killer would need to point the finger elsewhere. Muddy the waters, so to speak. And mud sticks.' The colonel took another swig from his glass as he finished speaking.

'My dear Colonel, surely not. No one would think ill of you. You and Hilda are very valued by the village,' Aunt Effie protested.

'Are you saying you wish to commission us to clear your name and that of your wife?' Kitty asked. She had some sympathy for the man as she could understand all too well what he meant.

There would always be whispers and Hilda might not be invited to certain clubs or outings. The annual village fair might even suffer. They could find themselves being subtly shunned by county society. If the killer were caught, however, then it would be of no matter.

'Just as an insurance, should the police not manage to capture whoever did this. I want mine and Hilda's names to be clear,' the colonel said.

Matt's gaze met Kitty's.

'Very well then, sir, Kitty and I shall see what we can do,' Matt agreed.

The colonel seemed satisfied with their response. Matt promised to write out their terms and conditions and deliver them to the Hall in the morning.

'Thank you both and thank you, Effie, for the drinks.' The colonel took his leave, wandering back out the same way he had come in. Kitty thought he looked worried.

CHAPTER SEVEN

The fine weather continued into the next day. Matt spent an hour after breakfast drafting a letter for the colonel outlining their fees, terms and conditions for undertaking the investigation.

'It will be a challenge to prove someone didn't do something rather than looking for whoever did do it,' Kitty observed as he folded the paper and placed it in an envelope.

'I'm not entirely certain we shall be able to separate the two,' Matt said. 'You are all right about this, aren't you, darling? I know this is our holiday.' He still had concerns about how Kitty truly felt about being involved in yet another murder investigation.

'I don't think we could have refused. Your aunt would have been most disappointed, and you know how I can't resist asking questions.' She flashed a mischievous grin and his spirits lifted.

'Then let's head up to the Hall before it becomes too hot outside. Bertie will enjoy the exercise.' Matt looked at his dog and smiled. Bertie had clearly heard his name and his plumed tail was already in motion in the expectation of a walk.

Matt put Bertie on his lead, while Kitty gathered her bag

and pinned a broad-brimmed straw hat trimmed with corn-flowers onto her blonde curls.

The air above the gravel path leading to the Hall shimmered with a fine heat haze. Matt noticed that the grass of the parkland had already begun to look less green, taking on a more yellow straw-like tinge. Kitty rested her hand lightly on the crook of his arm as they strolled along.

'Do we have a plan for today?' she asked.

'I'm not sure. We'll drop this off to the colonel and then we can see who is about.' Matt paused while Bertie investigated an interesting clump of daisies in the verge.

'Perhaps we can speak to Mrs Brothers and discover what those petty arguments with Miss Crowther were all about. Or even if they really were petty,' Kitty suggested.

'Yes, the colonel seemed to be holding something back there I thought.' Matt glanced at his wife as they continued their walk.

'I thought that too. And why is he so concerned about their reputation? I do understand it to an extent, but I don't know, he's hardly giving Inspector Woolley the opportunity to do his job,' Kitty said.

'I would have thought that the greatest source of gossip would fall around how the poison got into the tea and who gave it to Miss Crowther.' Matt had given the matter some thought after the colonel's departure the previous evening.

'Yes, and who else had Miss Crowther upset,' Kitty agreed.

There were a lot of questions to be answered if the colonel and his wife's names were to be cleared.

The drive rose on a slight incline towards the Hall before curving around a stand of trees. The house itself stood on the brow of a low hill. The gravelled area where Kitty had parked the previous day lay in front and to the one side of the house. A rather sporty-looking little dark-green car had been parked at a peculiar angle in front of the broad stone steps leading to the portico and front door of the Hall.

From the scuff marks on the stones and the position of the car Matt deduced that whoever had driven the car had clearly been in either a tearing hurry or in something of a temper.

'I wonder who that belongs to?' Kitty gave the car an admiring glance. 'It's a smashing motor.'

'I dare say we shall soon find out. Now, Aunt Effie said to go to the side door. No one uses the front it seems around here,' Matt replied, and they walked away from the mystery vehicle.

The side of the house was in shadow and felt cooler after the bright sunshine. A large wisteria covered the side and part of the front of the house wall. Matt wondered if this was where the wasps' nest had been treated. As they drew closer to the building the sound of raised male voices reached them from one of the open windows on the ground floor.

Matt felt Kitty press her fingers into his arm to signal him to stop and listen for a moment.

'No, Jamie, I refuse to invest in another of your hare-brained ventures. I'm not made of money, you know.'

'That's the colonel,' Kitty whispered.

'Talking to Jamie, the nephew,' Matt agreed.

'For pity's sake, Uncle Stanley, it's only a few pounds. It's a good investment.'

'That's what you said before and I've still to see a return on that. I said no and that's final. I suggest you turn your attention to learning to manage the estate.' The colonel sounded quite irate.

Jamie must have said something else in a lower tone that didn't reach where Kitty and Matt were standing in the lee of the house.

'And for heaven's sake keep away from the vicarage!' the colonel commanded.

Matt looked at Kitty.

'Curious,' she murmured.

The sound of a solid door slamming reached them, and they continued towards the dark-green painted side door of the house. Matt had just raised his hand to press the small brass button set into the stonework when the door opened, and Jamie appeared in front of them. He seemed somewhat discomfited by their unexpected appearance.

'Oh, hullo, have you come to see the old man?' he asked. Jamie looked flushed and out of sorts. The argument with his uncle had clearly affected him.

'Yes, the colonel's expecting us,' Kitty said.

'Well, good luck with that! He's in his study. Go on in, it's the second door on the left.' Jamie bounded away down the steps and disappeared around the corner of the Hall. A few seconds later they heard the throaty sound of a car engine roaring into life and the sporty little car shot off down the drive.

'Well, that answers our question about the ownership of the car,' Kitty remarked.

They entered the house and found themselves in a small hallway tiled in black and white. The walls were oak panelled and several paintings depicting scenes from India were displayed on the walls. No servants were in sight.

Following Jamie's instructions, they found the door to what they hoped was the colonel's study and Matt raised his hand and knocked.

'Come!'

At the colonel's command they entered to find him seated behind a large brass and mahogany desk. A pile of documents lay in front of him and the remains of two cigarettes smouldered in the large brass ashtray. A large portrait of the colonel in his younger years clad in dress uniform hung on the wall next to one of an equally youthful Hilda dressed in a dark-blue satin evening gown.

'Captain Bryant, Mrs Bryant, do come in and have a seat.'

The colonel had stood when they entered. He ushered them towards two slightly faded red velvet-covered chairs which were placed in front of his desk.

'We have the paperwork we said we'd bring, sir.' Matt handed over the envelope. He took his seat next to Kitty while the colonel opened and read the contents.

Bertie yawned and scratched his left ear with his hind foot while they waited.

Like his nephew earlier, Matt thought he could see that the older man was a little upset. Traces of plum still marked the complexion in his cheeks, and he took his time to focus on the information Matt had provided.

'Very good. That all seems to be in order. Yes, I'm happy to entrust you with the investigation.' The colonel shook hands with both of them before resuming his seat.

'Thank you, sir. We may have questions for members of your household, as well as yourself and Mrs Brothers as we try to establish the course of events leading up to Miss Crowther's murder,' Kitty said.

The colonel raised an eyebrow. 'Establishing our alibis, eh? Talk to whoever you like, my dear. There are no secrets here.'

Matt wondered how true that was.

'Speaking of alibis, do you have one, sir? For the period leading up to when we discovered Miss Crowther's body?' Matt jumped on the mention of an alibi.

'Me, well, no, not really. I mean, I saw lots of people, but I was busy setting up the duck race, keeping an eye on my tiger and whizzing around the stalls. It was a busy old day,' the colonel said.

'I think you told us before that you popped into the fortune teller's tent briefly after lunch to check that Miss Crowther had enough change?' Kitty asked.

'Yes, there was some confusion about the money floats for the stalls. Hilda had been most upset about it. Miss Crowther had been rather sharp with her I gathered. I was only there for a moment, and it was at the start of the event. She would have told a lot of fortunes after I saw her. It's always very popular you know, the fortune teller's booth.' The colonel stroked his moustache thoughtfully.

'Is Mrs Brothers aware of the commission, sir? Is she happy to answer any questions we may have?' Kitty asked.

'Hilda? Oh yes, she's as anxious as I am to be exonerated from all of this,' the colonel assured them in an airy tone.

'Is she at home now, sir?' Matt thought it might be as well to talk to Hilda Brothers while they were at the Hall. It would be interesting to find out what her relationship with the dead woman had really been like.

'Oh yes, she'll be in the orangery, I expect. She's often in there poking about with her plants.' The colonel gave them the directions and they left him to his work.

The orangery was on the other side of the house and so they followed the corridor into the large square entrance area with its magnificent venetian glass candelabra. Near the foot of the oak staircase stood the stuffed tiger that they had heard so much about.

The taxidermist had mounted the animal as if in mid-spring ready to attack. Its mouth permanently open in a silent roar displaying a fearsome set of teeth. Matt felt Kitty shiver as they passed it to take the other corridor leading towards the orangery.

The walls of the hallway leading to the orangery were hung with brightly coloured, embroidered Indian silks. The vibrant pinks, yellows and greens glowed against the oak panels displaying depictions of gods and goddesses. Matt recognised a few of the figures from his own travels. Lakshmi with her lamps, Ganesh with the elephant head, and Kali, the dark mother goddess.

The orangery was a large, white-painted wrought-iron and glass construction. Matt guessed it had been added to the Hall around the time of the Great Exhibition as so many of them were. Despite the vents in the roof being fully opened the air inside was humid and sticky. Huge tropical plants filled the space with greenery, leaving a narrow red-tiled path for them to thread their way through. The scent of damp soil and lilies filled the air.

'Mrs Brothers?' Kitty called.

'Down here.'

They followed the direction of the reply and the path led them to a small open space, where they discovered a wooden table and a couple of old chairs. Mrs Brothers was tidying up her gardening tools, her face pink and flushed from the heat.

'Hello, my dears. Stanley said that you would be along this morning.' Hilda placed a pair of secateurs and some worn gardening gloves inside a woven willow trug on the table.

'We thought we would see you and find out how you're feeling today,' Kitty said. 'It's all been the most frightful shock, hasn't it? And the colonel said the police had been asking lots of questions yesterday.'

Hilda shivered dramatically. 'Oh, Mrs Bryant, it was awful. I started to feel as if they really thought that I had done it. Taken the poison from the shed and placed it in Miss Crowther's tea myself. My having lost that wretched button inside the booth didn't help.' Hilda sat down on one of the chairs, a woeful expression on her plump face.

'You said you thought you must have lost the button in the morning when the stalls were being set up?' Kitty prompted.

Hilda's brow creased in concentration. 'Well, yes, I must have, mustn't I? I was so busy on the day, you know. Miss Crowther had me running here, there and everywhere. Stanley was too busy fussing over that wretched tiger and talking to the ringmaster about the elephant to be of any practical use. I know I was in her booth just before lunch because she was complaining about the floats, and quite nastily too. I'd counted the money for each stall out the day before with one of the other volunteers. Miss Crowther insisted hers was short, so I had to go and get more change. Such a nuisance when I still had the plant stall to finish setting up.'

'And you didn't return to the booth at any point after that?' Kitty asked.

'Well, only to add the extra shillings to the cash box, but that was before the fair opened.' Hilda took a large, white cotton handkerchief from the pocket of her green linen skirt and mopped her brow.

Matt too was starting to feel uncomfortable in the oppressive heat and Bertie had begun to pant. He would be glad to get back outside. At least Hilda's explanation tied in with the information her husband had provided.

'You hadn't realised that your button was missing?' Kitty asked.

'No, dear, if I had I would have gone and changed. I should have changed my clothes anyway but with all the rushing about I didn't have time,' Hilda said.

'Thank you, Mrs Brothers. We had better take Bertie back outside as he's feeling the heat in here,' Kitty said. 'Oh, by the way, I assume that you and Miss Crowther were on good terms?'

Matt saw the pink colour in Mrs Brothers' face deepen and her gaze shifted to a large clump of white lilies in a terracotta pot nearby.

'Well yes, most of the time. We had a few disagreements, of course. Nothing serious. She could be very annoying at times. Like with the change for the floats, but nothing that would cause me to murder her.'

Matt thought the woman's protestation sounded a little hollow. He was quite certain that Hilda Brothers, for whatever reason, wasn't telling the whole truth about her relationship with Miss Crowther.

. . .

'Well, that was informative,' Kitty said once they were back outside the house and out of earshot of any of the occupants. The cooler air was a welcome relief after the humidity of the orangery.

'I agree. The argument the colonel was having with his nephew sounded quite heated, didn't it? And I wonder what he meant by stay away from the vicarage?' Matt led Bertie over to a small ornamental pool with a fountain at the end of the terrace.

The dog lapped happily at the clear water burbling into the shallow bowl at its base.

'He could think that someone at the vicarage is responsible for Miss Crowther's death,' Kitty suggested.

'Or that he is too close to the vicar's daughter, Ruth?' Matt waited for the little dog to drink his fill.

'Hmm, and Jamie was clearly after money from his uncle this morning, and it sounded like it was not for the first time.' Kitty perched herself on the stone balustrade and tilted her chin upwards to try and catch what little breath of air was stirring.

'I know it's a reach but Miss Crowther said her float was short. Perhaps Jamie had helped himself to some of the money?' Matt sat next to her.

'She could have suspected him. It may have been that everyone's float was short but only Miss Crowther checked. Mrs Brothers said she had put them up the day before so he could have had access to them.' Kitty frowned. 'But then if she had accused him, surely he would have killed her in temper. Would he have gone away and fetched poison? Taken the risk that she might voice her accusations in the meantime?'

The scenario didn't quite ring true in her mind. Also, it was a big leap to go from hearing Jamie ask for money from his uncle to surmising that he was a thief. It could simply be that Mrs

Brothers had made an error when making up the float for the fortune teller's booth.

'What did you think of Mrs Brothers' claim that she and Miss Crowther had no real arguments?' Matt asked.

'She wasn't telling the truth, was she?' Kitty said. 'And I swear I could smell alcohol on her breath. I was much closer to her than you.'

'Hilda drinks?' Matt looked surprised. 'Interesting.'

Bertie finished at the fountain and Kitty stood to brush down the skirt of her pale-blue cotton summer frock. 'I think one of the gardeners has just gone towards the formal garden over there. Do you think it's worth talking to him?'

'It would be good to find out more about this shed where the killer found the poison,' Matt agreed.

'And if the missing key has been found?' Kitty slipped her arm through Matt's and they set off once more.

CHAPTER EIGHT

A flight of shallow stone steps led down from the terrace onto a yellowy-grey flagstone path lined with lavender, which took them to the more formal knot garden. This area was laid out with traditional low box hedging in intricate patterns, the centres of which were filled with roses, more lavender and other plants.

The gardener, a somewhat surly looking older man, had set down his wheelbarrow next to the central bed and was preparing to hoe inside the flowerbed. He paused in his task when he saw Matt and Kitty approaching, a wary expression crossing his weatherworn face.

'May I help you, sir, miss?' he asked as they approached.

'Are you the head gardener?' Kitty asked.

'Yes, miss. That I am,' he replied.

Matt reached into his coat pocket and drew out a business card from his silver card case. 'Colonel Brothers has asked us to assist in clearing the names of himself, Mrs Brothers and members of his household following Miss Crowther's murder on Saturday afternoon at the fair,' Kitty explained as the man took the card from Matt.

The gardener held it carefully between his dirty fingers. 'Oh aye.' He dropped the card into his trouser pocket.

Kitty pressed on. 'The colonel said the police believed that the poison used to kill Miss Crowther had been taken from a shed on the estate.'

The gardener sniffed. 'Aye.'

'The colonel also said the shed was usually kept locked, but the police found it open and that the key was missing from its usual place on a hook inside your cottage,' Matt said.

'That's right, sir,' the man agreed.

Bertie sniffed interestedly around the hems of the man's tattered moleskin trousers and Matt tugged at his leash to fetch him away.

'Has the key to the shed been found yet?' Kitty asked. The gardener was clearly a man of few words, and she suspected it was best to be as succinct.

'No, miss.' The man picked up his hoe as if ready to continue with his chores.

'Is the rack where the key is usually kept easy to access?' Matt asked.

The man scratched the side of his nose with a dirty thumbnail. 'I 'spect so, sir. I don't never lock the cottage see, no call for it until now.'

'And who would know where the keys were kept?' Kitty asked.

'Most everybody on the estate. The colonel and Miss Hilda, Master Jamie and the vicar's two, the vicar, 'bout most people, I reckon. Borrowed things see, tools and the like,' the man explained.

Kitty could see that it seemed as if half the village had access to the shed and to the keys whenever they wished. This information was not making the task of exonerating the colonel and his wife any easier.

'May I ask where you were on Saturday, during the village fair?' Kitty hoped he wouldn't take offence at her question.

'I were at the plant stall for a time making sure as Mrs Brothers don't get selling things as she hadn't ought to. Then I were at the produce stall as I had strawberries and some honey from the hives for they to sell there,' the gardener explained.

'You didn't return to your cottage or the shed at all during the afternoon, or ask anyone to collect anything from there?' Kitty guessed his tasks would have kept him busy all afternoon but thought it worth checking.

'No, miss. I stayed up on yon top field.' The man looked eager to get back to his task.

'Where is this shed?' Matt asked.

The man gave them directions to both the gardeners' shed and to his own cottage within the boundaries of the estate.

'Thank you.' Kitty fell back into step beside Matt as they made their way out of the formal garden and down some more steps into the park.

'The shed seems to be situated fairly close to the man's cottage from what he was saying. Not that he appeared willing to say very much.' Matt looked around for any buildings.

'Over there.' Kitty indicated a small grey-stone dwelling with a well out front and a stone outhouse at the rear. The cottage was tucked away in a corner of the field under some trees. Three beehives were sited along the perimeter of the garden next to neat rows of bean canes and soft fruit bushes. A well with an iron pump handle was at the front of the cottage.

An ugly rusty-brown corrugated-iron shed stood about sixty yards away from the house. Bertie trotted along over the tussocky grass as they approached the shed. His tail held high as he sniffed interestedly at the ground. They stopped near the shed and looked back across the field towards the Hall to orientate themselves.

'This is to the side of Quixshotte Hall and the fair was held in the area at the front. That large oak tree and the pine copse is the area where Bluebelle the elephant was kept. I think if you were near the elephant then you would be able to look down the field to see the fortune teller's booth, but perhaps not the refreshment stand,' Kitty said as she gazed across the grassland.

Matt strode off to examine the door of the shed. 'Yes, it would be the one spot on the field that would let you see the fortune teller's booth clearly. There is a new bolt and padlock been fitted on this door. I can see where the original lock would have been. That must have been the one that the missing key opened. The colonel has wasted no time in making certain that nothing else can be taken.'

Kitty walked down the front path to the cottage and peered inside the front window. It seemed to be one of the simple one-up one-down style of workers' houses common to the area. The ground floor comprised of the kitchen, scullery and living area, while she presumed the upper floor, accessed by a wooden ladder, must be the sleeping quarters.

As she squinted through the grubby glass window, she could just about make out a row of hooks on the back of the whitewashed back door where she assumed the missing key to the shed had been kept.

The cottage's location was certainly secluded. Even on a day as busy as Saturday she would have been surprised if any members of the public would have ventured to this corner of the field. Someone would only walk down this far if they were after something in particular.

'Would anyone take any notice of someone coming this way on Saturday, do you think?' Kitty asked as she turned to look back across the parkland.

Matt returned from his examination of the shed to join her at the cottage. 'Unlikely I would have thought. They could come the way we came, via the formal gardens, or they could have left from the field. I don't know if anyone would have noticed, they would be focused on the stalls and the elephant.'

Kitty frowned. 'I wonder why they didn't hang the key back on the hook or lock the shed back up after taking the poison.'

Matt shrugged. 'In too much of a hurry? I expect they would simply take what they wanted and leave. The police said the tin of poison had been hidden not far from the refreshment stall in some bushes.'

'We should go and take a look to see if we can work out where that was. They must have concealed the tin somehow to hide it once they got closer to the fair.' Kitty quickened her pace to keep up with Matt's longer strides as they set off towards the site of Saturday's festivities.

It proved harder than Kitty had anticipated to locate where the refreshment stall had been sited now the area was completely empty of tables and there were relatively few land-marks that they could use as markers.

'These must be the bushes,' she said, pointing to a small scrubby area of rhododendrons. Their lower branches had been snapped off and the sticky remains of their earlier pink flowers looked somewhat battered. The grass was completely flattened around them as if trodden down by numerous pairs of heavy boots.

Bertie poked his head deep into the heart of the bushes and began to scrabble at the soil with his front paws. A shower of dirt shot out and Matt tugged at the lead to try and extricate the spaniel.

'Bertie!' Kitty remonstrated in a sharp tone as something hard hit her ankle making her wince.

'Was that a stone?' Matt asked as Kitty bent to rub at her foot while glaring at an unrepentant Bertie.

Kitty looked around to see what had struck her. She spotted the glint of metal amongst the freshly dug soil. 'No, in fact, I rather think this may be the missing key.' She pulled a handkerchief from her handbag and carefully picked up the metal object.

'Inspector Woolley's men missed that,' Matt remarked drily as Kitty stowed the key away.

'It must have been right in the centre of the bush. It was pure luck that Bertie found it. The killer could have disposed of it at the same time as they got rid of the poison,' Kitty said, feeling a little more kindly towards her dog now it appeared he had unearthed a clue.

'Where do you think the refreshment stall was exactly?' Matt studied the area looking for some sort of marker.

'It was across to the side and much further down the field. There was another group of shrubs not far from the stall. I remember when I gave that child the bear that his perambulator was near the edge of them in the shade.' Kitty walked forward with Bertie trotting after her.

There was another small group of bushes further down the hillside at the point where the ground levelled out.

'Around here then?' Matt asked as he joined her to examine the well-trodden grass.

She nodded and they turned to look back at the bushes where the poison had been left.

'You can't really see much from here, can you? The ground rises and the shrubs hide anyone from view,' Kitty said.

The refreshment stall had been at the end of the row to give room for tables and chairs for people to take their ices and cups of tea. The field was flatter at that point providing a level area. Because of the fall of the ground, the site where the poison had been left would not have been a place where the public would have gone. It was also shielded from the view of anyone at the stall.

'It explains how the killer managed to remain unobserved as they disposed of the tin and the key.' Matt sounded thoughtful as he continued to study the site.

'How would they then get the poison into the cup and ensure that only Miss Crowther drank it?' Kitty asked.

She had been pondering this part of the conundrum as they had been walking across the field.

'Hmm, the cups the stall were using were all quite mismatched, weren't they? I noticed some had a floral design like cabbage roses and others were white or decorated with birds.' Matt gave Bertie's leash a gentle pull to signal to the dog that they were ready to move on.

Kitty fell back into step beside her husband as they walked back over the parkland to where they had entered the grounds at the top of the drive.

'You mean you think the killer had picked out a particular cup for Miss Crowther that they could introduce the poison into?' she asked.

'It seems likely that's what would have happened. They must have transferred enough of the poison into some other container and then tipped it into her cup when no one was looking.' Matt glanced at her.

Kitty could see how that was a possibility. 'Perhaps, but then they either have to take it to her themselves or ensure that someone else delivered it to her. I doubt they would risk killing the wrong person. If I recall they were pouring tea from that large white enamelled teapot they had and then people added their own milk and sugar at the table.'

'So, it has to be someone who was responsible for pouring the tea or for delivering it to Miss Crowther?' Matt suggested.

They had arrived now at the entrance to the driveway ready to continue on to the Dower House.

'Or we have to consider that someone entered the fortune teller's booth and slipped the poison into the tea after it had been delivered. There was no milk or sugar in the tent, so someone knew how she took her tea, or she added it herself at the stall. That to me seems to be the strongest case. The killer would have been certain then that no one else would have the tea except Miss Crowther,' Kitty said.

Matt smiled at her. 'That's very true. They would have to have either delivered the tea themselves or have observed someone taking it into the tent. They would then have come up with some pretence for entering the booth.'

'Which means it must have been someone she knew. She had put up her closed signs and I think she was the kind of lady who would have given short shrift to anyone entering the tent who she didn't know well.' Kitty was warming to her hypothesis.

'I think you may be right. They would have had to have distracted her or engaged her in conversation somehow to give them the opportunity to add the poison to the cup,' Matt agreed.

'We need to know who delivered the tea and who entered the booth,' Kitty said.

'I suspect the answer to both those questions may be hard to work out, and no doubt Inspector Woolley will be following the same lines of enquiry as us.' Matt took her arm as she stumbled on a tussock of grass.

The Dower House was now in sight and Bertie had picked up speed eager to return to the comfort of a cool stone floor and a big drink of water.

'Heavens, look at the time.' Kitty looked at her watch, the morning seemed to have flown by.

'We had better hurry or we shall be late for lunch, and no doubt Aunt Effie will wish to hear about our morning.' Matt grinned at Kitty as they quickened their pace.

They made it to the dining table with only a minute to spare. Aunt Effie was already seated in her customary position at the head of the table. Bertie, having drunk his fill had positioned himself near Aunt Effie's feet hidden by the tablecloth, presumably in the hope that some of the food might come his way.

'Do sit down, my dears. I thought you were going to be late.' Aunt Effie shook out a large white linen napkin and spread it on her lap.

'Sorry, Auntie. It took us a little longer than we thought to walk back from the Hall in the heat,' Matt apologised as the servants placed their first dish in front of them.

Kitty picked up her spoon and sniffed appreciatively. The watercress soup smelled delicious, and the morning's exercise had given her quite an appetite.

'I trust you had a productive outing?' Aunt Effie asked after the servants had left the room.

Matt quickly told her what they had discovered.

'Aunt Effie, you know Hilda Brothers much better than Matt or me. Has she ever had a problem of any kind with drink?' Kitty asked as she placed her spoon back into the empty china bowl.

'Hilda? I don't know. I had never considered it, but I suppose she could have. Her behaviour is a little odd at times. She does like a drink whenever there is a party or a dinner.' Aunt Effie patted the corners of her mouth delicately with her napkin. 'What makes you ask, Kitty dear?'

Kitty tucked the information away in the corner of her mind. 'I thought I could smell whisky this morning when she was close to me in the orangery, so it crossed my mind.'

'Well, now I think about it I suppose it may explain some of the times she has missed an event and the colonel has made an excuse on her behalf. It happens not infrequently. I think I just assumed she had migraines or a digestive issue.' Aunt Effie looked thoughtful.

'There are some very lovely mementos in the house of the Brothers' stay in India, pictures and silk hangings. They must have been terribly fond of it. I'm surprised they decided to return to England rather than remain there when the colonel retired. Is this the area where their family came from?' This was something else she had wondered. *Why had they returned to England and why to this particular area?*

The servants had returned to clear the soup bowls and to serve the main course of minted lamb cutlets with new potatoes and peas. Once they had gone Aunt Effie came back to Kitty's question.

'I believe the colonel comes from somewhere near Leeds. Hilda is from London originally. As for their return from India, well the colonel wished to retire, and I suppose they thought it better to move home sooner rather than later. I rather think the colonel saw the Hall for auction in some catalogue or paper and decided to take a look. Although...' Aunt Effie's brow wrinkled as she tried to recall the events of some years ago.

'Although...' Matt prompted gently as he added extra mint sauce to his lunch.

'I have a feeling there was a bit of a whisper of some scandal or other. Something that was hushed up about why they left India. Hilda misses their life there even now, I think. She always sounds so wistful when she speaks of it.' Aunt Effie dug into her lamb chop with gusto.

Conversation reverted back to other subjects and Bertie benefitted from a few slivers of lamb reaching him from Aunt Effie's plate. Once the main course was cleared the servants returned with frosted glass dishes of lemon sorbet topped with fresh strawberries.

'Begging your pardon, madam, but a messenger just delivered this note for you.' One of the maids passed a small cream-coloured envelope to Aunt Effie.

Kitty noticed it was embossed on the back with the address of the Quixshotte Arms.

Aunt Effie set down her spoon and opened it as the maid departed.

'Oh, how marvellous. I sent an invitation to Inspector Woolley to join us for dinner tonight and he has agreed. Although he has added a caveat that he cannot discuss the case.' She folded the note back up and replaced it in the envelope, beaming at their stunned expressions.

'That was very good of you.' Matt looked suspiciously at his aunt who had resumed her consumption of her sorbet.

'Well, everyone knows the landlord's wife is a dreadful cook and he can hardly dine elsewhere if the others are suspects and a poisoner is on the loose.' Aunt Effie winked at him, causing Matt to choke on his dessert at his elderly relative's mendacity.

CHAPTER NINE

'I sometimes wonder if your aunt should have made a career as a detective or working for the brigadier in Whitehall,' Kitty remarked to Matt as they left the dining room to sit for a while on the terrace in the shade of the umbrella. She could picture Matt's aunt engaging in a spot of espionage for her husband's former employer.

Matt chuckled. 'I think you have a point. She is quite remarkable, isn't she?' He sat down on his favourite lounger and lifted his feet as he lay back.

Bertie, looking very pleased with his own lunch of titbits and leftovers, settled down happily in a pool of deep shade on the cool stones of the terrace.

Kitty took her seat at the table. 'We do need to talk to the occupants of the vicarage if we are to fulfil the colonel's commission. They seem too close to the case for us to ignore them. It's so difficult when one really doesn't know any of them terribly well.'

Their introduction had been fleeting during the fair and they had only said a few words to Reverend Drummond as they had left the church yesterday. They could hardly just turn up on the vicarage doorstep and start asking awkward questions about Miss Crowther's demise.

'I agree. I expect that Inspector Woolley is probably talking to them all again today in any case. Ruth and her brother seemed to be running the stall for the most part, with their step-mother assisting them. I suppose that with the history of ill-feeling between Lilith Drummond and Miss Crowther then it would be natural for him to concentrate his endeavours there first.' Matt adjusted his hat, so the brim shaded his eyes and Kitty suspected her husband was about to settle for an after-noon nap.

'Perhaps we may learn something to our advantage during dinner this evening. Who knows, the inspector may have found enough evidence by then to make an arrest.' Kitty decided that, frustrating as it may be, there was little else they could do for the time being.

Instead, she fetched her detective story from her room and decided to make up for the reading time she had lost on the previous evening during the colonel's visit.

After a pleasant and leisurely few hours, Kitty went upstairs to bathe and dress for dinner. As she placed her handbag on the chair in her bedroom, she suddenly realised that neither she nor Matt had sent a message to Inspector Woolley to say they had discovered the key to the shed.

There seemed little they could do about it now as the inspector would be calling shortly for pre-dinner drinks, so they would be able to pass it on to him then. She hoped he wouldn't think that they were interfering or hindering his investigation.

She dressed for the evening in a new pale-green shantung silk gown shot through with splashes of gold and cerise. When she had been packing for the trip, Alice had assured her that it was very flattering and a perfect match for her gold evening sandals. She had still to write to her friend to tell her about the events at the fair. Something she resolved to do first thing tomorrow.

Matt called her into his bedroom before they went downstairs so she could assist him with his cufflinks. Kitty always considered her husband to look quite dashing, if a little rakish, when in evening attire. It was a relief to see him looking well again after what had happened in Devon.

'Did you realise that we forgot to let the inspector know about the key?' Kitty said as she secured the crisp-white starched cuff of his shirt with a monogrammed gold cufflink.

'Blast.' Matt picked up his dinner jacket. 'So we did. Do you have it with you now?'

Kitty nodded. 'I transferred it into my evening purse.' She indicated the small gold silk bag she had brought into his room with her.

'Good show, we'll hand it over as soon as he gets here.' Matt shrugged into his dinner jacket and dropped a kiss on the top of her head.

Inspector Woolley had already arrived and was seated on the terrace with Aunt Effie when they went downstairs. Aunt Effie had her usual glass of sherry in hand, while the inspector appeared to be enjoying a whisky.

Matt gave his and Kitty's requests for drinks to the butler and joined the others.

'It's such a fine evening, far too nice to go inside just yet so I thought we would have drinks out here,' Aunt Effie declared.

'This weather is set to continue, I believe, for a few more days,' the inspector said.

The butler returned and served Kitty with a Cosmopolitan cocktail and Matt with a whisky.

'Dinner will be ready at seven thirty, madam,' the man announced and left them to continue to talk.

'I'm afraid that we have a confession to make, Inspector,' Matt said as he and Kitty took a seat at the terrace table.

'And an apology,' Kitty said.

'Oh?' The inspector's expression immediately became wary.

Kitty delved into her evening bag and took out the key, still safely wrapped in her handkerchief. 'We were at Quixshotte Hall this morning and Bertie went digging in the rhododendrons where you discovered the poison container. He found this.' She placed the key on the table.

The inspector lifted a corner of the cloth. 'That looks very much as if it might be the missing key to the gardeners' shed. Have either of you touched this at all?' he asked.

Kitty shook her head. 'No. Bertie dug under the bush, and it flew out and hit my ankle. I thought it was a stone at first. When we saw it was a key, I picked it up with my handkerchief and kept it safe.'

The inspector dug in the pocket of his evening jacket and produced a small brown envelope. He carefully tipped the key inside and sealed it, being sure not to touch the key itself.

'I doubt there will be any prints on this, but you never know. There were none on the poison container, not even the gardeners' fingerprints, so someone had been very careful.' The inspector tucked the envelope inside the inner breast pocket of his jacket.

Kitty glanced at Matt. This was another useful snippet of information.

'I think it's only right to tell you, sir, that the colonel has commissioned us to ensure that his and Mrs Brothers' names are cleared from any hint of wrongdoing concerning the death of Miss Crowther,' Matt said.

The inspector raised his eyebrows at this. 'I see.'

Kitty wondered what he knew that they didn't about the case and the colonel and Mrs Brothers. *Was Hilda the main suspect after all?* 'I think he is concerned about any damage to their reputations since the murder happened on his land. Do you have any objections to this, sir?' she asked.

'No, not at all. So long as you bring any new information to me and do not compromise the investigation.' Inspector Woolley eyed her levelly.

Matt's aunt steered the conversation onto gardening, something it seemed the inspector was fond of. Although his interests lay more in potatoes and rhubarb rather than flowers.

Kitty sipped her cocktail and listened, aware that her husband was amused by her growing frustration at not being able to talk about the investigation.

'Patience, darling,' Matt whispered in her ear when their companions were engrossed in a debate about leeks.

The butler announced that dinner was ready, and they went through to the dining room. Aunt Effie took her place at the head of the table while Kitty was seated on one side beside the inspector, with Matt opposite her.

'Are you comfortable at the Quixshotte Arms, Inspector?' Aunt Effie asked as their first course of crabmeat cocktail was set in front of them.

'Yes, the rooms are very airy, and the landlord has been most accommodating.' The inspector started on his food.

'Lilith Drummond was a landlord's daughter,' Aunt Effie mused. 'I rather think that was why she thought Miss Crowther disapproved of her suitability as a wife for Reverend Drummond. Plus, as I think I said before, I fancy Miss Crowther thought she may have had a chance with the vicar at one time after the death of Martha, his first wife.'

Kitty glanced at the inspector. He seemed to be stolidly making his way through the first course unmoved by Aunt Effie's disclosures.

'How did Reverend Drummond meet Lilith?' Matt asked.

'Oh, my dear, it all sounds terribly romantic. Reverend

Drummond's first wife Martha was a lovely woman but delicate. Her health never really recovered after she had the twins.
She had rheumatic fever when she was a child, and it damaged
her heart, she had been warned that a pregnancy might be very
dangerous. Then, with them being twins, well, I think the
damage was probably done then. The children were only about
six when poor Martha succumbed. A chest infection was too
much for her heart. It was a bad winter that year. I think that
was when Miss Crowther thought she might win the vicar over
to her.' Aunt Effie paused to take a sip of water.

After a moment she continued her story. 'Miss Crowther set
about doing what she did best, organising things and, well,
attempting to play mother to the children. I don't think the children took to her though. She was not a terribly endearing
person and not especially maternal. The vicar, of course, was
oblivious to all of this. He had a very good nanny who saw to
the day-to-day things and Miss Crowther took care of the parish
matters. Then he was called to a symposium in Leeds.'

'Where he met Lilith?' Matt asked.

Aunt Effie set down her cutlery. 'Yes, the story I heard was
that he and several other members of the clergy had been
staying at a hotel near the city centre. Lilith's father had a
public house across the road, and they met by chance one day in
the street. Reverend Drummond literally walked right into her
and knocked her shopping flying. He stopped to assist her in
gathering up the spilled items. Their eyes met and they fell in
love. They married about six weeks after that meeting.'

'How romantic,' Kitty said. She could see that Miss
Crowther wouldn't be at all pleased by that development, but
the vicar had been married to Lilith for a number of years now.
The twins were quite grown up. Could that have been the start
of the ill feeling between the two women though?

'Lilith is quite unsuited to the life of a vicar's wife. She has
no interest in chairing committees or arranging flowers. Miss

Crowther fulfilled most of the duties which Lilith should have done. Organising the Sunday school, visiting the sick and so on. In fact, I wonder what will happen about all that now? Unless the reverend's daughter, Ruth, takes it on.' Aunt Effie settled back a little in her chair as the staff removed their first course and proceeded to serve turbot with fresh greens and creamed potatoes.

'We saw Mrs Drummond at the refreshment stall at the fair. She didn't appear to be terribly happy about being there,' Kitty said as she sniffed appreciatively at the beautiful fish dish in front of her.

'I dare say she was only assisting on the stall at all because she couldn't get out of it. I think last year she had a migraine,' Aunt Effie said drily as she applied pepper to her potatoes.

'Does the vicar not mind that Mrs Drummond has chosen to take a back seat from the parish activities?' Matt asked.

Aunt Effie shrugged. 'Not at all. I doubt he has even noticed since Miss Crowther did all the work. He seems to think Lilith is as delicate as his first wife, Martha. Wraps her up in cotton wool and treats her like a piece of Dresden china. Reverend Drummond has a private income, you see, as well as his stipend from the church and what Lilith wants, Lilith gets. Nothing but the best for her.'

'It's an interesting dynamic,' Matt observed as he cut into his fish.

'Do you think Ruth will wish to take on any of the parish duties? It's a lot to expect of such a young girl,' Kitty asked, recalling the pretty young woman who had served them on Saturday. It seemed to her grossly unfair if everything were to land on Ruth, and Frank, Ruth's twin, were to get off scot-free just because he was a man.

'She was talking of training to be a teacher and already assists with Sunday school,' Aunt Effie said. 'But, just lately, she has been very thick with Jamie Martin, the colonel's nephew.'

'What of her brother, Frank?' Matt asked.

'There is talk of him going to Oxford in the autumn. He's a very bright boy.' Aunt Effie placed her fish knife and fork down neatly on her empty plate. 'I presume you've met the family, Inspector?'

Inspector Woolley had maintained a discreet silence throughout the meal so far. Kitty was in no doubt though that he had been taking in all the information.

'Yes, I was at the vicarage today.' He placed his own cutlery down on his plate having finished his fish.

'I do hope young Ruth is all right? She was on that refreshment stall for most of the day. A most conscientious young woman. I hope she is not blaming herself in any regard for what happened to Miss Crowther?' Aunt Effie enquired innocently, before taking another sip of her water.

'I believe Miss Drummond is unaffected by Miss Crowther's death.' The inspector dabbed at the corners of his mouth with the starched white linen napkin.

His expression was bland as he spoke, and Kitty suspected he had seen through Aunt Effie's attempt to subtly acquire information about the progress of the case.

The plates were cleared, and a glass bowl of Eton mess was set before them.

'Frank Drummond is also very friendly with Jamie Martin, I believe?' the inspector remarked as he picked up his spoon.

'Yes, young people together, you know. Frank, like most boys, likes motor vehicles and Jamie, most unwisely I feel, has a very sporty little car. They often spend time either repairing or improving it, I'm not quite sure which.' Aunt Effie tucked into her dessert.

'It is a very nice car, we saw it this morning while we were at the Hall. Quite an expensive model.' Kitty had wondered how Jamie had come to own it.

'Yes, he bought it himself, I believe. He had it when he

arrived at the Hall. Hilda said that when his mother died, she left him some money. Not a fortune but if managed wisely it would have lasted for some time. Jamie, however, spent most of it on that car and some unwise speculations apparently.' Aunt Effie's tone was full of disapproval at this.

'Miss Crowther mentioned something about Jamie when she called here before the fair, about him having been wild,' Kitty recalled.

Aunt Effie scraped the last of the cream and meringue from her dish. 'Yes, a few brushes with the law and I rather think he was let go from his place of employment. Hilda claimed it was the upset from losing his mother.'

'It seems he is widely regarded as being groomed to inherit the estate?' Inspector Woolley finished his own dessert.

'Yes, that is the expectation, the Brothers have no children and Jamie is their only living relative on either side.' Aunt Effie looked a little regretfully at her empty bowl. Kitty hid her smile behind her napkin, Matt's aunt was rather fond of desserts.

The servants returned and cleared the dishes, leaving a platter of crackers with a selection of cheese on the table.

'We shall take coffee in the lounge,' Aunt Effie instructed.

'Very good, madam,' the butler agreed and left them to help themselves to cheese.

Kitty declined the cheese course and concentrated on finishing her glass of wine. Considering they had been requested not to discuss the investigation she felt they had learned quite a lot about the other people involved in the murder.

'Miss Crowther doesn't seem to have been a very popular lady, for all her good deeds,' Inspector Woolley remarked as he loaded a biscuit with butter and a thick slice of Wensleydale.

'I fear you are correct, Inspector. She did have a good heart and was terribly kind in many ways. Unfortunately, she was also very nosy and fond of bestowing her opinions on others, even when those opinions were clearly unwelcome. She also had a sharp tongue.' Aunt Effie nibbled thoughtfully on a small stick of celery.

'Was there anyone else in the village besides the occupants of the Hall or the vicarage who she had crossed swords with lately?' the inspector asked after licking his lips appreciatively to collect the last crumb of cheese.

Aunt Effie thought for a moment. 'It's very difficult. There were lots of small things you see. She would accuse the grocer of having faulty scales and the post mistress of listening in on telephone calls at the exchange, or the milkman of failing to leave the right order. She did have an argument with Doctor Masters too a few days ago. I have no idea what it was about. She was fond of diagnosing herself with various illnesses though and I think she had a small fondness for him. She would give him gifts, jars of jam and home-baked cakes, that sort of thing. He certainly didn't seem to reciprocate her attentions.'

Kitty looked at Matt. His aunt hadn't mentioned Doctor Masters' name in connection with Miss Crowther before. It might explain the unpleasant note she thought had been present in his voice when they had left the church on Sunday. Or had Miss Crowther uncovered one of the doctor's secrets?

Cheese course concluded they adjourned to the lounge for coffee. Kitty played hostess, pouring the beverage from a tall, elegant silver coffee pot into angular modern cups painted in vivid oranges, reds and greens.

'Thank you, my dear.' Aunt Effie accepted her drink and settled down comfortably on a large chintz-covered armchair opposite the inspector.

'Thank you, Mrs Bryant.' The inspector took his drink from Kitty and added two sugars and some cream to his cup.

'I hope you have enjoyed dinner, Inspector. We have all attempted to be most restrained with our curiosity about the case,' Aunt Effie said.

The inspector smiled. 'Thank you, Miss Bryant. That restraint has been most appreciated. Indeed, the background information you have provided over dinner has been very helpful. It's always a difficult thing as a stranger in a small community to obtain information. Who is friends with whom and who bears a grudge? The petty loves and jealousies and the history of relationships. One never knows which of those may be relevant to a case at first, but it all helps to build a picture.'

Kitty could appreciate the inspector's words. She knew what it was like in a close community, having lived in a small town for all of her life. There were so many things that went unspoken because everyone else knew them. And, of course, a stranger would have no idea what those things were.

Matt stirred his coffee. 'I suppose that is one of the biggest problems with this case. Miss Crowther was tolerated, even mildly disliked in some quarters, but to poison the woman, well, someone had to have had a really strong motive.'

Inspector Woolley sipped his coffee and set his cup back on the saucer. 'Quite so, Captain Bryant. Someone went to a great deal of trouble to steal the key and put poison in Miss Crowther's tea. It was not a crime of passion where she was struck on the head or strangled in the heat of an argument. No, this was premeditated and cold-blooded murder.'

A shiver ran down Kitty's spine at the inspector's words. He had only voiced what she already knew to be true but even so, hearing it said aloud was surprisingly chilling.

CHAPTER TEN

The following morning was another bright, sunny start. No clouds were visible in the azure blue sky and the air was already warm.

'I should like to walk to the village to post this letter to Alice before it gets too hot.' Kitty waved the neatly addressed envelope in Matt's direction as they finished their breakfast. She had written to her friend before coming downstairs.

'Capital idea. We can take Bertie,' Matt agreed.

The walk from the Dower House along the lane to the village would take them past the church, the vicarage, Miss Crowther's cottage and the doctor's house. Kitty suspected that Matt shared her hope that they might run into someone connected with the village fair on the way to the postbox.

Kitty could have given her letter to Aunt Effie's butler who would have sent a maid to post it along with the rest of the outgoing mail from the house. This way, however, she got some exercise and the opportunity to do a little more sleuthing.

She pinned on her wide-brimmed straw hat and set off with Matt and Bertie. The lane was a pretty, wide, tree-lined avenue and the postbox was situated on the village green opposite the

Quixshotte Arms public house and a small tea room. There was a blacksmith's a general store, a butcher's, a greengrocer's and a bakery alongside the post office. The area was usually busy with village life.

Despite the fairly early hour and the dappled shade from the trees it was still quite warm as they walked. Bertie trotted ahead of them on his leash, his nose to the ground and his plumed tail high in the air.

'I wonder if we shall see anyone of interest to our case this morning?' Kitty asked as they approached the start of the village and the first couple of cottages came into view.

'Let us hope we shall be lucky.' Matt smiled at her. 'Last night was quite a valuable evening. We seemed to learn a great deal about the people involved in the case without asking too many questions. We also gained some insight into the inspector's thoughts about the case, despite him remaining quite tight-lipped.'

The vicarage was situated beside the church. A well-proportioned house in the Georgian style it reminded Kitty of a doll's house, set back on a nicely maintained lawn with a couple of apple trees.

Reverend Drummond was wheeling a bicycle out through the black wrought-iron front gate as they approached. He looked as if he had spilled yolk from his breakfast egg on the front of his black surplice. His straw hat was somewhat battered, and the pockets of his loose brown jacket were weighed down with books and other objects. He peered absent-mindedly at them over the top of his spectacles as they approached.

'Good morning, Reverend. Another fine day today,' Kitty greeted him cheerfully. She wondered if he would recall who they were.

'Yes, yes, indeed, very fine.' He blinked at her and pulled the gate shut behind him with a clang.

'We enjoyed the service on Sunday,' Matt said as he discreetly tugged Bertie away from his investigation of the vicar's ankles.

'Oh good, thank you. Are you the people staying with Miss Bryant? At the Dower House?' The vicar looked hopefully at them as if he had just placed who they were.

'That's right, sir, Miss Bryant is my aunt,' Matt confirmed.

'Bless me, then you must be the people who found our poor Miss Crowther on Saturday?' The vicar looked at Kitty and then at Matt.

'We were, sir. A most unfortunate event,' Kitty said.

'Terrible, quite terrible. I hope it was not too distressing for you both. Hardly what one expects when one is on holiday.' Reverend Drummond sounded concerned.

'No, sir, it was something of a shock. We had only been talking to Miss Crowther a couple of days before when she called at my aunt's house. Miss Crowther seemed to do so much for the community, was she well liked in the village?' Matt asked.

'What? Oh yes, I should say so. Such a generous soul, as you say, she was always volunteering her services. She was very kind to my family and myself when I lost Martha, my first wife. Most kind. Without her and my darling Lilith I'm not sure how I should have managed.' The vicar seemed lost in his memories of the past.

'I'm so sorry for your loss. My aunt has said she wonders how everyone will cope now without Miss Crowther,' Matt said.

'Yes, she does indeed leave quite a vacancy. I expect Ruth will assist in some things. That's my daughter, she's a good girl, Ruth.' Reverend Drummond blinked and swatted at a fly that had ventured too near to his spectacles.

'Aunt Effie said you had twins.' Kitty felt a little irked on

Ruth's behalf that already an expectation seemed to be heading towards the girl.

'Yes, that's right. Frank and Ruth. Frank is a very bright boy. We expect him to have a place at Oxford in the autumn.' The vicar beamed at Kitty.

'I heard Ruth also has a place at a teacher training college? You must be very proud of both of them,' Kitty said.

'Oh yes, yes, of course.' The vicar's expression indicated that he had forgotten his daughter's plans.

Kitty could see from the reverend's response that he had not considered that his daughter might not be around to fill the hole left by Miss Crowther.

'And your wife must also be a great asset to the parish.' Matt followed Kitty's lead.

'Darling Lilith is very delicate. She does what she can to help, but I would not wish her to exhaust herself. She found assisting at the fair quite tiring. It's fortunate that Ruth is able to assist with some of the duties involved in running the parish.' The reverend smiled happily at them.

Kitty felt quite sorry for Ruth. She hoped that the girl would be able to extricate herself from the mesh of responsibilities if she truly did wish to pursue a life and career of her own.

The vicar prepared to mount his bicycle.

'We met Mrs Drummond briefly on the refreshment stall at the fair. Did you enjoy the day, Reverend?' Kitty asked, knowing that neither she or Matt remembered seeing Reverend Drummond that afternoon.

'Now, where was I? I seem to recall intending to go to the village fair. Ruth had asked me to bring something from the vicarage.' The vicar frowned as he stood astride the bicycle. 'Ah yes, chutney, that was it. She had made some chutney for the fair in the autumn and wanted me to bring it to the stall. I think I arrived late, just before the brass band. I've always thought them very stirring for the spirit, brass bands.' Reverend Drummond beamed at them once more, clearly delighted that he had recalled his whereabouts at the fair. 'Well, if you'll excuse me. I promised to call on a parishioner at the local hospital.'

Kitty and Matt stood back with Bertie as the vicar pushed off and wobbled precariously away.

'Well, he is rather eccentric, isn't he?' Kitty remarked.

'Certainly, he appears to be very vague. Very fond of his darling Lilith.' Matt sounded thoughtful.

'Yes, and perhaps at the expense of his daughter.' Kitty's tone was dry.

She had scarcely finished speaking when they heard the sound of running feet on the stone path leading to the vicarage and Ruth appeared, panting at the gate.

'Oh bother, I've missed him.' She had a small object wrapped in greaseproof paper in her hand.

'Your father? He's just set off on his bicycle. Forgive me, it is Miss Ruth Drummond, isn't it? Matt Bryant and my wife, Kitty. We met briefly at the fair,' Matt said.

'Oh yes. I think Mrs Brothers mentioned you were staying at the Dower House with your aunt.' Ruth had an open and engaging smile. Her long dark hair was confined today into a neat bun at the nape of her neck.

'Father was supposed to take this with him to Mr Perks at the hospital. It's a piece of fruit cake. Still...' She shook her head in mock despair.

'Forgive me, but the vicar does seem to be a little absent-minded,' Kitty said.

Ruth rolled her eyes. 'Frank and I think he would forget his head if it were loose. He's frightfully clever you see, and his head is always full of, well, scholarly things. It means he isn't terribly good at the day-to-day things.'

'He was saying how clever you and your brother Frank are. You must both take after him.' Kitty watched the girl flush a deep pink.

'That's very kind of you to say so, Mrs Bryant. My late mother was also something of a bluestocking. Frank is hoping to go to university in the autumn and I, well, I would like to become a teacher.' Ruth smiled shyly as she spoke.

'How wonderful,' Kitty said. 'I do hope the events on Saturday were not too distressing for you? It was the most frightful shock about Miss Crowther.'

The girl shuddered. 'Awful. I can't believe that she was murdered, not that I cared for her very much. Oh dear, that sounds mean, doesn't it? But she could be so dreadfully intrusive. Always poking her nose in everyone's business and giving her opinions. I wouldn't have wished her dead however.'

'I wonder who saw her alive last? I suppose it must be whoever took her a cup of tea?' Kitty made her question sound casual.

'It was so busy on the refreshment stall I'm not certain who took it, if any of us did. That's what I told the police. It wasn't me, I was serving the strawberries and cream. Frank was waiting on the tables, but I don't think he had time to take a cup to the fortune teller's booth. Lilith, my stepmother, was supposed to be helping but I think all she did was set out the teacups and pour out. She certainly never left the stall.' Ruth shrugged her slender shoulders. 'It's a bit of a mystery. I know some cups had been poured ready for the stallholders and set on a tray to one side. The ladies from the bookstall had collected their drinks. We had given everyone a time you see when they were to collect them. Once the gates opened and everyone came in, we knew we would be swamped. It's the same every year so we ask people to come to the stall.'

The conversation was interrupted by the throaty purr of a familiar dark-green motor car approaching from the direction of the Hall. Jamie Martin pulled his car to a stop next to Kitty and Matt.

He nodded a hello in Matt and Kitty's direction before addressing Ruth.

'What ho, Ruthie! Are you game to come out for a drive? It's been ages since we've gone anywhere.'

The girl's cheeks pinked up again. 'I don't know, Jamie. It's frightfully busy at the moment now Miss Crowther isn't here to run things.' Ruth looked longingly at the car.

'Rot. Let Lilith do something for once. Grab your hat and let's go. If Frank is about grab him as well. We can go for a run, have a picnic,' Jamie urged.

Kitty saw the girl hesitate for a moment.

'Oh, hang it all. Give me two minutes.' Ruth turned and hurried back towards the vicarage.

'I think it might do Ruth good to get away,' Kitty said to Jamie. 'This business at the fair is quite distressing and Miss Crowther seemed to be involved in so many things.'

'Creepy Crowther we used to call her. I hated her, don't mind admitting it. I didn't kill her, mind you.' Jamie smiled disarmingly as Ruth came flying back up the path holding on to her hat.

'Frank is out,' Ruth explained breathlessly as Jamie leaned over and opened the car door for her.

'Have a nice day,' Matt said as he closed the car door behind Ruth.

He and Kitty waved as Jamie roared away with Ruth beside him.

'It would seem that Jamie has no intention of obeying his uncle and staying away from the vicarage,' Kitty said as the car disappeared from sight.

'No. He appears to be very good friends with both of the Drummond twins. He also freely admits to disliking Miss

Crowther.' Matt smiled at her, and Kitty saw the dimple flash in his cheek.

Kitty had taken Matt's arm ready to walk on when Lilith Drummond came hurrying down the vicarage front path. Dressed in a pale-blue silk dress, it looked as if she were intending to go out on a social engagement of some kind. A piece of notepaper was in her hand and a faint flush outlined her high cheekbones.

'Excuse me, have you seen my stepdaughter, Ruth, at all?' Lilith asked.

'I think she's gone out for the day with a friend. You've just missed her,' Kitty said.

'Well really! I expect it's with Jamie Martin. He is as irresponsible as the twins.' Lilith sounded quite put out. 'She was supposed to be taking the ladies' Bible class this afternoon. Normally Miss Crowther would have done it but...' The woman broke off as if suddenly realising that she didn't quite know who she was talking to.

'Now Miss Crowther is dead I expect things will have to be organised differently,' Matt said. 'I believe we met briefly at the village fair? Captain Matthew Bryant and my wife, Kitty. I'm sure you know my aunt Effie.'

Lilith's brow cleared and she simpered at Matt. 'Of course, I knew I recognised you both from somewhere. I'm so sorry to be bothering you with my domestic difficulties.'

Up close, Kitty could see that the older woman made good use of cosmetics to enhance her complexion and her large, dark-brown eyes. 'Not at all, Mrs Drummond. Miss Crowther's death must have been most upsetting.'

Lilith waved a beautifully manicured hand. 'My dear Mrs Bryant, you have no idea. The police were here all day yesterday asking all kinds of questions. Who served the tea? Had any of us argued with Miss Crowther?'

'How awful for you. I assume you were on good terms, with

her managing so many of the parish affairs?' Kitty said innocently.

'Well, good is not quite the term I would use. We tolerated one another, I suppose. I won't pretend that we were friendly. She was the most dreadful snob you know. Always looking down her nose at anyone she considered below her socially.' Lilith tossed her dark bobbed head.

'Oh dear,' Kitty sympathised.

'One doesn't like to speak ill of the dead, but, well, a lot of people in the village disliked her,' Lilith said.

'Enough to poison her?' Matt asked.

This earned him a sharp look from the vicar's wife. 'Not me, but I daresay there are those in the village who might have felt that way.' She turned away and made her way back inside the vicarage. Her heels beating a tattoo on the stone flags as she walked.

CHAPTER ELEVEN

'Whew, I think I may have hit a nerve there,' Matt remarked as they continued their interrupted stroll towards the village centre.

'Perhaps other people have already been suggesting that Lilith may have had a motive for Miss Crowther's death. There certainly appears to have been several years of ill feeling between them,' Kitty said as they rounded the corner and walked towards the bright red pillar box situated outside the post office.

Kitty slipped her letter to Alice inside the box along with another cheery postcard for her grandmother, which made no reference to murder. Matt knew that she had no desire to alarm her beloved Grams with talk of crime and death.

'Since we are on holiday, despite us agreeing to take on the colonel's commission, shall we stop for a lemonade before we return to Aunt Effie's?' Matt asked. He indicated towards the couple of wooden tables which had been set up in the shade of a large oak tree on the edge of the green.

'That sounds delightful,' Kitty agreed.

They walked across the grass to the seating area. Kitty took

Bertie's leash and sat down while Matt went inside the quaint tea room to order their drinks.

A couple of ladies were seated inside taking tea and Matt passed them to locate the owner, who was busy behind the small well-scrubbed wooden table that served as a counter. He ordered two lemonades and stepped back out into the sunshine to join Kitty in the shade.

Bertie had happily found the large ceramic brown bowl containing fresh water which had clearly been placed for any passing dogs. Suitably refreshed, he lay at Kitty's feet and started to inspect his front paws.

'This is most pleasant.' Kitty smiled at Matt as he took his seat opposite her. Looking around, he had to agree with her. The village green was roughly triangular in shape with roads bordering all sides. A small pond was in its centre, the water reflecting the colour of the sky to make the water appear a soft blue green. Two small white ducks paddled nonchalantly around the reeds which bordered the one side of the pond. A colourful painted sign hung from a white wooden frame announcing the village name and featuring the Quixshotte coat of arms.

The shade from the oak tree beside the table provided a welcome relief as the sun had climbed higher in the sky since they had set off.

'Here you go, sir, miss.' The owner of the tea room, an older lady clad in a respectable dark-print frock covered by a white apron, placed two tall glasses on the table before them.

'Thank you. I was just saying to my husband what a delightful spot you have here,' Kitty remarked to the woman.

'Thank you, miss, that's most kind of you. Quixshotte is a nice place, though I expect as I'm biased as I've lived here all my life.' The woman smiled back at Kitty, clearly pleased with the compliment.

'Like my aunt Effie, then,' Matt said as he picked up his

glass.

'Oh, you must be the nephew. Miss Bryant had said as you were coming to stay at the Dower House on a little holiday,' the woman replied.

Matt noticed the corners of Kitty's mouth curving upwards in a smile at this remark. It was always interesting the way gossip spread around a village.

The woman had tucked the now empty round wooden tray under her arm. 'Were you the people who found poor Miss Crowther at the fair on Saturday?'

'Yes, I'm afraid that we were. Such an awful thing to have happened,' Kitty said.

The tea room owner tutted indignantly. 'Oh, indeed it was, miss. Things like that don't happen here like that normally. We're all good, respectable folk. Miss Crowther were very respectable too. Lived in the cottage just over yonder she did.' She nodded her head towards a small stone cottage at the end of a short row of similar buildings. A small dark-blue motor car was parked outside. 'Now barely cold she is and that distant cousin of hers, that Margery, is already in there picking over her stuff. Kept her house nice, did Miss Crowther, some lovely bits of china, she had. That back room was a shrine to her brother Kenneth mind. She never got over him dying out in India the way he did.'

'How tragic. I believe she mentioned him to us. What happened to him?' Kitty asked.

'Well, he were in the army and it were said as there had been an accident with a loaded gun. I'm not so sure as it were an accident mind. Between me, you and the gatepost I think that were to save face. I think as he took his own life, the way it were all sort of hushed up. Unhappy he was, so Miss Crowther said at the time. Proper cut up about it all though she was. Especially with him being buried out there as well and her with no grave even to mourn him at over here. Had a nice service though in memory of him like, and there's a brass plaque in the church. You can go and see it if the church is unlocked.' The woman brightened at this recollection.

'Poor Miss Crowther, and now to meet such a terrible end,' Kitty remarked.

''Tis that. Wicked, that's what it is, wicked.' The woman shook her head in disapproval.

A young couple rode up to the tea room on bicycles, so the friendly woman made her excuses and walked away to serve her new customers.

'Could this cousin, this Margery, have had a motive?' Matt asked. 'If she inherits Miss Crowther's cottage and all its contents?'

'I wonder where she is from and if she was already here during the fair? Although I expect Inspector Woolley will have already looked into anyone who might have gained financially from Miss Crowther's death.' Kitty sighed and took a sip of her drink.

'It's still got to be worth looking into. Most crimes of this nature are down to love or money,' Matt said.

The lemonade proved to be cool and refreshing and he enjoyed the feeling of sitting in the dappled shade with Kitty looking at the peaceful scene before them.

'That looks like Doctor Masters over there, I expect his morning surgery must be finished,' Kitty said as the doctor emerged from his surgery only to walk the short distance along the street before turning into the vicarage gate.

Matt watched as the doctor's pale linen jacket disappeared from view as he neared the house. 'I wonder who he is calling on and why. Mrs Drummond appeared quite well a moment or so ago when we met her.'

'Perhaps he is requesting visits from the vicar for some of the parishioners who are unwell,' Kitty suggested.

'Possibly,' Matt agreed.

The tea room had a good view of the comings and goings around the green. It struck him that Miss Crowther would have had a similar view from her side of the triangle. Perhaps this was why Miss Crowther had often been called nosy? She would have seen everything that occurred in the village centre.

Miss Crowther's house had a low, wrought-iron fence in front of a postage stamp sized green square of lawn. A wooden tub with summer flowers stood to the side of the white front door. Her view of the green was excellent.

He finished his drink and waited for Kitty to finish hers.

'Do you need anything from the shops before we walk back?' he asked as she drained the last sip of lemonade from her glass.

'No, I don't think so. I bought some sweets at the fair.' She smiled at him as he untied Bertie's lead from where he had secured him to the leg of the table.

A bright red and yellow poster sun-faded and a little ragged at the edges was attached to a nearby tree. Kitty walked over to see what it said.

'It's an advertisement for the circus. It gives the list of all the different villages where they are opening and the dates.' Kitty studied the poster.

'Don't tell me you would like to go to the circus?' Matt asked. He knew the elephant had fascinated her. However, she'd been less enthusiastic about the snakes and the monkey.

'No, well, yes, a trip to the circus might be nice. I've never seen one and we are on holiday. They seem to have gone to a village called Barnsover,' Kitty said.

The tea room owner had come out to collect their empty glasses. ''Tis about ten miles away, Barnsover, if you'm thinking of following after the circus.'

'Oh, thank you.' Kitty smiled her thanks at the woman who promptly disappeared back inside.

Matt could see the cogs turning inside his wife's head. 'This visit to the circus. It wouldn't just be to see Bluebelle again?'

Kitty rested her hand on the crook of his arm. 'I am very fond of Bluebelle, but maybe, just maybe, her keeper may have noticed something that afternoon while he was minding her. He's the one person on the field who would have had sight of the fortune teller's booth.'

Matt nodded. 'And possibly someone approaching the refreshment stand from the direction of the gardener's cottage.'

They started to walk back towards the Dower House.

'So, a visit to the circus might be in order? It said the performance starts at six. I'm sure your aunt will understand if we say we won't be in for dinner. I can easily drive us to Barnsover if it's not far.'

Kitty looked at him with a definite gleam in her eyes.

'Very well. If nothing else, you will have seen a circus at last,' Matt agreed with a laugh.

Aunt Effie readily acquiesced to ask her cook to keep them a supper plate for after their return from Barnsover.

'It's a much larger village than Quixshotte, more of a small market town really. The circus always has the same field, on the main road going in. You can't miss it.'

She also happily agreed that Bertie could stay with her for the afternoon since Kitty was unsure if dogs would be permitted. She also thought Bertie would dislike the noise and heat of the marquee. He would also prefer Aunt Effie's generosity when it came to dispensing tasty treats.

Matt looked up the route, while Kitty tidied her hair and re-pinned her hat ready to drive across the Dales after lunch.

'It seems a straightforward route.' Matt showed her the map. They decided it would be best to try and speak to the man who had been looking after the elephant before the performance.

'It may be quieter and less crowded,' Kitty said as she

opened her car door and climbed in.

'I still think that you're keen on the elephant,' Matt teased as he took his place beside her.

'So long as I don't have to deal with the snakes.' Kitty gave a mock shudder as she started the car and they set off along the quiet country roads.

The road to Barnsover took them through picturesque countryside. Deep valleys lined with grey drystone walls were dotted with sheep. Cow parsley frothed at the edge of the verges; the white flowers interspersed with splashes of red from the wild poppies. The green of the fields was fading to a gentle yellow after the prolonged spell of hot weather.

Matt was in charge of navigation and with the roof down and a warm breeze brushing their faces it was a delightful way to spend an afternoon.

'I can see the top of the marquee,' Matt said as they crested the top of a hill past a white painted fingerpost that said Barnsover ¼ mile.

Kitty saw he was right. The huge white tent with red and yellow pennant flags was right ahead of them, just as Aunt Effie had said. They briefly lost sight of the circus as the road dropped down but picked it up again as they drew closer to the field.

'I think you can turn in at the gate, Kitty. There seems to be an area for parking over there.' Matt indicated with the map where she could leave her car. They bumped their way through the open gate and across the grass to the designated spot.

Kitty turned off her engine and looked around with interest. The big top was in the centre of the field and seemed enormous now they were up close to it. Near the entrance to the tent was a small red and yellow painted booth with a sign saying tickets and programmes. Opposite the ticket booth was a small array of stalls all set up to sell items designed to attract the public, ice cream, doughnuts, sweets and small stuffed animal toys.

The air smelled of food and the faint scent of animals. At the far side of the field under a stand of trees were the brightly painted wagons which housed the performers and their families.

'There's your friend.' Matt nudged Kitty's elbow and she saw the elephant was secured in the shade near the wagons, much as she had been at the fair. A variety of large metal cages on wheels were also parked in the shade. Kitty wondered what other acts were part of the circus. The poster at the tea room had mentioned tightrope walkers, clowns and an escapologist.

There were people milling about near the wagons, so Kitty tucked her hand in the crook of Matt's arm, and they headed towards the collection of caravans. As they drew closer to the enclave a large dog tied to a rope near to the closest wagon started to bark.

The sound alerted a tall, thin man with sharp eyes who appeared from inside the wagon. 'The performance starts at six. Tickets are on sale from five thirty onwards,' he said stepping into their path.

'Thank you, sir, we shall indeed purchase tickets for tonight. My wife is very much looking forward to seeing the show. We saw your magnificent elephant on Saturday at the fair at Quixshotte Hall,' Matt said.

A wary expression crossed the man's face. 'Yes, some of our artistes were there on Saturday,' he said.

Matt produced his business card and handed it to the man. 'Colonel Brothers has asked us to look into the death of Miss Crowther on his behalf. I'm sure you have heard there was a murder that afternoon in the fortune telling booth.'

The man took the card with an air of reluctance. 'I did hear about that, yes. Not that it had anything to do with us.'

'No, I'm sure no one would ever think that anyone connected with such a reputable circus could possibly be involved,' Kitty assured him quickly.

The man seemed slightly mollified by her assurance. 'I should hope not,' he said.

'On the afternoon of the murder, Bluebelle's keeper was the one person on the site who could have seen down the field towards Miss Crowther's tent, as well as the gardeners' shed where the poison was kept. It would help immensely if we could speak to him for just a moment,' Kitty said.

The man looked at her and Matt, then back at the card as if weighing up if he should allow them to go ahead. Kitty's heart thumped and she held her breath.

'You can ask him, but he had enough to do keeping them perishing kids away from our Bluebelle.'

Kitty released her breath. 'Thank you, we do appreciate it.'

'Jimmi!' The man turned and shouted in the direction of the wagon closest to where the elephant was chained up. 'Jimmi Choudhury.'

A moment later, a man appeared who Kitty recognised as the person who had been in charge of the elephant at the fair. He looked quite different out of his uniform, now dressed in ordinary working men's clothes with a flat cap low on his brow.

'This lady and gentleman want to ask you about the fair on Saturday when that woman was murdered.' The first man passed Matt's card to Jimmi Choudhury, the elephant keeper.

Jimmi took the card carefully and glanced briefly at it before giving it back to the other man. 'You'm not from the police then?' he asked.

'No, my husband, Captain Bryant, and I are private investigators employed by Colonel Brothers who organised Saturday's event.' Kitty suspected from the way the man had looked at the card and his subsequent question that he couldn't read.

Jimmi licked his lips nervously and looked back to the first man as if seeking reassurance that he could speak to them.

Kitty saw the taller man give a barely perceptible nod.

Their conversation had drawn the attention of a small knot of circus folk who stood silently at a distance watching them.

'How can I help? I was busy all day looking after Bluebelle so I didn't have time for much else,' Jimmi said.

Kitty gave what she hoped was a reassuringly confident smile. 'Your elephant is beautiful, and we saw you were doing a splendid job with her on Saturday.'

Jimmi visibly perked up at Kitty's admiration for his animal. 'Bluebelle is my life, she is.'

'It's true. He'd do anything for that elephant,' the other man said.

'When we went back to the field yesterday, we realised that the only place that had any view of the gardeners' shed, where the poison was kept, as well as the fortune teller's booth was the spot where Bluebelle was tethered,' Matt said.

Jimmi shifted his weight from one foot to the other as if he wanted to bolt from the conversation. 'Like I said, I was busy with Bluebelle. There was a lot of people, and the kids was bothering her. Good-natured she is but it's a lot to ask of her being up close for too long like that.'

'We know the fair was very busy and you were looking after your elephant, but please take a minute to think if you saw anyone at all on the grassland coming from the side of the field away from the stalls,' Kitty said.

Jimmi fidgeted and looked back to the taller man again. 'I don't know.'

Kitty could see he was prevaricating. She glanced at Matt before trying again. 'Please, Jimmi, this could be very important.'

The man scratched the side of his head, knocking his cap slightly off-kilter. 'I weren't looking that way very much. I had to keep watching the kids. Some of them threw pebbles at my Bluebelle.'

'But you did see someone?' Kitty asked.

'I saw a man walking that way, quick like. An older man, tall he was, dressed in dark clothes. I didn't take much notice.'

Kitty looked at Matt. The description could fit any number of people. However, an older man could rule out Jamie and Frank. That's if this mystery man were the only person to have approached the fair from that direction.

'And looking down the field, towards the booth? I know you were looking that way more often because that's where the crowd were standing behind the ropes.' Kitty pressed on with her questions.

The man shrugged. 'There were lots of people, miss. The fortune telling were popular.'

'But at one point during the afternoon, Miss Crowther took a break and you must have seen that no one entered the tent?' Matt said.

Jimmi fidgeted with the arms of his jacket. Kitty was aware that the small crowd of circus onlookers had grown larger the longer their conversation had gone on.

'It was quieter round by her booth after a certain point, yes. I noticed she went out and put up a sign and people stopped coming. I remember that as it made me fancy a cup of tea then too. The colonel, he was one as went in during the afternoon, just after she put out her sign. I saw him in them funny clothes he had on. Then there was lady in a big hat, before lunch she went in and was inside for a bit. I didn't get a good look at her because I had to see to Bluebelle. Then I saw you two with a dog and then a man in a light jacket.' Jimmi looked quite pleased with himself as he recounted the last part. He had obviously suddenly recalled where he had seen them before.

'Did you see anyone enter the booth carrying a cup?' Kitty asked.

Jimmi shook his head. 'No, miss. Only Miss Crowther, the lady that was killed. It had to be her because of the turban and the cloak. She carried her own cup.'

CHAPTER TWELVE

A ripple of excitement ran through Kitty. No one else had mentioned seeing Miss Crowther herself outside the booth. If she had fetched her own cup of tea, then the likelihood that it had been tampered with at the stall surely had to be so much higher. Unless someone had entered her tent later and Jimmi hadn't seen them.

'You saw Miss Crowther carrying a cup of tea? In her turban and cloak?' Kitty repeated the question to be certain she had understood Jimmi correctly.

'That's what I said, miss. She was a tall lady and the jewel holding the feather in the top of her turban flashed as she were walking back to the booth, and it caught my eye.' Jimmi fidgeted again, clearly anxious for the conversation to be over.

A loud roar sounded unexpectedly from the cages near the wagons.

'Thank you, Jimmi, you've been most helpful. The police may wish to speak to you about this as it's important. Do you know what time this would have been?' Kitty asked, wondering which animal had made the noise.

'I don't have a watch. It was after people had stopped going in the booth though. A bit before the band started up,' the man said.

Matt joined her in thanking Jimmi and the tall man for their time. 'We'll be back in an hour or so to buy our tickets.' He shook hands with both men.

'I'll have a couple put by for you at the box office. Front row,' the tall man said.

'That's most kind of you, sir. We look forward to seeing the show,' Matt replied.

Kitty took Matt's arm once more as they walked back across the field towards her car.

'Let's go into Barnsover, we may be able to find a tea room for an hour before we come back to see the performance,' Matt suggested.

Kitty acquiesced and following Matt's guidance with the map, drove the short distance into the centre of Barnsover which turned out to be a bustling place. She found a space to park near the large stone cross which marked the centre of the town and where the small market was just starting to pack up their stalls for the day.

'There's a nice-looking tea room over there.' Matt indicated a smart frontage shaded with a gold and white striped canopy. Pots of pink geraniums stood on either side of the open door and the interior looked cool and inviting.

After the uniformed waitress had taken their order, Kitty drew off her white cotton gloves and sighed.

'I thought we were trying to find evidence of the colonel and Mrs Brothers' innocence but now, well, everything seems much more complicated.'

Matt reached across the table to squeeze her hand. 'I know, it does, doesn't it? Still, Jimmi does seem to have confirmed what the colonel and Hilda have already told us.'

'I never really considered that Miss Crowther could have collected her tea herself. I wonder that Ruth or anyone else didn't notice her. As that man, Jimmi said, she was very distinctive in that outfit.' *How had the poison ended up in that cup?* Kitty was growing more and more baffled by each piece of evidence they uncovered.

The waitress returned and set a tray of tea in front of them. Matt had also ordered them a cream bun each. Kitty suspected that he thought they had earned it after all their sleuthing.

'Then there was the older man Jimmi saw crossing back from the direction of the gardeners' shed. I suppose that could have been anyone, even the head gardener himself. Even so, I can't help wondering who it could have been and why they were there.' Kitty placed the metal tea strainer over the top of one of the china cups and poured the tea.

Matt nodded as he bit into his bun. He chewed and swallowed before speaking. 'Yes, at least it tells us that someone was over there that afternoon. It could have been the murderer, it may have been a witness. It's very irritating that he didn't see anyone enter Miss Crowther's tent who resembled the person he witnessed returning from the direction of the shed.'

A shiver danced along Kitty's spine as she added milk to their tea. 'I agree. Surely the colonel wouldn't have engaged us if he and Mrs Brothers were involved in Miss Crowther's death, would he?'

Matt's brow creased into a frown. 'I don't know. He might just want to know what kind of evidence was being gathered against him or Hilda. It could be a kind of insurance.'

This was something Kitty hadn't considered. 'It still comes down to a lack of motive, though, doesn't it? Inspector Woolley is right. Who hated Miss Crowther enough to want to poison her?'

Matt took a sip of his tea. 'Maybe not hate,' he said slowly. 'Perhaps Miss Crowther had discovered something about someone. Something they didn't want anyone else to discover.'

Kitty looked at him. 'The one thing everyone agrees upon is

that Miss Crowther was nosy. Her cottage was in a prime spot for seeing everything in the village. She was on lots of committees too. Although she claimed to have the sight, your aunt said she actually enjoyed fortune telling because she knew a lot about everyone in the village.'

Matt had the last bite of his cream bun while Kitty's mind raced.

'Are we looking for secrets then? Secrets that someone would kill to keep?' she asked.

'I think that has to be the motive. Miss Crowther wasn't wealthy, no one has mentioned money and I'm sure they would have done so by now. She had her cottage which seems to have been left to her cousin, but money doesn't seem to be a factor in her murder. Whoever killed her didn't take any of her silver jewellery.' Matt dabbed the corners of his mouth with the pale-pink napkin.

'And although Miss Crowther appears to have had unrequited crushes on various gentlemen there has been no serious talk of a suitor,' Kitty mused.

As she finished her tea and cream bun, her mind was still considering everything they had learned.

'First thing tomorrow we must call on Inspector Woolley and tell him what we have discovered today. He will probably wish to speak to Jimmi himself,' Matt said as they left the tea room and returned to Kitty's car.

'I'm sure he will,' Kitty said as she started her car ready to drive back to the circus. 'I hope Jimmi will be happy to talk to him.'

'Yes, he was rather cagey, but sometimes show people have a difficult relationship with the police,' Matt agreed.

The road was busier as they drove back to the big top. More vehicles, both motorised and horse drawn, were travelling in the same direction. As they got closer to the field, they saw more people approaching on foot too.

Kitty drove carefully through the gate and found a place to park, near where she had stopped before. Her heart raced with excitement as she and Matt joined the queue for tickets from the box office. It would be her first visit to a circus. A man in black and white striped trousers wearing a bowler hat walked amongst the crowd on stilts, teetering above their heads as he shouted through a megaphone.

'Roll up, roll up, see the greatest show on earth, ladies and gentlemen, boys and girls. See the amazing Flying Cordinis defy gravity. Meet Bluebelle the elephant. Be amazed by the daring expertise of Signor Denone and his lions.'

Kitty realised that must have been the lions she had heard roaring earlier and she hoped they were safely locked inside a cage. Two clowns dressed in lurid clothes with their faces painted ran in and out of the ticket queue. They squirted water at the waiting children from large flowers on the lapels of their bright jackets causing squeals and ripples of merriment.

The smell of toffee and fried foods filled the air and there was a buzz of excitement.

'Two tickets, front row have been put aside for you, sir. Best seats in the house.' The booth attendant had evidently been told to look out for them and the tall man had kept his word. Kitty wasn't too sure about being so close to lions and she hoped the snakes and the monkey wouldn't come very close to her either.

Matt thanked the man and paid him before they made their way inside the huge marquee. Kitty was relieved to see that inside the sawdust strewn centre there was indeed a caged area which she assumed must be for the lions.

The seating area they had been allocated was right at the front on wooden chairs. All around the interior of the circular marquee were tiered wooden bench seats. The ones at the back, closest to the canvas walls of the marquee were quite high up.

The seats were filling rapidly and a smartly dressed gentleman accompanied by a woman in a very splendid hat and two young children joined them in the front row. As the man sat down, Kitty saw he was wearing an ornate gold chain and guessed he was probably the mayor of Barnsover.

There was a buzz of excited chatter inside the marquee and various circus staff moved amongst the crowd selling programmes and refreshments. Matt bought them a programme.

'A souvenir. You can show Alice and your grandmother when we go home,' he said.

The tent filled up rapidly and after a few minutes there was a drumroll and the crowd hushed.

'Ladies and gentlemen, boys and girls, Big Top Circus welcomes you to the greatest show on earth!' The tall man they had met earlier was in the centre of the ring, resplendent in a red coat with gold brocade and a shiny black top hat, a whip in his hand.

The crowd burst into enthusiastic applause as behind him the various performers appeared in their costumes, glittering and sparkling. Bluebelle was dressed in her red and gold brocade, as was Jimmi. The clowns cavorted about, spraying the children with more drops of water causing a chorus of excited squeals.

The ring emptied and the ringmaster announced the first act, Mystero and his monkey. Kitty watched as the man performed a series of magic tricks aided by his animal assistant. This was swiftly followed by the snake charmer who paraded about the edge of the ring showing his very large snake to the audience. Kitty recoiled when he came close to them but the mayor, keen to impress his children and perform his civic duty, gingerly stroked it.

After the snakes, the ringmaster announced his own act, the lions. Kitty watched in trepidation as the man handed his hat and coat to a glamorous young lady and entered the cage where the lions sat on gaily painted drums.

There was a chorus of oohs and ahhs from the audience as the ringmaster put the animals through their paces, with great showmanship and whip cracking. The act culminated with him placing his head in one of the lion's open jaws.

'Oh my goodness.' Kitty pressed her hand firmly on Matt's arm.

'Don't worry, darling, it's Bluebelle, your favourite next,' Matt reassured her and she relaxed back from the edge of her seat.

Her spirits rose as Jimmi and Bluebelle made their way back into the ring. The elephant performed various balancing tricks and made the children laugh at some of her naughty antics. She had clearly been trained to tap Jimmi on the shoulder with her trunk and then pretend to be looking the other way.

As he walked the elephant around the edge of the ring, Bluebelle stopped and took Matt's hat from his head, placing it on top of her own head. This made the audience roar with laughter as Jimmi pretended to remonstrate with Bluebelle until she lifted the stolen hat and replaced it on Matt's head once more.

Kitty applauded as loudly as anyone, entranced by the elephant's cleverness.

'Find me after the show. I remembered something else I need to tell you,' Jimmi murmured under the cover of the applause as he led his animal away.

There was little time to wonder what he could have meant as the escapologist was introduced. Kitty's heart was in her mouth when the man was fastened into a straitjacket and hoisted high above the ring with the rope set alight.

'Oh, this is much more stressful than I could ever have imagined,' Kitty said, sighing with relief as the man made good his escape before the rope burned through.

Comic relief followed with the clowns capering about the

ring making the crowd roar with laughter at their slapstick routines.

The final act was the Flying Cordinis, a family act of high-wire walkers and acrobats that had Kitty holding her breath as they flew through the air high above her head, being expertly caught and flipped by various members of the act.

The circus ended with all the performers returning to the ring to take their bows, before the audience started to make their way out of the marquee.

'Well, darling, did you enjoy your first trip to the circus?' Matt asked as he took Kitty's hand and they prepared to leave.

'It was quite something. Alice would have loved it, and Dolly,' Kitty said.

'Now we have to go and find Jimmi and see what it is that he has suddenly remembered,' Matt said.

Dusk had fallen while they had been watching the show and the light had faded. The sky had turned violet with streaks of pink and orange. The birds in the hedgerows surrounding the circus field were tweeting and twittering as they prepared to settle in their nests.

There were streams of people and various vehicles leaving through the gate. Kitty guessed that the very shiny, expensive-looking car which glided past belonged to the mayor. The peaked cap chauffeur behind the wheel obviously signified someone of importance was inside.

Matt slipped his arm around her waist and steered her out of the crowd towards the wagons on the far side of the field. She could see a fire had been lit there now and oil lamps hung in the wagon windows, spilling rich yellow light into the dusk.

'I hope the lions are all safely back in their cages,' Kitty said as they walked across the grass.

'I'm sure they are. The circus seems to take very good care of all their animals,' Matt assured her.

To her relief no roars greeted them this time as they drew

nearer to the spot where Bluebelle stood contentedly eating her supper in the deepening shadows.

'Where is Jimmi?' Matt looked around for the elephant keeper.

'He's not likely to be far away from Bluebelle.' Kitty looked around, trying to see if she could spot Jimmi's slight figure amongst the other circus folk near the brazier.

They reached the tree where the elephant was shackled without any sign of the animal's faithful keeper. Kitty peered into the darkness beside the wagons which were furthest away. No bright lights were at their windows and that area was quiet.

'Matt! I heard something, over there.' Kitty clutched at her husband's arm and listened again. She was certain that she had heard something from that direction. 'I'm going to look.'

'Kitty, wait.' Matt overtook her as she hurried forward. The sound was louder now she was closer to the caravans. Somebody, or something was groaning.

Matt halted suddenly and stooped over a dark shape lying on the ground. 'I think it's Jimmi, he's been hurt.' Matt swiftly pulled out his cigarette lighter and by the light of the flame Kitty could see blood trickling down the elephant keeper's forehead.

'Oh no. I'll fetch help.' Kitty hurried back towards the wagons to alert the performers. Her heart thudded as she stumbled over the rough ground to a group surrounding a fire in a brazier.

As soon as she explained what had happened, a band of men raced back to where Matt was crouched over Jimmy.

Kitty made to follow but someone called out to her. 'Here, my love, you come sit here.' An older lady ushered her to a vacant spot on a wooden bench near the fire and a tin mug of something was pressed into her hand.

Kitty suddenly realised that her legs were shaking, and she accepted the seat gratefully. She hoped that Jimmi would be all right. It looked to her as if someone had been waiting for him under the cover of darkness and had attacked.

There was a hubbub of chatter in various languages all around her and more lamps were carried out from the wagons. A moment later the men reappeared along with Matt carrying Jimmi on a makeshift stretcher. They set him down carefully in the light near the fire and the women rushed forward with water and cloths to tend to him.

Matt came to sit beside Kitty. 'He's all right, I think. It looks as if he's been hit over the head by someone lurking near his wagon.'

Kitty breathed a sigh of relief. 'Poor man. Thank goodness he's all right though, I really thought we were too late.' Tears prickled her eyes, and she fumbled in her handbag for her handkerchief.

The ringmaster approached them, still clad in his shiny black boots and gold-braided coat. He looked worried. 'You came back to see Jimmi again?'

'Yes, he told us he'd remembered something when we were in the marquee. He asked us to meet him after the show. When we got here, we found him on the floor over there.' Kitty looked in the direction of Jimmi's wagon.

The ringmaster frowned. 'Whatever he thought of could have killed him. Did anyone follow you here? Or know you were coming tonight?'

Kitty shook her head. 'No, the lady in the café in Quixshotte and Matt's aunt knew, but they only thought we were coming to see the show.'

Jimmi was now being propped up on a pile of cushions and the lady who had tended to Kitty was forcing him to sip something. Kitty sniffed her own mug and guessed it was brandy.

'We need to talk to him, and I think Inspector Woolley who is investigating Miss Crowther's murder will also need to be involved.' Matt's gaze met that of the ringmaster.

'Our people are wary of the police,' the man said.

'I appreciate that, but Jimmi was fortunate not to be killed. At the very least he will have a bad head for a few days, I think.' Matt looked to where the elephant keeper was being fussed over by a group of performers.

Kitty could see two of the Flying Cordinis, wearing cloaks over their glittering costumes, tending to the injured man. She saw him murmur something to one of the women and she looked towards Kitty and Matt.

'Jimmi wants to speak with you,' the girl said as she approached the fire. She had a faint accent as she spoke. Possibly Italian, Kitty thought. She had a good ear from looking after guests at the Dolphin.

Kitty set down her untouched mug of brandy and went with Matt to see the injured man. Close up in the lamplight she could see the gash on his scalp, the blood already drying in his thinning hair. The skin surrounding the cut was raised and swollen and starting to bruise.

'What happened?' Matt asked.

'I had seen to Bluebelle and was on my way to the wagon to change and light the lamps. Somebody was waiting in the shadows, a man. I didn't see his face. The next thing I knew I was on the floor with my head split open.' Jimmi flinched as he spoke. The effort of talking clearly painful.

'And you didn't see anything to indicate who the man may have been? He didn't speak?' Kitty asked.

Jimmi went as if to shake his head and stopped, screwing up his face as the movement hurt him. 'No, nothing. Just a black shape out of nowhere. I never even had time to react.'

There was a ripple of anger and concern from the performers as Jimmi spoke.

'You said you had remembered something earlier, something important about Saturday?' Kitty asked as Jimmi closed his eyes.

CHAPTER THIRTEEN

Kitty waited anxiously for Jimmi to answer her question, while the ringmaster asked some of the circus members to step back, giving them more space.

'The lady that was killed at the fair, that Miss Crowther. I knew her brother. It came to me after I spoke to you that I hadn't said anything to anyone. It had been at the back of my mind, bothering me, ever since it happened,' Jimmi said.

'Kenneth Crowther? He was killed in India in an accident some years ago. She doted on him. The back room at her cottage was kept as a virtual shrine.' Kitty was surprised.

'That's because she didn't know what he did. They didn't tell her.' Jimmi closed his eyes again. It was clear the effort of telling the story was taxing his strength.

Kitty looked at Matt, feeling badly for questioning Jimmy. She hoped that someone had sent for a doctor.

'Do you know what happened to Kenneth Crowther?' Kitty asked.

'I was born in India and lived there for many years. Kenneth hanged himself while waiting to be court martialled. I was one of the guards watching him. He'd attacked a woman in the town while he was drunk.' Jimmi's voice was faint. 'I didn't realise until Miss Crowther said her brother had died in India who she was. She talked to me about India and Kenneth when I was at the fair with Bluebelle.'

'I take it you didn't tell her about any of this, the court martial or taking his own life?' Matt frowned as he asked the question.

Kitty wondered how any of this could fit into Miss Crowther's murder or why Jimmi had been attacked.

'No, nothing. Like you said, she loved her brother, I could tell from how she spoke. I just said as I'd met him out there.' Jimmi licked his lips and Matt offered the man another sip of brandy from the mug that was thrust towards him by one of the Flying Cordinis.

Jimmi's eyelids closed once more, and Kitty wondered if this was the end of the story or if he was simply too exhausted to say anything more. Silence fell for a moment then Jimmi made a sudden grab for Matt's sleeve to pull him closer. 'Colonel Brothers, ask him about Kenneth Crowther. He was there.' Jimmi released Matt's arm and fell back on his cushions, his energy now completely spent.

There was a bustle of conversation, the crowd parted and a man came hurrying towards them carrying a medical bag.

'The doctor is here.' The ringmaster reappeared at Kitty's side and she and Matt stepped away to allow Jimmi to be looked after.

'We should go and let Jimmi get some rest. We'll let Inspector Woolley know what's happened here tonight,' Matt said to the ringmaster.

'We'll make sure Jimmi is safe, one of the Cordini family will stay with him.' The ringmaster glanced back to where the doctor was examining the prone body of the elephant keeper. 'Jimmi is a former soldier, like many. He was born in India and he and Bluebelle joined us from another circus in Germany. I don't know what his connection is fully with Colonel Brothers or the woman who was killed. I dealt with the negotiations for our people to appear at the fair. Jimmi didn't mention that he knew the colonel until after I'd agreed the deal and he saw him at the Hall when we were setting up.'

Matt nodded. 'Did the colonel mention to you anything about knowing Jimmi at all?'

The ringmaster shook his head. 'I don't know if they ever met. Jimmi just saw him at a distance and recognised his name. That's what he told me. Said the colonel had been in charge of the brigade in Kashmir.'

'A brigade is around six thousand men. I doubt the colonel would have known Jimmi personally.' The frown which had been creasing Matt's forehead deepened.

'I do hope Jimmi makes a good recovery,' Kitty said. She liked the elephant keeper and was grateful to the man for trying to tell them what he knew, despite being attacked.

They bade farewell to the ringmaster and set off across the field towards Kitty's car. The area had grown dark now and her car stood alone next to what she presumed must be the doctor's motor. All of the other vehicles had departed, the stalls had closed, and the crowd had long gone back to their homes.

'Poor Jimmi,' Kitty said as she opened her car door and took her place behind the wheel.

'I think he was lucky he wasn't killed. That was no doubt his assailant's intention,' Matt said as he climbed into the passenger seat next to her.

'I rather fear that instead of proving the colonel's innocence we seem to be uncovering more things which could incriminate him.' Kitty started her car engine and turned on her headlamps ready to drive out through the gate onto the road.

'I wonder who attacked Jimmi tonight and why? It has to be connected to Miss Crowther's death in some way, but how?' Matt said as Kitty eased her car into the dark lane.

'Well, we worked out that Jimmi was probably the only person on Saturday with a view towards the gardeners' shed and clear down the field to the fortune telling booth. Perhaps someone else realised that too and decided to ensure that Jimmi wouldn't be able to tell anyone if he did see someone where they shouldn't have been?' Kitty suggested.

'It's a possibility,' Matt agreed.

Kitty was forced to put the puzzle of Jimmi's attacker to the back of her mind while she concentrated on finding her way back to the Dower House along the dark country roads. Her headlamps illuminated a narrow corridor between the hedgerows and drystone walls with moths dancing crazily in the beams of light.

She was relieved when she reached a stretch of road she recognised, and they entered Quixshotte village.

'Stop here at the pub,' Matt requested. 'I'll go inside and see if Inspector Woolley is available.'

Kitty pulled her car to a halt outside the now closed tea shop on the village green. Light spilled from the open leaded-windows of the public house and the sounds of laughter and conversation accompanied it. Matt opened the car door. 'I won't be long.'

The night air was still warm, and Kitty switched off her car engine while she waited, taking care to turn on her parking lamps. She had no desire to be fined for having an unlit vehicle.

The lights were on inside the vicarage, and she hoped that Ruth had enjoyed her outing with Jamie. Lilith had certainly been none too pleased about her stepdaughter's defection. Perhaps she had been forced to cancel her own plans to take the ladies' Bible class.

Suddenly, she saw the gate to the vicarage garden open and Frank Drummond step out. He glanced back at the house and closed the gate quietly. It seemed to Kitty that he was hoping not to be seen and she wondered where he was going.

Frank walked away quickly in the direction of the Dower House and Quixshotte Hall. Kitty wasn't sure what other buildings lay along the lane in that direction. She knew of a couple of farms and some small cottages but where else Frank might be headed, she had no idea. It seemed most likely that he planned to meet Jamie Martin, but he clearly didn't seem to want any of the occupants of the vicarage to see him, judging by the way he had furtively ducked under the hedge.

'Very curious, now what are you up to, I wonder?' Kitty murmured to herself.

Miss Crowther's cottage was in darkness, and the car that had been outside earlier had gone. Her cousin must have departed for the day. Kitty realised that if Miss Crowther had been upstairs in her house, she would have seen Frank leaving the vicarage in this manner. *Had he done this before?* Would Miss Crowther have dropped hints to Frank about what she knew? Or challenged him?

Deep in thought, she didn't notice Matt return until he opened her passenger door and got back into his seat.

'Gracious, you made me jump.' Kitty pressed a hand to her heart, startled by his sudden appearance.

'Sorry, darling. I've seen Inspector Woolley and updated him. He's going to go and see Jimmi tomorrow to take a statement.' He gave her a curious look. 'What's wrong?'

'Nothing. Well, I just watched young Frank Drummond sneak out of the vicarage. He obviously didn't wish to be noticed.' Kitty started her car and switched on her headlamps once more. 'Keep your eyes peeled, he set off towards Quixshotte Hall.'

The drive back to the Dower House only took a couple of minutes but there was no sign of the vicar's son along their route.

'He must have either gone elsewhere or knows some shortcuts through the woods to reach the Hall, if that was his destination,' Matt said as Kitty drew to a halt back at the house.

'I suppose so. I was wondering if Miss Crowther often noticed him sneaking out. She had a good view of things from her cottage,' Kitty mused as she switched everything off.

Matt crossed around the nose of the car to open Kitty's door. 'That's a very good point. She had a bird's-eye view all over the village from her house.'

* * *

Matt's stomach growled as he followed Kitty inside the Dower House. He hoped his aunt had remembered to ask her staff to save them a cold plate for their supper. The cream bun they had eaten in Barnsover before the circus performance seemed a long time ago.

His aunt was seated in the drawing room listening to a play on the radio when they entered. Bertie was sprawled contentedly at her feet.

'Hello, darlings, did you have a lovely time? I expect it was quite thrilling seeing the circus acts.' Aunt Effie sat up expectantly in her armchair as Bertie bounded up to greet them wagging his tail happily.

'Oh yes, it was very exciting. I had my heart in my mouth several times,' Kitty assured her.

'Well go along to the dining room and have your supper. Then you can come back and tell me all about it,' his aunt said.

One of the maids was just setting two places at the end of the long mahogany table as Matt and Kitty entered the dining room accompanied by the ever-hopeful Bertie.

'This looks marvellous. I am quite famished.' Kitty looked appreciatively at her plate as Matt drew out her chair for her to take her seat.

'Me too,' Matt agreed.

By mutual agreement they requested beer to accompany their meal from the maid and settled down to their supper.

'It's certainly been a most eventful day,' Kitty said as she applied butter lavishly to a thick slice of crusty white bread.

'Yes. Not exactly the restful holiday we were expecting.' Matt smiled apologetically at her.

The incident at the circus had left him feeling quite out of sorts. Perhaps because it revived memories of the attack he had sustained during their last case. He helped himself to pickles and wondered what Kitty was thinking. He could tell from her expression that she had something on her mind.

'Matt, do you think we should continue to work for Colonel Brothers?' she asked eventually when her plate was almost empty.

He looked quizzically at her.

'It's just that we know now that he went into the fortune teller's booth. Jimmi saw him and the colonel did admit it himself. Then there is this story about Miss Crowther's brother. He would have known about the court martial surely? And why Kenneth Crowther had been charged. Suppose Miss Crowther discovered he had been involved? She could have blamed him for her brother's death and tried to make trouble.' Kitty patted her lips with a napkin before picking up her drink.

'I could see that if Miss Crowther discovered his involvement after all this time, she might be angry with the colonel, but if anything, it would give her a reason to attack him, not the other way around.' Matt rested his cutlery down on his plate.

Kitty frowned. 'She may have threatened to expose him. To tell the world he was responsible for Kenneth's death. It would certainly make things very awkward socially for the family. He told us mud sticks.'

'But enough for him to kill her?' Matt queried.

'What if he attacked Jimmi to silence the one other person who knew the truth about Kenneth Crowther? The colonel might have realised that Jimmi was the only person who could have given Miss Crowther any information,' Kitty said.

Matt shook his head. 'It doesn't work. Jimmi swears he didn't tell Miss Crowther about what actually happened to her brother, and it seems she was killed before she could really ask any questions of the colonel.'

The maid had left them an apple pie and a jug of cream on the sideboard. Kitty cleared their plates and served them both dessert.

'That brings us back to someone realising that Jimmi may have noticed something from his position on the field with Blue-belle.' Kitty picked up her spoon.

'It would seem that way to me. Darling, if working for the colonel bothers you, we can stop all our involvement in the case. Leave it all to Inspector Woolley. He seems a sound enough chap.' Matt looked across the table at his wife.

She smiled. 'No, I think we're in too deep to be satisfied with abandoning ship at this point. I think we were on the right line earlier today when we said there were a lot of secrets hidden in this village. One of those secrets is the reason why Miss Crowther was killed and why Jimmi was attacked. We just need to find out what.'

Matt laughed. 'That's my girl.'

'I take it that we shall be speaking to the colonel again tomorrow?' Kitty asked.

'We need to find out what he knew of Kenneth Crowther's case and if Miss Crowther ever approached him about her brother. After all, we know that Jimmi says he didn't tell her, but what if she knew already?' It was something Matt had been considering while he ate his apple pie.

'It would be helpful too if the colonel had an alibi for when Jimmi was attacked,' Kitty said.

.   .   .

They finished their supper and returned to the drawing room where the radio play was just finishing. Bertie curled himself up near the open French windows. Aunt Effie switched the wireless off as they sat down. Kitty described the events of the day, leaving his aunt aghast with the news of the attack on Bluebelle's keeper.

'So, Kenneth Crowther did take his own life? How dreadful! I am glad poor Emily Crowther did not discover any of this. She adored her brother and would have been devastated.' Aunt Effie shook her head sadly. 'I shall of course keep all of this to myself. And you say Colonel Brothers may have known all of this? All this time and never breathing a word, goodness me.'

They stayed with Aunt Effie for a while, mulling over the case and the characters of those involved. Kitty told Aunt Effie about seeing Frank Drummond sneaking out of the vicarage.

'I expect he went through the woods to the Hall. There is a path you know that goes around the back to the trade door. Up to no good with Jamie no doubt. You know what boys can be like,' Aunt Effie remarked drily.

'Perhaps, at least Ruth escaped for the day thanks to Jamie,' Kitty said. 'Her stepmother and her father seem to already be assuming that Ruth will take on Miss Crowther's role in the community.'

Aunt Effie's brows rose at this. 'Oh dear, poor Ruth. Still, she was always quite feisty as a girl, she may not be as compliant as they think. Perhaps Lilith may be forced to participate more in the parish duties now.'

Matt sat and listened to Kitty and his aunt debating the matter. He wished he could shake the pressing sense of foreboding that had been gradually enveloping him ever since they had left the circus.

He resolved to ensure that his bedroom door was locked, and that Kitty had the key. He knew all too well from past experience that when these feelings occurred, a bad night almost always followed, and he had no wish to upset the household. The trauma of the battlefield could be forgotten or held at bay during the day but night-time was a different matter.

It was the reason he and Kitty had separate rooms. He had been known to destroy items in his room or to go walking about the house during those terrible, vivid dreams. Along with the physical injuries to his shoulder and chest, the mental scars were also still present. Memories of men and horses suffocating in the thick mud of collapsed trenches and the horror of gunfire and explosions. He could only hope that the night would pass swiftly, and he would feel better again with the dawn.

CHAPTER FOURTEEN

Kitty woke early the next morning and unlocked the door that linked her room to Matt's. He had given her the keys to his room when they had retired for the evening. She tapped quietly and opened the door a crack to peer inside. Matt was still asleep in the oak framed bed. His sheets lay in a tangled heap half on the floor, his sleeping position speaking of a disturbed night. He had put away most of his belongings when he had gone to bed, so the room appeared to have escaped any serious destruction.

Satisfied that all was well, she left him to rest and returned to her own room. Sometimes Matt walked in his sleep. The terrible memories of his time on the battlefield driving him to seek an escape. It was why he couldn't bear even now to be in enclosed spaces.

It was at times such as these that she missed the days when she had been a single woman living at the Dolphin Hotel. Alice would have brought her tea and toast and sat beside her on the bed for a natter. They would have discussed Miss Crowther's murder and the attack on Jimmi and her friend would have given her good advice. She wondered what Alice would make of the letter she had sent to her and smiled to herself as she pictured her friend reading it.

It was another bright and sunny day and the heat had already begun to creep into the house by the time Kitty was dressed and downstairs for breakfast. Matt joined her just as she was eating her bacon and eggs. She noticed faint smudges underneath his bright blue eyes but otherwise she was relieved to see that he appeared unscathed.

'Shall we call on the colonel after we have finished breakfast?' Kitty asked as he took a seat at the table.

'Why not? I hope Jimmi is feeling better this morning. I daresay Inspector Woolley will go out to the circus to talk to him first thing.' Matt helped himself to toast.

Kitty hoped the elephant keeper was recovering. She had been relieved when the doctor had arrived. She could only hope that whoever had attacked Jimmi wouldn't be tempted to try again. Although if word got around that the police had already spoken to him then his safety might be more assured.

'I thought that perhaps after we had seen the colonel that we might take a picnic and go and see some more of the countryside,' Matt suggested as he applied marmalade to his toast.

'Oh, yes. That would be nice.' Kitty's spirits rose at the suggestion. Despite the murder they were supposed to be on holiday after all. She knew that the events of yesterday had unsettled Matt and she had no wish to see his health become adversely affected by the case. A picnic sounded like a tip-top idea.

'I'll telephone the Hall and see if the colonel is available to see us if you speak to aunt Effie's staff to organise the picnic?' Matt suggested.

Kitty beamed. 'That sounds like a plan. Shall we try to leave here at ten? We can drive to the Hall and go straight off from there.'

Matt smiled back at her. 'Capital, make sure you ask the staff to pack Bertie's lunch too, or he'll try to have ours.'

The colonel said he would be happy to see them, and Aunt Effie's staff packed a generous wicker basket full of food and cold bottles of beer for their lunch. With Bertie safely seated in the back of Kitty's car and their picnic strapped to the boot, they set off for the Hall.

Kitty parked her car in the shade next to Jamie's shiny dark-green sports car and she, Matt and Bertie rang the bell at the side door they had used previously. A uniformed maid appeared and took them down the corridor to the colonel's study where they had met him the previous day.

The colonel was seated behind his desk studying a document. He rose as they entered and covered whatever he was reading discreetly with a blank sheet of paper before shaking their hands.

'Good morning, Captain Bryant, Mrs Bryant, have a seat.' He waved towards the empty chairs in front of his desk. 'What news? Has the inspector made an arrest yet?'

'I don't believe he has made any arrest just yet. However, we think he has some new lines of enquiry that he may be following up,' Matt replied cautiously as he took a seat next to Kitty.

'Oh?' The colonel looked expectantly in their direction.

'We wanted to see you this morning, sir, to update you on our progress. Our own investigation has unearthed a few more questions and Inspector Woolley may also be in touch with you to clarify a few points,' Matt said.

Kitty saw a wary expression flit across the colonel's craggy face. 'Well, anything I can do to help. What do you need to know?'

'We visited Big Top Circus over at Barnsover yesterday. We spoke to Jimmi, the elephant keeper.'

Kitty watched the colonel's face as Matt explained. The colonel remained impassive, but Kitty could see the wariness was still in his eyes.

'I don't follow you? Is he a suspect in Miss Crowther's death?' the colonel asked.

'We went to ask him if he had noticed anyone arriving on the field from the direction of the gardeners' shed or if he saw anyone entering the fortune telling booth after Miss Crowther closed for her tea break. He had a unique position on the field to observe both places,' Kitty said.

'Oh right, yes, I suppose he would from the copse, it's the highest point on the field.' Colonel Brothers appeared to relax slightly, his shoulders dropping.

'You told us that you entered Miss Crowther's booth to check that the money in the float had been corrected?' Kitty wanted to clarify the statement the colonel had made previously.

'Yes, that's right.' Colonel Brothers shifted his weight in his seat.

'Do you recall when you entered the fortune telling tent, sir?' Matt asked. The colonel had told them that he had visited at the start of the afternoon, but Jimmi had said it was later, when Miss Crowther was taking her break, which would put him in the frame for her murder.

'I, erm, well, I...' The colonel seemed to sense that they had picked up on the discrepancy in his statement.

'Please think carefully, sir.' There was a steely note in Matt's tone.

'Dash it all, it was a busy afternoon. I had a lot to do. I had set up the duck race and sales were going well. We were almost out of ducks when I recalled I had an extra box at the refreshment stall that had become mixed up with the crockery boxes. I went to fetch them and popped in to check up on Miss Crowther. Hilda had said there had been some bother over the float money. Hilda had been quite upset by it.' The colonel looked uncomfortable, and his complexion had pinked.

'And this was when Miss Crowther was on her break?' Kitty asked.

'Yes, the notice was on the front of the booth, and she was just putting the money tin out of sight. She was cross that no one had brought her tea to her even though the arrangement was that the stallholders collected their own refreshments. In fact, she was very short with me, quite angry about it. I think she felt that after having done so much to set up the day, it was the least they could have done. I said I would tell them at the stall. She was perfectly well and hadn't had any tea when I left her.' The colonel glared belligerently at them.

'What did you do then, sir?' Matt took up the questions.

'I carried on to the refreshments area. I told Lilith that Miss Crowther was on the warpath as she hadn't had her tea. Lilith said they were busy, and she would have to fend for herself. I felt I'd done all I could so I picked up the box of ducks and went back to the stream.'

'Can you recall who else was at the stall, sir?' A frisson of excitement ran through Kitty as she posed the question. The colonel could hold the key to who had opportunity to introduce the poison into Miss Crowther's cup.

The colonel's bushy eyebrows knotted together in thought. 'Well, Lilith obviously, Ruth, Frank, oh and Jamie was hanging around as usual. I told him to get back to my tiger. I believe Doctor Masters had appeared too. It was very busy.'

'Why did you say that you saw Miss Crowther in her booth earlier in the afternoon, sir?' Kitty was curious about why the colonel had lied in his previous statement.

'Did I? Well, perhaps I was confused. Like I said, it was a busy day. Hilda and I were run off our feet and I did cross paths with Miss Crowther a number of times as we were setting up,' the colonel blustered.

Kitty was forced to accept his response, even if she suspected that he was not being entirely truthful in his answers. She wondered which version of events he had given the inspector. Was Miss Crowther alive when he had entered the booth? Had they argued? Had he slipped poison into her tea? They would have to ask Lilith if she recalled the conversation and if Miss Crowther had collected her tea after the colonel had picked up the box of celluloid toy ducks.

But they knew from Jimmi that finally Miss Crowther had fetched her own tea. So someone on the stall had served her. Surely one of their witnesses must recall Miss Crowther or speaking to her at the refreshment table. Clad in her distinctive fortune telling robes and jewelled turban she would have stood out in the crowd. Why had no one mentioned seeing her?

'There is something else, sir,' Matt said as the colonel began to stir in his chair as if eager to see them out.

'Oh, what's that, then?' The colonel stilled and waited for Matt to continue.

'Jimmi Choudhury was attacked last night at the end of the circus performance. He had seen to Bluebelle and was returning to his wagon when an unknown person jumped him and hit him over the head with something heavy.' Matt, like Kitty, was once again watching the colonel closely.

'Good Lord. Is the man all right?' This time shock was evident in the colonel's voice and on his face.

'We believe so, yes. Although he was very lucky. It seemed clear that whoever attacked him intended to kill him,' Matt continued.

The colonel slumped in his seat as if devoid of the power of speech for a moment.

'Jimmi told us that he had been a member of your brigade,

sir, out in India. He had been one of the guards detailed to look after Kenneth Crowther.' Kitty held her breath as Matt spoke.

The colonel covered his face with his hands leaning his elbows on his desk. 'I never told Miss Crowther the truth about Kenneth.'

Kitty breathed out silently and locked her gaze with Matt's. Her voice was gentle as she asked, 'Would you tell us what happened?'

Colonel Crowther rubbed at his face, then leaned back in his seat, his watery gaze resting on Kitty. 'It was a long time ago now, my dear, and not a very edifying tale. Kenneth Crowther was indeed a member of my brigade. I did not know him personally. A report came in from the local town. An Indian man of quite some importance complained that a soldier had attacked a member of his household. A young woman. She was rescued by another local man who heard her screams. Kenneth Crowther was identified as the culprit.'

The colonel sighed and rubbed his face once more as if trying to clarify his recollections of the event. 'Crowther had been drinking and had grabbed at the girl in an alley near the marketplace. He was clearly identified by witnesses, and he had scratches on his hands and neck where the girl had fought back. We clapped him in the brig and a date for his court martial was set. Crowther went to pieces. He begged the guards not to tell his sister back in England of his disgrace. If found guilty, which seemed inevitable, he faced a sentence and dishonourable discharge from the army.'

'Jimmi said that Kenneth took his own life?' Kitty said.

'He was found hanging in his cell. He'd fashioned a noose out of a sheet. He left a note pleading with us not to let his sister know the particulars of his death. It was passed to me and I asked my sergeant to write to Miss Crowther saying Kenneth had met with a firearms accident. It seemed the kindest thing to do in the circumstances.' The colonel blinked and produced a slightly grubby handkerchief from his trouser pocket, before loudly blowing his nose.

'When did you realise that Miss Crowther was Kenneth's sister?' Kitty asked.

The colonel tucked his handkerchief away. 'A couple of months after we moved here. Miss Crowther was invited to the Hall for tea, and she admired all the things we had from our time in India. She said her brother had died in an accident and was buried there. Like me, he was a military man. I never told her the name of my brigade, nor did Hilda.'

'You never let on to her at all, after all these years, that you knew what had happened to Kenneth?' Kitty was astonished that they had managed to keep the secret for so long.

'No, Miss Crowther would ask where we had lived in India and so on but we moved around a lot and after the first few years she didn't ask. I don't display any of my militaria in the house. Hilda and I both thought it would be difficult, for Miss Crowther, if she discovered that I had been Kenneth's commanding officer.' The colonel frowned and sighed.

'Did you recognise Jimmi as one of your men, sir?' Matt asked.

Colonel Brothers shook his head. 'No, as I'm sure you're aware, Captain Bryant, as a military man yourself, it is quite difficult to know all of your men by name once you are higher up the chain of command. It had also been a long time since I left India. The elephant keeper, Jimmi Choudhury, made himself known to me on the morning of the fair when I went to see the elephant.'

'Did you warn him about Miss Crowther?' Kitty asked.

The colonel sighed again. 'I did. I asked him not to let on that I had been Kenneth's commanding officer or to tell her the truth behind Kenneth's death. You have to understand that Miss Crowther believed her brother to be a hero. An upstanding soldier. She has spent the years since his death building him up in her mind and his reputation around the village. He said she had been talking to him about Kenneth. Fortunately, he had realised that she was in the dark about the circumstances of her brother's death and had kept quiet.'

Colonel Brothers fell silent for a moment before continuing, 'The Indian theme for Saturday was something Miss Crowther supported. She said she would never be able to visit India or her brother's grave and the theme made her feel a little closer to him, even after all this time. Although she did not approve of the elephant.'

'I'm afraid I must ask you where you were yesterday evening between six and nine?' Matt said. 'I expect Inspector Woolley will ask you the same question.'

'Have I an alibi for the time you said he was attacked, you mean? Yes, Hilda and I were both at home. There was a play on the radio.' The colonel sounded resigned. 'I have to say, now that I'm thinking about all of this, Miss Crowther was well, rather distrait when I stopped by the booth. As if she had something weighing on her mind. She was snappy and cross, barely answering me but it was hot in the tent, and she wanted her tea, so I thought nothing of it at the time.' He looked at Kitty.

'But now you think that there was something else going on?' Kitty said softly.

He nodded slowly. 'I could be mistaken. I remember saying that I would ask about her tea at the stall, and she said that she could sort it out herself. She was not such a fool as everyone took her for. At the time I assumed she was just cross because she was thirsty, but now, well, something so terrible makes you question everything.'

There seemed little else to say so Kitty and Matt said their farewells and walked back along the hall with Bertie and out of the house onto the terrace. Mrs Brothers was standing near the stone steps leading down into the rose garden. A large woven-willow basket was over her arm and a pair of secateurs in her other hand. She was wearing the mushroom hat once again and a pair of sunglasses with round, dark lenses.

'Mrs Brothers, good morning!' Kitty called to her, and the woman turned slowly in their direction as they approached.

'Oh, good morning.' Hilda peered over the top of her sunglasses and Kitty noticed the whites of her eyes were bloodshot and tinged with yellow. 'I was just cutting a few fresh flowers for the house. They don't last long you know in this heat.'

She had a few long-stemmed pink roses in her basket and a couple of sprigs of lavender. 'Have you just been to see Stanley? Is there any news of an arrest yet?' She swayed as she spoke, and Kitty placed a hand on the older woman's arm to steady her.

'Come and sit for a moment, Mrs Brothers. I fear this heat is overcoming you.' Kitty led Hilda to a nearby white-painted wrought-iron bench in the shade of the wisteria.

'Yes, it's very hot again today. Not like the heat one gets abroad though. That was more of a dry heat.' Hilda attempted to smile at them. 'I shall be perfectly all right in a moment.' She set her basket down on the floor and the gardening gloves that had been placed on top of the flower stems shifted slightly to reveal the corner of a silver hip flask.

Matt glanced at Kitty, and she knew he too had noticed it.

'There have been no arrests as yet, I'm afraid. We were just telling your husband that Jimmi, the elephant keeper, who was here on Saturday was attacked at the circus last night after the performance,' Kitty said.

Mrs Brothers took off her glasses, tears brimming in her eyes. 'Oh dear, was he badly hurt?'

'He should make a good recovery as far as we know. He was very lucky,' Kitty said as she proffered the older woman a clean handkerchief from her handbag.

'He was in India too, you know. One of my husband's men,

recruited locally. I was talking to him on Saturday.' She sniffed miserably.

'He told us about Kenneth Crowther's death and that you had to tried to spare Emily Crowther from the details, as her brother had wished,' Matt said.

Hilda rocked forward on the bench. 'We never said anything to her, not for years. She should never have known.' She burst into a flood of tears and mopped at her eyes with Kitty's handkerchief.

'Mrs Brothers, what do you mean?' Kitty crouched down next to Hilda and took her hand. Once again, she could smell a faint odour of stale alcohol on Hilda's breath.

'It was my fault she found out.' Hilda sobbed.

CHAPTER FIFTEEN

Kitty looked up helplessly at Matt, stunned by this latest revelation. He lifted his shoulders slightly in response.

'Mrs Brothers, what do you mean, she found out? Did Miss Crowther finally discover what happened to her brother in India?' Kitty asked.

Hilda sniffed. 'I'd gone to her booth as I said to sort out the float. I knew the floats had been correct when I'd made them up, but she didn't believe me. Emily Crowther could be very cutting, and she implied that well, that I had been...' her voice tailed off before she sucked in a breath and ploughed on '... drinking, and that was why they were wrong. We started to argue and then she had to make a nasty remark about Jamie. She said he had probably taken the money and I should watch him sneaking around. She said he was dishonest and untrustworthy. I could have ignored it and risen above it like I had a thousand times before, but then she said something about why good people like her brother had to have died and men like Jamie were alive.'

Hilda paused once more to dab at her nose. 'I lost my temper, Mrs Bryant. I said something about if she only knew the truth about her beloved Kenneth. That he wasn't the saintly figure she had made him out to be.'

'Oh, my goodness, what happened then?' Kitty's mind reeled. If what Hilda was saying was true, then it possibly provided an even bigger motive for the colonel to have killed Miss Crowther and to have attacked Jimmi.

Miss Crowther would have been furious at their deception and would have had no compunction in socially destroying the colonel and Mrs Brothers and their nephew. Even though Kenneth had done something terrible, Kitty had no doubt that Miss Crowther would have framed things to blame the colonel and his wife.

'I knew I had said too much, and I tried to leave the tent. She was furious and caught hold of the sleeve of my dress to stop me. I bitterly regretted having said anything. I just wanted to get out of there. That must have been when I lost the button. She said that after the fair ended that she would get to the bottom of it all.' Hilda wiped her eyes once more.

'Did she say anything else?' Kitty asked.

Mrs Brothers sat up a little straighter, her lips pursed angrily. 'She called after me that not only would she find out what I meant, she would see to it that everyone in the village would find out the truth about everything. She said that I should be careful about what I said about Kenneth as she knew all about Jamie and his unsavoury proclivities. I walked away as quickly as I could. I'm sure half the field must have heard her. Thank heavens we hadn't opened to the public.'

Kitty's knees ached from where she was crouched, and she stood up. Bertie nudged her leg with his nose as if eager to be off.

'Please don't upset yourself, Mrs Brothers. But I'm afraid I have to ask, do you know what Miss Crowther meant by everyone finding out the truth about everything?' Matt asked.

The older woman slipped her sunglasses back onto the

bridge of her nose. 'I don't know exactly. Probably she would tell everyone about this.' She waved her hand towards the basket where the corner of the flask was now glinting in the sunlight. 'And no doubt once she had ferreted out that Stanley had been her brother's commanding officer, she would twist everything to portray her beloved Kenneth as a wronged man and Stanley as the villain of the piece.'

'And the comment she made about Jamie?' Kitty asked in a gentle tone. She was certain that Miss Crowther knew something about him that both the colonel and his wife did not wish to have made public.

Mrs Brothers rose and picked up her basket. 'I don't know. Probably something about his past. Many people know that he went a little wild when my sister passed away. I feel rather foolish now, telling you all this.'

'Not at all, Mrs Brothers. It must have been upsetting having this weighing on your mind,' Kitty said. She had a growing suspicion about Jamie which, if she was correct, was supported by Miss Crowther's comment.

'Thank you. Now, if you'll excuse me, these roses will start to wilt if they are not placed in water soon.' Hilda nodded brusquely at them and marched away down the terrace.

'Well, that was a turn up for the books!' Matt exclaimed as they watched Hilda's plump figure disappear down the steps into the lower garden.

Kitty took Matt's arm and they started to walk back towards Kitty's car with Bertie tugging impatiently at his leash.

'I wonder who else was there to hear Miss Crowther threatening to spill everyone's secrets?' Kitty mused.

'Anyone who was on or around the refreshment stand would have been in earshot I would have thought. Ruth, Frank, Lilith maybe,' Matt agreed as they reached Kitty's car.

He stowed Bertie on the back seat and secured the dog safely, before taking his own seat on the passenger side.

'At least we know now how Hilda lost that button, assuming she was telling the truth.' Kitty started her car. 'And after seeing that hip flask it confirms our suspicions about her secret drinking.' She reversed carefully around Jamie's car ready to set off for their planned drive and picnic.

'It certainly gives both Hilda and her husband a motive to murder Miss Crowther. I wonder exactly what Miss Crowther knew about Jamie that they didn't want made public?' Matt glanced at Kitty.

Kitty frowned as she drove steadily along the country lane towards the village. 'I think it has something to do with the vicarage and the Drummonds. Frank was definitely behaving very furtively last night, and we heard the colonel warning Jamie to stay away from there when we were at the Hall the other day. That mention of Jamie's *proclivities* was quite telling I thought.'

'We shall need to speak to Inspector Woolley again later, when we get back.' Matt spread his arm along the back of Kitty's seat. 'For now though, let's go and enjoy our holiday and our picnic.'

Kitty laughed. 'Yes, no more talk of murder for a while. You had better find the map though as I have no idea where I'm going.'

Matt dutifully obeyed and after a delightful drive through the rolling countryside they ended up at a green and sheltered valley with a small stream running through the middle. Picturesque stone ruins of a long-deserted abbey provided a welcome spot of shade as they enjoyed their meal. Bertie splashed in and out of the shallow water chasing the large white butterflies that danced past on the faint summer breeze.

A few hours later, feeling relaxed and refreshed they returned to the Dower House.

'That looks rather like a police vehicle,' Matt said as they turned into the driveway.

Kitty parked her red car next to the larger black one. 'I think you're right. Perhaps Inspector Woolley is here.' She jumped out of the car while Matt unfastened Bertie and they hurried into the house to see who the mystery caller might be.

'Miss Bryant is on the terrace with Inspector Woolley, Mrs Bryant, Captain Bryant,' Aunt Effie's butler informed them as they entered the Hall.

Kitty paused only to take off her hat and tidy her hair before walking swiftly to the terrace at the back of the house. When she arrived, Matt was shaking hands with Inspector Woolley and Bertie was crunching on a biscuit under the table.

A jug of iced lemonade and some glasses had been placed ready and Aunt Effie was engaged in serving the inspector with refreshments.

'Mrs Bryant, I was just saying to your husband that I had called to update you both on Mr Choudhury's progress. He received a couple of stitches in his scalp and has something of a headache today but is otherwise unscathed it seems.' The inspector shook hands with her as he spoke.

'I am so pleased to hear that, Inspector.' Kitty took a seat, relieved the elephant keeper was recovering from his ordeal.

'Actually, we have learned some more new information for you today, sir,' Matt said as he too took a seat on one of the rattan loungers. He proceeded to share what they had learned at the Hall with the inspector.

'Hmm, this does shed some new light on matters.' Inspector Woolley made a series of notes inside the notebook he had taken from his pocket.

'Dear me, poor Hilda.' Aunt Effie shook her head and tutted at these latest revelations.

'Did any of the circus people see who may have attacked Jimmi?' Kitty asked.

The inspector tucked his notebook away. 'I'm afraid not, Mrs Bryant. There were a lot of people around leaving the performance, and that area of the field had grown quite dark.'

Kitty was unsurprised by this, but it would have been useful if someone had seen the attacker.

'In the spirit of sharing, and, obviously, this is confidential, I have just re-interviewed Mrs Drummond.' The inspector looked at Matt and Kitty.

'Lilith? Did she recall seeing Miss Crowther collecting her cup of tea from the stall?' Kitty asked eagerly. She wished she could have been present during the interview. The occupants of the vicarage to her seemed to hold the key to the puzzle of what had happened on Saturday.

Inspector Woolley looked keenly at her. 'That's the thing, Mrs Bryant. She emphatically denies seeing Miss Crowther at the refreshment stand, even though Mr Choudhury says he witnessed her there.'

'What about Ruth? Or Frank? Or even Jamie? I believe he was there for a time that afternoon. Surely one of them must have seen her?' Kitty was puzzled. Miss Crowther would have been hard to miss in her distinctive clothing.

'Mrs Drummond stated that she was very busy at that time as everyone had come from the other stalls to collect their drinks, as well as the public wanting strawberries and cream. She recollected pouring several cups of tea and setting them out on a table to the side of her for the stallholders.' The inspector picked up his glass of lemonade and took an appreciative sip.

'What about Ruth or Frank? Did they see Miss Crowther?' Matt asked.

'Miss Drummond says she was clearing tables and organising the washing up as they were running low on crockery, so she didn't take much notice. Frank Drummond said he was serving the strawberries and cream and waiting on the tables. They were so busy at that point Doctor Masters came to help them, as Jamie had to return to assist the photographer with the tiger at the entrance.' Inspector Woolley accepted an iced fancy biscuit from the plate Aunt Effie offered him as he finished speaking.

'So none of them admit to either seeing or serving Miss Crowther?' Kitty was astonished. 'Surely one of them *must* have seen her. I don't think that Jimmi could have been mistaken.'

'My thoughts exactly, Mrs Bryant. When pressed, Miss Drummond did say she thought she saw Miss Crowther walking back towards her tent.' The inspector nibbled at the edge of his biscuit while Bertie moved closer to the policeman in case he should drop any crumbs.

'I see.' Kitty accepted a glass of lemonade from Aunt Effie and sipped it thoughtfully. 'With what we know now, I wonder if any of them heard Miss Crowther's argument earlier that day with Mrs Brothers?'

'I rather think that will have to be a question for tomorrow, Mrs Bryant, along with fresh statements from the colonel and his good lady wife.' Inspector Woolley finished his drink and turned to Matt's aunt. 'Thank you very much for the refreshments, Miss Bryant, most welcome on a day like today.' He rose as he spoke and nodded to Kitty and Matt. 'I understand this weather is set to break in the next day or so. I expect the farmers will be thankful for a drop of rain.'

Matt stood and went to see him out.

'That was all quite fascinating stuff. One thinks one knows one's neighbours, and it just goes to show, doesn't it? You can never truly know anyone completely,' Aunt Effie remarked as she topped up her own drink.

'That's very true, Aunt Effie. I thought after this morning that perhaps things looked bad for the colonel and Mrs Brothers, but now I am all confused again. It very much sounded as if the Drummonds had something to hide too,' Kitty said.

She wondered if the inspector had drawn the same conclusions that she had made about Miss Crowther's comment about Jamie. It would be too awful for both Jamie and the colonel and his wife if the inspector felt it may have provided the young man with a motive for murder.

Aunt Effie snorted. 'Well, if push came to shove the twins certainly wouldn't feel as if they had to protect Lilith. They tolerate her but they certainly wouldn't cover for her. They might do it for each other, however. Twins often do, don't they?'

Kitty nodded slowly. Matt's aunt made a good point. She wondered though about the attack on Jimmi. Lilith surely couldn't have been responsible for that and as Matt's aunt had just pointed out, Frank was unlikely to have helped her. She, too, couldn't see how Frank could have returned to the vicarage in time for her to witness him sneaking out again if he had attacked Jimmi.

Matt came back to the terrace to join them and took his favourite place on the lounger, swinging his legs up on the footrest and tugging a faded yellow-silk cushion behind his head. 'I think the inspector may be right about the weather. There are a few clouds building up over there.' He shaded his forehead with his hand and squinted into the distance.

Aunt Effie and Kitty followed his gaze. Where the sky had been a clear blue with the odd tiny wisp of cloud now there was a distinct bank of grey starting to form over the distant hills.

They passed the rest of the afternoon and evening relaxing and talking about what they should do for the rest of their holiday. All thoughts of the murder were put to one side. Instead, Kitty focused on her hand at cards as she played with Matt and Aunt Effie. Even so she couldn't help wondering what the next day would bring when Inspector Woolley had spoken to everyone once more.

CHAPTER SIXTEEN

Kitty rose the following morning feeling rather dull and dreary after a restless night's sleep. The clouds had accumulated overnight, and the air inside the house was muggy and sticky. Matt greeted her with a kiss on her cheek when she joined him at the breakfast table. Bertie was already tucking into some sausages in a dish near Matt's feet.

'I think this rain may arrive by this evening, the weather has definitely taken a turn,' Matt said as she took her place at the table.

'Yes, it certainly looks like it,' Kitty agreed, pouring herself a cup of tea from the china teapot.

'The post has been already. I think you may have a letter from Alice.' Matt inclined his head towards the small, square white envelope next to her place setting.

Kitty grinned as she recognised Alice's neat handwriting, her spirits lifting. 'Oh, how lovely, I wonder what she has made of Miss Crowther's murder?'

Suddenly feeling much more cheerful, Kitty used a clean butter knife to slice open the envelope.

Dear Kitty,

I am so glad as you and Captain Bryant are having a good time with Miss Bryant. I'm glad too as Captain Bryant is doing so much better after that dreadful fire. Although I can't believe that you've become entangled in another murder case. Please do be careful, I know how trouble always seems to find you in these matters. I was so jealous when you said as you had seen a real elephant up close. My word, what a thing. I've only ever seen them at the pictures.

By the bye I think you may have lost Rascal, your kitten, to your grandmother. I've never seen her so taken with anything as she is with that little cat. I haven't said anything about the murder to her. I thought as you would like to tell her that yourself when you get back to Dartmouth. Enjoy the rest of your holiday and please stay out of mischief.

With much love, your friend, Alice x

Kitty read the letter aloud to Matt. 'What do you think of that?'

Her husband chuckled. 'I think Rascal may be doing your grandmother the power of good.'

Kitty filled her plate with toast. Matt was right, she had been concerned of late about her grandmother who had seemed, to Kitty at least, increasingly frail. If Rascal was bringing some colour back to her beloved Grams life, then she was quite happy to let the kitten stay at the Dolphin. She would see it often enough when she visited.

They had decided the previous evening to take Bertie on a walk through the woods on the Quixshotte estate. Aunt Effie had suggested a route which was probably the one Frank Drummond had taken the night Kitty had seen him sneaking out of the vicarage. It might even give them a clue about where he had been heading that night.

Aunt Effie had said it was shaded and pretty and would bring them out by a series of small waterfalls which fed down into the river where the colonel had held his duck race. It sounded a pleasant way to spend the morning and Matt was keen to explore.

Once breakfast was over, they put Bertie on his leash and set off along the lane. It was slightly cooler under the canopy of the trees but there was little breeze. They reached the turn that Aunt Effie had told them about and followed a small rabbit path into the woods.

Bertie trotted ahead of them, his nose to the ground happily sniffing for rabbits and squirrels. Kitty strolled along next to Matt enjoying the sounds of birdsong above their heads and the otherwise stillness of the woods.

After about ten minutes of walking the path opened out into a clearing. A group of large grey stone boulders stood in the middle. It was clearly a popular place for walkers to pause and smoke, judging by the number of cigarette stubs scattered near the lowest of the stones.

'This looks as if it might be the local trysting spot,' Matt said. He indicated the sets of initials carved in the side of one of the upright stones.

Kitty laughed as she noticed the hearts and dates combined on the rock. 'Some of these look really old.' She ran her fingertip lightly over one of the moss-covered carvings.

Others there looked much more recent. A letter J linked to an F with a heart and two elaborate L's curling around each other in a fanciful font that must have been carved over several visits.

'Do you wish to add us to the stone? A memory of our honeymoon?' Matt asked, the dimple quirking in his cheek as he teased her.

Kitty shook her head, laughing. 'No, I don't think so. I think our holiday here will be memorable enough without needing to carve a note in a rock for posterity.'

Matt kissed her tenderly. 'I agree, although I'm not sure Miss Crowther's demise is perhaps the best romantic remembrance.'

'True. I wonder if this was where Frank was heading on the night I saw him? I assumed he was going to the Hall, but I suppose he could have been meeting someone here,' Kitty said.

'A lover's tryst, you mean?' Matt asked. 'It's certainly a possibility on a fine summer's night.'

They continued on along the path that led out on the far side of the clearing. The way took them down the side of the hill and ahead they could hear the gentle bubbling of running water trickling over stone.

The ground grew damper underfoot as even the sunlight failed to penetrate the thick layer of trees above their heads as they descended into the floor of the narrow ravine. Ferns surrounded them and the tree trunks were green with moss and lichen. Even the recent spell of hot weather had failed to affect the plants growing there.

Eventually they reached the stream and the ground opened out to reveal a small stream of clear water tumbling down over a series of rocky shelves to reach the small pool at the base of the cliff, before continuing on its way to join the wider river further down.

Kitty gazed around trying to get her bearings, while Bertie snuffled and splashed at the edge of the stream.

'This is quite magical. Where is the Hall from here?' Kitty asked.

'I think if we had taken the other path out of the clearing where the boulders were then we would have come out near the door at the side of the Hall. I can only guess that there is another path from there that probably brings you to the top of the cliff face above the waterfall,' Matt said as he peered around for signs of another path.

'It's quite high up there. I thought from what Aunt Effie said that it would be smaller.' Kitty scrambled a little way up the side of the cliff to get a better view downstream.

Matt smiled and held out his hand to help her get back down. 'I know. It is quite amazing. I expect the water must be even more spectacular after a period of rain. The rivers and streams are all quite low at the moment.'

He unclipped Bertie from his leash to allow the dog to frolic in the water while he and Kitty paddled happily in the icy water, laughing together at the sudden cold shock after the heat of the day.

After a short rest sitting on the large river rocks, they put their shoes back on and set off once more. This time following the path beside the stream until they reached the iron kissing gate which gave them access back into the parklands.

Matt reattached Bertie's lead in case there were any deer or other animals nearby and they re-entered the less wild part of the estate. The notice for the duck race was still attached to a small wooden stake near the low stone bridge spanning the river. Someone had clearly missed it when the fair had been packing up.

Kitty wandered onto the bridge and looked down the stream. The water was quite fast-flowing at this point. She could see how the myriad of small pastel-coloured celluloid toy ducks would have been swept along by the current. A net would have been strung across the water further down to catch the ducks and stop them from escaping and bobbing off into the ornamental lake with its vast stone fountain.

A spot of yellow and pink at the side of the river caught her eye and she noticed that one unlucky duck had not made it to the net, having been trapped in the reeds on its way to the finish line. She could envisage Colonel Brothers in his nautical garb issuing instructions to whoever was at the finishing point to wade out and catch the winning duck so the prize could be awarded.

How had such a happy, carefree day ended so tragically?

The faint but unmistakeable rumble of thunder sounded overhead as she left the bridge to rejoin the path. 'Matt, I think we need to get back,' Kitty called to where her husband was persuading Bertie to keep away from the reeds where the ducks had their nests.

'I know, I heard it. We had better hurry if we don't wish to get caught in the storm,' Matt agreed.

They walked back along the driveway and had almost reached the Dower House when Jamie's familiar green sports car roared up from the direction of the village. The roof was down, and he wore a cream-coloured flat cap at a rakish angle. He braked when he drew level with them.

'Good morning,' he called across to them. 'Been out exploring the estate?'

'Yes, through the woods and down by the stream. It's very beautiful. Aunt Effie said your uncle wouldn't mind,' Kitty replied.

Jamie laughed, showing perfect white teeth. 'Since I assume neither of you are poachers then Uncle Stanley will have no objection. I say, I've just come from the village and there is a right to-do going on at the vicarage.'

Matt glanced at Kitty. 'Why? Has something happened?' he asked.

Jamie shrugged. 'I'm not sure quite what's going on. I ran into Ruthie, and she said she thinks that inspector chappie is going to arrest Lilith.'

'Lilith? What for Miss Crowther's murder?' Kitty was a little astonished by this. She had considered the possibility but had discounted it once she'd realised that Lilith couldn't possibly have attacked Jimmi.

'That's what Ruth seemed to think. Her father is up in arms about it. I've never seen the vicar angry before. He never usually notices anything around him to be fair,' Jamie said.

'He does seem to adore Lilith,' Kitty said.

Jamie laughed. 'That's an understatement. He worships her. Lilith can do no wrong.' He put on a saintly, pious expression.

'Perhaps Ruth is mistaken,' Kitty suggested.

Jamie shrugged once more. 'I don't know. She seemed pretty certain. What a thing though, eh? I must admit I never pictured Lilith as the poisoner. I mean I can see her dropping the stuff into Creepy Crowther's cup, but she would be far too lazy to go and fetch the poison herself. I doubt she would even know what to look for; she isn't terribly bright.'

'Yes, it's all a puzzle. Still, I'm sure Inspector Woolley knows his own business best,' Kitty said.

'Well, I'd best push on. Aunt Hilda is expecting me back in time for lunch and the old girl has been a bit sensitive lately.' Jamie gave a farewell wave and a toot of his car horn before roaring off towards the Hall.

'We should hurry too,' Matt said.

Another rumble overhead added urgency to their journey, and they quickened their pace to reach the Dower House before the first of the rain started.

'Do you think Ruth was right, with what she said to Jamie? That Lilith is about to be arrested?' Kitty asked once they were safely inside the hall of the house.

Matt unclipped Bertie's leash and hung it up on the dark-oak hallstand. 'I don't know. It sounded from what Jamie said as if she was pretty certain. We know Lilith had a motive as she and Miss Crowther did not get on.'

'And she was in charge of the tea on Saturday. She could have directed Miss Crowther to the poisoned cup,' Kitty mused.

'But then who attacked Jimmi and why?' Matt said as they hastened along the hall to the dining room.

Matt's aunt was about to take her seat at the table as they arrived. 'I hoped you would be in time for lunch, and not a moment too soon. It seems we are about to have some of the rain the inspector forecast.'

Kitty took her place at the table with Matt opposite her. Bertie assumed his favourite place beside Aunt Effie. He knew now who was most likely to pass him something tasty.

The dining room grew dark as the storm rumbled overhead. Raindrops as large as pennies beat against the now closed French windows and Aunt Effie asked the servants to put on the electric lights.

'We just ran across Jamie Martin. He was returning from the vicarage and he seemed to think Lilith Drummond was about to be arrested,' Matt told his aunt once the servants had withdrawn.

'How extraordinary. I can imagine Lilith doing something to Emily Crowther out of spite but poisoning her seems quite a stretch. And surely she cannot have attacked that man at the circus? Does the inspector think that was coincidental?' Aunt Effie paused and took a sip from her glass of water. 'The reverend will be devastated.'

'Jamie said he was furious that Lilith was even a suspect.' Kitty frowned at Bertie who was gobbling up a large chunk of ham from Aunt Effie's main course.

Lightning lit the room, immediately followed by a loud crack of thunder that sounded as if it were right over their heads.

'Gracious me, you were fortunate not to have been caught out in this. I asked the gardener to put your car in the garage, by the way, Kitty dear, so it will be quite safe.' Aunt Effie beamed at her while not-so secretly giving Bertie the last of her ham.

'Thank you, that's most kind.' Kitty glared at the unrepentant Bertie who now looked completely innocent as he sat under the table.

'I wonder if we shall hear any more on the matter of Miss Crowther's murder today,' Matt said as he placed his cutlery down on his empty plate. 'I suppose if the inspector does arrest Lilith the news will travel quite quickly.'

'In Quixshotte? Oh absolutely, my dear, you can be sure of that,' his aunt agreed.

CHAPTER SEVENTEEN

They passed the afternoon in a desultory fashion. Matt completed a crossword and Kitty stretched out luxuriously on the sofa with a box of chocolates and her detective novel. Bertie dreamed in front of the empty fireplace, his paws twitching as he chased rabbits in his sleep.

The storm finished rumbling and banging and rolled away. By four o'clock the sky had cleared back to a clear blue and the birds had resumed their chorus in the garden. Kitty drafted a reply to Alice's letter and sealed the envelope ready for the post.

'I think I might walk down to the village to catch the evening post now the rain has stopped,' Kitty said.

She felt restless after an afternoon of enforced idleness and her innate curiosity meant she longed to know what had happened at the vicarage. Not that she was guaranteed to see anyone, but she thought it worth taking a chance.

'Would you like me to come with you?' Matt asked, the twinkle in his eyes told her he had guessed her real motive for suggesting a walk.

'No, it's all right. I can take Bertie.' Kitty smiled back at her husband. She knew that Matt was still not fully fit from the effects of the smoke he had inhaled on their last case. She thought he looked quite tired from the long walk they had already taken earlier. He had also had a disturbed night's sleep.

Bertie's ears had pricked up at the mention of another walk and he wagged his tail in happy anticipation. Kitty hoped the lane would not be too muddy after all the rain that had come down knowing how much Bertie loved puddles. She changed her shoes for some sturdy brogues and set off for the village with the dog.

The air felt fresher but already the ground was steaming as the late afternoon sun dried the puddles left by the storm. She was relieved to see that providing she kept Bertie out of the hedgerow, the muddy patches were easy to avoid.

All seemed quiet in the village as she rounded the corner near the green to walk past the vicarage gates. There was no sign of Inspector Woolley's large black police vehicle either outside the Quixshotte Arms or in the vicarage drive.

She posted her letter to Alice in the red pillar box near the post office and turned round ready to walk back to the Dower House. The tea room had closed for the day, the shops were shut and everywhere appeared deserted.

'Mrs Bryant, it is Mrs Bryant, isn't it?' She turned around again on being hailed by Doctor Masters who had appeared unexpectedly behind her.

'Good afternoon, Doctor, yes, but do please call me Kitty.' She was intrigued about where the man had come from and why he had called to her.

'I trust there were no ill effects after the shock of discovering Miss Crowther on Saturday afternoon?' he asked. 'We didn't have much chance to talk when I saw you and your husband at church on Sunday.'

'No, it was rather distressing to discover her, but we had only met Miss Crowther before on one occasion, so she wasn't someone we knew well. My husband and I are private investigators so, sadly, poor Miss Crowther was not our first murder case,' Kitty explained.

Doctor Masters was quite a good-looking man, Kitty thought, and dressed very smartly in a heather-green tweed suit. She wondered if he had come from his practice or if he was on the way there to open up ready for the evening's clinic.

'It was a shocking business. Quixshotte is such a quiet village, the last place one would expect a murder to occur. The police have confirmed that the poison found in Miss Crowther's tea was from a pesticide that the colonel's gardeners kept in their shed.' Doctor Masters' brow furrowed.

'So I believe. The key to the shed was taken from the head gardener's cottage, I understand. Someone must have disliked Miss Crowther very much to have gone to so much trouble, don't you think?' Kitty remarked.

The crease in the doctor's brow deepened. 'Yes, I suppose they must have.'

'I mean, my husband and I don't really know anyone here terribly well, but do you know of anyone who could have fallen out with Miss Crowther, or who might have wished ill upon her?' Kitty asked.

'As no doubt Miss Bryant will have told you, Miss Crowther was something of a busybody. Her house was that one there.' He indicated Miss Crowther's now vacant cottage. 'It was in a prime spot to spy on everyone in the village. She also used to snoop all the time. My receptionist caught her several times trying to read various people's medical cards when she was in the surgery. She always pretended she wasn't, of course. She had arguments with Lilith Drummond, which are well documented but not serious. She also argued with the Drummond twins and Jamie Martin, the colonel's nephew.'

'Oh?' Kitty's ears perked up.

'Yes, I caught the tail end of quite a vicious sounding exchange on the Friday evening before the fair. Miss Crowther was outside her house talking to Jamie. He was in that flashy car of his. I think he must have just dropped Ruth or Frank back home. I heard her say something like, "Don't think that I don't know what's going on. It's disgusting. I intend to speak to someone once this business with the fair is over."' Doctor Masters shrugged. 'I have no idea what it was all about. Jamie looked furious as he drove off.'

'I see. I presume you have told Inspector Woolley about this?' Kitty asked.

'Yes, this morning. I had called to see Lilith and found the inspector interrogating her, quite harshly I thought.' The doctor looked quite thoughtful.

'And you had no quarrel with Miss Crowther yourself, other than obviously her snooping around the medical records?' Kitty asked.

'Nothing in particular, Mrs Bryant. The only issue I had, was, well, personal. It is a little embarrassing. I am a bachelor and Miss Crowther was a single lady. Her attentions were flattering towards me but misguided. I was the recipient of many gifts, hand-knitted items, cakes, that sort of thing. I was forced to gently discourage her affections. She was somewhat upset.' The doctor shifted uncomfortably.

'Jamie met Matt and I on our walk back to the Dower House this morning. He said he thought that Mrs Drummond might be arrested?' Kitty tried to keep her tone casual as she changed the topic of conversation.

The doctor's brows raised. 'I must admit that I thought so too when I arrived at the vicarage. The reverend was furious at the suggestion that Lilith might have been involved in Miss Crowther's death. He insisted it was quite preposterous and I agreed with him. However, the inspector said he had a few more enquiries to make.'

Kitty was intrigued by the physician's version of the morning's events. 'Of course, I expect you know Mrs Drummond quite well. Is she one of your patients?'

'What? Oh yes, well, Lilith is a delicate woman. The reverend asked me to keep a close eye on her health. I think after he lost his first wife it has made him very cautious about protecting Lilith,' Doctor Masters explained.

'I see, I suppose it would. Have you known the family for a long time?' Kitty asked.

'I came here about ten years ago. So yes, I've known the family for some time. Long enough to know that Lilith would not have killed Miss Crowther,' Doctor Masters said.

'Let us hope that Inspector Woolley's enquiries bear fruit and he discovers who really did murder her soon.' Kitty turned slightly, ready to walk back to the Dower House.

Doctor Masters fell into step beside her. 'Forgive me for asking, Mrs Bryant, but are you and your husband investigating the case?'

Kitty peeked up at him from under the brim of her straw hat. 'Not as such. We have a private commission on a related matter.' She picked her words cautiously. She didn't want to be thought of as a gossip by spreading Colonel Brothers' affairs about the village.

'I see. Thank you, Mrs Bryant. I had better say goodbye just here, I'm afraid. I must go and set up for my evening surgery.' He paused at the entrance to a narrow path leading to a large stone built bay-fronted villa which lay behind the cottages.

'Good evening, Doctor, it was nice talking to you,' Kitty answered politely.

Kitty walked on, her mind busy with everything the doctor had just told her. It was clear to her that Doctor Masters was quite partial to Lilith Drummond. He certainly appeared to be a regular visitor to the vicarage. She wondered if Miss Crowther had noted the doctor's frequent visits to the house and had drawn a similar conclusion.

Then there was the reported argument with Jamie Martin. She had begun to get an idea of what that may have been about, especially after the walk she and Matt had taken that morning. If her suspicions were correct, was that why the colonel had told Jamie to stay away from the vicarage? It was all terribly interesting, but she couldn't see how it added up to murder.

Matt listened attentively to her story when she arrived back at the Dower House. 'So, Lilith is not yet under arrest?'

'It seems not, but from the way the doctor described what happened, I can only assume that Inspector Woolley is making quite a case against her. It sounded as if her arrest might be imminent from what Jamie and the doctor said,' Kitty said. 'I find the doctor's concern for her quite interesting, don't you?'

Matt chuckled. 'You think they are lovers?'

'I think it a strong possibility, or that the doctor would like them to be. It's certainly ethically dubious since she is his patient, and she is a married woman. Miss Crowther could have caused quite a stir if she had discovered their affair. And I'm pretty certain that she would have. Doctor Masters told me she had a bit of a crush on him and she had no love for Lilith.' Kitty perched herself on the edge of the leather sofa in the drawing room.

Matt busied himself at the drinks trolley. 'A cocktail before we dress for dinner?' he asked. 'I think your sleuthing deserves a reward.'

Kitty laughed. 'I won't say no. If the doctor and Lilith are lovers, that alters the complexion of the case considerably. They could be working together. She could have poisoned Miss Crowther and he could be the mystery man who collected the poison and attacked Jimmi.'

'Hmm, that is a possibility.' Matt handed her a glass. 'I wonder if that is the premise Inspector Woolley is working upon. This so-called interrogation of Lilith might have been done to try and shake something into the open.'

Kitty took an appreciative sip of her drink. 'True. Perhaps the inspector heard rumours. Staying at the Quixshotte Arms he is bound to pick up taproom gossip. I wonder what the vicar makes of it all. Surely, he must have suspicions about his wife's friendship with the doctor,' she mused.

Matt took a seat opposite her. 'We are jumping to an awful lot of conclusions here,' he reminded her.

'I know,' Kitty agreed. Whilst Matt had a point, she was pretty certain that she was right. The doctor had been hanging around Lilith at the refreshment stall on Saturday. He visited the house frequently under the guise of Lilith's supposed poor health. Not that anyone seemed to know what, if indeed anything, that diagnosis meant.

Kitty wished she could think of a ploy to speak to Lilith herself. It was so frustrating when one was just a visitor somewhere. They also had to be mindful of not upsetting the local police or causing any ill feeling towards Matt's aunt after they had gone home.

Dinner that evening was a quiet affair. Kitty told Aunt Effie what she had learned in the village.

'Well, my dear, the doctor is quite a sought-after bachelor locally you know and Lilith is a handsome woman. The dear vicar lives in a world of his own, so if anything untoward were going on between them, then he would be the last person on earth to suspect it.' Aunt Effie had been quick to pick up on the inference in Kitty's narrative of events.

'Has Doctor Masters always been single?' Kitty asked.

'Yes, well so far as I know. He came here when the previous doctor sadly passed away. I think Leo Masters had been a student of his at some time in the past. He came to the village originally just to help out. Our previous doctor was very elderly and was a bit of a dodderer I'm afraid towards the end. It caused quite the stir having a younger, good-looking single man taking over the practice.' Aunt Effie sounded thoughtful.

'I can imagine.' Kitty smiled at Matt's aunt.

'He was much in demand for bridge evenings and tennis parties. He is also quite a good dancer, so I'm told.' Aunt Effie rose from her place at the table ready to return to the drawing room for coffee. 'He is generally well thought of in the village.'

Kitty and Matt sat on the sofa while Aunt Effie poured them coffee from a tall silver coffee pot. Bertie settled himself on the floor next to Kitty and promptly fell asleep. The weather outside had settled back into a fine clear evening and the French windows had been reopened a crack allowing the air to circulate.

'I wonder what will happen about Miss Crowther's funeral?' Aunt Effie mused thoughtfully as she settled back in her chair, dainty coffee cup and saucer in her hands.

'Oh yes. I think I see what you mean. If the vicar's wife is a suspect, or even worse is arrested, it would be most odd for the vicar to officiate at the victim's funeral,' Matt said.

'I suppose this cousin of Miss Crowther's will be in charge of organising everything?' Kitty said.

'That would be Margery Addersley. She's a widow, lives towards Barnsover way. She and Emily did not get on at all well together. They tolerated one another at best. They would meet once a month for lunch but it was really an opportunity to snipe at one another,' Aunt Effie said. 'Margery was very intolerant of Miss Crowther's hero worship of Kenneth, and Emily was always slightly jealous of Margery's marriage. Margery was married to an older man, a farmer. He died a few years ago and left her quite well off, I believe.'

It occurred to Kitty that although they knew that Margery had benefitted financially from Miss Crowther's death, they didn't know quite what Miss Crowther had to leave. 'Was Miss Crowther well off?' Kitty asked.

'She owned her cottage. It had been her parents' home and then obviously she and Kenneth lived there. When Kenneth died, it became Emily's. She had a small private income, I believe. Her mother had married beneath her.' Aunt Effie smiled apologetically. 'That was how it was always phrased. Her mother had been a Miss Tilley of Tilley's Cottons. They owned mills near Bradford. Whereas her husband Herbert Crowther was a foreman at one of the mills when they met.'

'Perhaps that was why she looked down on Lilith Drummond?' Kitty suggested.

Aunt Effie looked surprised. 'I hadn't thought of that, but yes, I believe you are right. Emily was very conscious of the connection with the Tilleys and fond of mentioning it. Lilith was a publican's daughter.'

'The lady at the tea room said Margery was clearing the cottage. So, I suppose she must have inherited it.' Matt sipped his coffee thoughtfully.

Aunt Effie gave a slight shrug. 'Well unless Miss Crowther bequeathed everything to charity, then there isn't anyone else.'

'I wonder if she had a will,' Matt pondered.

'Yes, she had. I only know because we were talking one day at a bridge evening. We were having supper. Doctor Masters was there, and the Drummonds, Colonel Brothers and his wife, oh and a Miss Pargetter. She was a visitor staying with the colonel, an elderly lady, very deaf but a bridge fiend. There were enough of us for two tables.' Aunt Effie paused for breath and Matt shot Kitty an amused glance.

'Anyway, what was I saying? Oh yes, wills. Colonel Brothers was saying that Jamie would be coming to live with them and if he showed aptitude, he would inherit the estate. Miss Crowther said that she had recently made her own will as she had heard of someone in a neighbouring village who had died intestate, and everything had gone to the man's estranged brother, a drunken wastrel. She said she had no intention of leaving her things to someone who would not appreciate the legacy,' Aunt Effie said.

'How interesting. I wonder who would have drafted the will?' Matt said.

'Oh, I assume that would be Mr Shepherd, he's the local solicitor. I'm sure she would have seen him. I expect the police will have already looked into the matter,' Aunt Effie remarked as she finished her coffee.

'It would be nice to know who inherited and if there might be a financial consideration of which we are unaware.' Matt was thoughtful.

Kitty could see his point. It was usually one of their first considerations in a case. Who benefitted from the death? Even so, she couldn't see that Miss Crowther's cousin would have a motive if she was already financially comfortable.

It was all very puzzling.

CHAPTER EIGHTEEN

The latest spell of fine weather continued to hold into the next day. Although Matt noticed considerably more clouds in the sky than when they had first arrived at his aunt's house ten days earlier.

They had originally intended to leave for Devon after a fortnight's holiday with his aunt. Matt suspected, however, that if Miss Crowther's murderer had not been arrested by the time their departure date arrived, Kitty might press for an extension. Not that his aunt would object to having them stay for longer. She was very fond of Kitty and enjoyed the company of what she flatteringly called 'young people'.

His aunt had decided to join them for breakfast that morning. She generally preferred to take a breakfast tray in her room and rise later in the day. Bertie as usual was under the table primed and waiting for some sausages and a bit of bacon to come his way.

'Good morning, Aunt Effie.' Matt greeted his aunt with a kiss on her cheek as he took his seat next to Kitty. His wife had already started on her breakfast.

'What are your plans for today?' Aunt Effie enquired as Matt loaded his plate with bacon and eggs.

Matt looked at Kitty. He knew her all too well. After dinner the previous evening when they had been discussing the case, he could tell that she was thinking about everything that had happened since they had discovered Miss Crowther's body.

'I'm not sure. It looks fine out at the moment, but the forecast on the wireless yesterday said we might get more storms later.' Kitty set her cutlery down on her empty plate with a satisfied sigh.

'You have no more sleuthing plans?' his aunt asked with a twinkle in her eye.

'I rather think we are at something of an impasse at the moment. We were commissioned by the colonel to clear him and his wife of any wrongdoing in the matter. With the inspector seemingly close to a breakthrough there appears to be little more that we can do,' Matt said.

His aunt raised her eyebrows. 'Hmm, well if you were thinking of staying close to home today, I recommend a walk around the village churchyard. It's very old you know and there are some interesting stones there. At the rear of the churchyard there is another gate leading into the lane. It is a very pretty walk that takes you around the back of the village behind the doctor's house and then round onto the green. You could always take tea at the tea room again,' his aunt suggested innocently.

Matt bit back a smile as he looked at Kitty to see what she thought of the suggestion.

'Bertie does enjoy a good walk.' Kitty patted the edges of her lips with a white linen napkin.

'That sounds a capital suggestion then, Aunt Effie, thank you,' Matt agreed.

They set off after breakfast with Bertie trotting happily ahead of them, clearly delighted to be out and about. The air was a little cooler and Matt thought the holiday had done Kitty good. She looked fresh and charming in her pale-blue floral cotton dress with her wide-brimmed straw hat shading her face. She had been so pale when they had left Devon and he knew she had been worrying about him.

He had to admit that he too felt much better for their holiday. The recurrence of problems that had been sparked after the attack on the elephant keeper had receded. He was also no longer plagued by the aggravating cough that had dogged him since their last case and he felt stronger.

They followed his aunt's directions and walked past the vicarage into the centre of the village. The police car was back outside the Quixshotte Arms, he noticed, as they entered the churchyard via the wooden lychgate.

When they had attended church on Sunday with his aunt there had been little time to take much notice of the exterior of the church, or to appreciate its setting. He suspected that Kitty too had been preoccupied with the events at the fair. Now though he could see that the surroundings of the grey stone church with its square belltower were well maintained.

The more recent graves were set on the one side closer to the stone wall surrounding the grounds. The older graves were closer to the church with more of them at the rear of the church. The grass had been recently mown and everywhere was in order. The oldest stones were tilted at various odd angles. The inscriptions weatherworn and covered with moss.

He couldn't help but be reminded of the churchyard many miles away near London where his first wife and baby daughter had been laid to rest. They had been killed by a bomb during the war and it had taken him a long time to get over the loss. Kitty too seemed to sense his thoughts and slipped her hand into his.

They wandered along the stone-flagged path between the gravestones. It gave way to a narrower gravel-covered section that led out of the churchyard via a small metal gate into a quiet lane. Elms and oak trees cast a pleasant, dappled shade and overhead the crows called to each other in raucous voices.

The lane itself was more of a track, clearly used mainly by horses and carts judging by the ruts in the surface and the hoof prints. Mixed in with these were the recent marks of a set of tyres. Someone had driven a motor vehicle along there recently, as the impressions could only have been left after the ground had been softened by rain.

They started to stroll away from the village centre along the curve at the back of the cottages. Aunt Effie had said it led behind the vicarage and the doctor's house, eventually leading them back to the main road where they could complete the loop to take tea on the green.

Bertie had paused to investigate an interesting clump of dandelions when the peace and quiet was shattered by the sound of a feminine scream from somewhere just ahead of them around the bend.

Matt and Kitty hurried forward pulling Bertie away from his discovery.

'Who is it?' Kitty said, panting, as the screams continued, rising in volume as they reached the corner.

Matt was faster than his wife and ahead he saw the sleek lines of a black motor car parked in the lane, its passenger door wide open. Next to the car stood the woman who was screaming. Lilith Drummond dressed in a smart pastel-pink summer frock with matching hat and jacket.

'Mrs Drummond! Whatever is the matter?' Matt hurried forward with Kitty hard on his heels.

As Matt drew closer, he saw the woman's face was paper white beneath her make-up and she was trembling visibly. Inside the car he noticed there was an occupant in the driving seat. A man who seemed unmoving and impervious to Lilith's ear-shattering screams.

The vicar's wife suddenly seemed to realise they were there and tore her gaze away from whoever was inside the car.

'Blood, there's blood!' Lilith's knees buckled and Matt was forced to release Bertie's leash in order to dart forward to catch her.

'Mrs Drummond, what's happened?'

He saw that the white cotton glove on her right hand was indeed stained dark red on the fingertips. Kitty snatched up Bertie's lead before he could run off and peered into the driver's side of the car.

'It's Doctor Masters. It looks as if he's been stabbed.' Matt could tell from the expression on Kitty's face as she spoke that it was obvious the doctor was dead.

Lilith was a dead weight in his arms, and he looked around for somewhere he could set her down safely. A high brick wall bordered the lane where the car was parked, and a pale-blue wooden door stood partially open.

Kitty noticed it at the same time and pushed it aside to reveal the kitchen garden area at the far end of the vicarage's back garden. To his relief there was a small wooden bench next to the lettuces. With Kitty's assistance and Bertie's hinderance he managed to get Lilith onto the bench.

'Doctor Masters is dead, stabbed with what appears to be a kitchen knife. The driver's window is down and the knife is at an angle in his chest,' Kitty related to Matt as she perched herself on the bench beside Lilith and started to chafe the unconscious woman's hands in hers in an effort to rouse her.

'You think he had the window down to speak to someone and they leaned in and stabbed him?' Matt was quick to pick up the inference in Kitty's description.

'Yes, that's what it looks like to me.' She glanced up the garden to the distant blank walls and windows of the vicarage. 'It seems no one has heard Lilith screaming.'

The woman groaned and Matt could see Lilith was starting

to rouse. 'I'll head to the vicarage and send someone down to help you and I'll fetch Inspector Woolley from the pub.'

Kitty nodded her agreement as Matt secured Bertie's leash to the handle of a nearby garden roller before setting off on his mission.

Kitty didn't have to wait long before Ruth Drummond came running towards her down the garden path. Her eyes wide with alarm and her dark hair secured in its usual braid.

'Mrs Bryant, your husband said there had been an accident, he's gone to fetch the police inspector. What's happened?' Ruth stopped dead as she noticed the stain on her stepmother's glove.

'Doctor Masters is dead.' Kitty could see a hint of colour creeping into Lilith's ashen face as she spoke.

'What? How? Where?' Ruth looked towards the open door in the garden wall as if she were about to dart through the opening into the lane.

'Please, Miss Drummond, do stay here. The police will be here in a moment and your stepmother has had the most frightful shock.' Kitty looked at the girl.

There was the sound of more voices approaching from the direction of the house and Frank Drummond appeared, along with his father.

'Lilith?' The vicar took in the scene with a gasp and bent over his wife who opened her eyes at the sound of his voice.

'Please could you assist Mrs Drummond into the house so she can recover.' Kitty looked at Frank and the vicar as she spoke.

'Yes, of course, come, Lilith, my poor darling. Frank, come and help me.' The vicar and his son took Lilith between them and supported her tottering steps back through the rows of green beans back to the vicarage.

Ruth remained with Kitty and Bertie, who had been

surveying the comings and goings with interest and barks. The girl's gaze was fixed on the open garden door as if she both longed and feared to step through it into the lane.

'What's happened, Mrs Bryant?' Ruth asked.

'Doctor Masters has been killed, stabbed to death in his car.' Kitty caught hold of the girl's arm as she made a small involuntary move towards the gateway.

'The doctor? But why? I don't understand.' The girl's face grew paler, and Kitty feared that Ruth too might faint.

'Sit here for a moment. Matt will be back with the police any minute now. There is nothing that can be done, and we must not trample all over the place in case there are any clues to whoever did such a wicked thing.' Kitty gently steered the girl onto the bench and sat beside her.

Ruth leaned forward once she was seated, burying her face in her hands. 'I feel quite sick.'

'Take some deep breaths,' Kitty advised as she rubbed the girl's back gently.

There was the sound of male voices and more approaching footsteps from the back of the house. Matt, Inspector Woolley and a uniformed constable appeared. The inspector and the constable rushed past them and out into the back lane.

Matt halted at the bench. 'Has someone taken Mrs Drummond inside?' he asked.

Kitty nodded. 'Frank and the vicar are with her, she has just come round.'

'That's good. Miss Drummond, are you all right?' He looked at Ruth.

The girl removed her hands from her face and straightened up. 'Thank you, Mrs Bryant, Captain Bryant. I feel a little better now.'

'Please, call me Kitty. I think it best if we go inside and wait for the inspector to join us when he is free,' Kitty suggested.

She placed her arm around the girl's shoulders as they

stood. Matt untied Bertie from the garden roller and they made
their way up the long garden path and in through the back door
of the vicarage.

Kitty noticed that the French windows at the rear of the
house were closed, which would explain why Lilith's screams
had not been heard. The back door itself opened into a small
lobby with a red-tiled floor. Another door opened off it presumably leading to the scullery and kitchen.

Ruth led them through a boot room and into the end of the
main hall of the house, before opening a door into the drawing
room. Lilith was lying propped up with cushions on a large red-
leather chesterfield sofa. Her husband was at her side minis-
tering to her tenderly with brandy. Frank was standing in front
of the marble fireplace staring into the empty hearth, a troubled
look on his face.

Lilith had removed her bloodstained gloves and Kitty
noticed they had been placed on a small rosewood occasional
table beside the sofa.

'My poor darling, here take another sip.' The vicar urged his
wife to take more of the brandy he was holding to her lips.

Frank Drummond turned to his sister. 'Lilith said Doctor
Masters is dead.'

Ruth glanced at Kitty and Matt.

'Yes, that's correct,' Matt answered instead of Ruth.

The girl sank down on a nearby armchair, wrapping her
arms around herself. Lilith emitted a low groan.

'What's happened? Captain Bryant rushed into the house
and said Lilith had been taken ill in the garden and there had
been an accident.' Frank sat on the arm of his sister's chair and
looked to Matt for an answer.

'Doctor Masters has been murdered. It looks as if he has
been stabbed while he was waiting in his car in the lane at the
back of the house,' Matt said.

'Stabbed?' Frank echoed.

Kitty watched an array of emotions pass across the young man's expressive face. Disbelief, concern, relief. It was so swift she couldn't be certain of what she saw.

Lilith started to sob quietly.

'Oh, my darling, don't distress yourself.' The vicar produced a large white-cotton handkerchief from his jacket pocket and proffered it to his wife.

While Lilith hiccoughed and dabbed at her eyes and nose the vicar straightened up and glared at Matt. 'My wife is very delicate and has clearly suffered a great shock.'

'Of course, sir,' Matt agreed in a mild tone.

Kitty took a seat on a small dark-green velvet-covered stool. Bertie flopped down at her feet. 'I expect the police will be in soon to talk to us.'

Lilith closed her eyes and pressed the back of her hand to her forehead. 'I don't think I can face talking to that dreadful man again today. I can't believe it, Leo dead, it's just too awful.' Her voice was barely a whisper.

Kitty saw Ruth exchange a glance with her twin and Frank rolled his eyes.

'I don't think you will have much choice I'm afraid, Mrs Drummond. You will have to be brave,' Kitty soothed.

She suspected from the twins' reactions that Lilith was used to avoiding anything she deemed to be unpleasant. However, she was certain that the inspector would insist on getting Lilith to answer at least a few of his questions.

'Nonsense, Lilith is a delicate woman. I'm sure the inspector will understand how distressing this is for her.' Reverend Drummond blinked at Kitty from behind his glasses, his cheeks pinking with indignation.

'I'm sure this is dreadfully shocking and upsetting for everyone, but a man has been murdered. Someone who was your friend and neighbour, as well as your physician. I'm sure Mrs Drummond will wish to do her best to ensure that whoever committed this terrible crime is caught,' Matt replied.

'It was so awful, the blood...' Lilith whimpered and blew her nose daintily.

There was the sound of male voices in the hall, then the drawing room door opened, and Inspector Woolley entered. His seemingly mild glance taking in the scene before him.

'Now then, it seems that a shocking crime has taken place in the lane at the rear of the house. I understand from Captain Bryant that Mrs Drummond made the terrible discovery?' He took out his notebook and looked at Lilith's semi-prone figure.

'Inspector, I'm not sure that my wife is well enough to answer your questions right away.' The vicar had moved to stand between Lilith and the policeman as if to shield her physically from his gaze.

'I appreciate your concern, Reverend, but a murder has been committed and time may be of the essence if we are to catch the culprit.' Inspector Woolley stepped around the vicar and took a seat on the edge of the other armchair opposite Lilith.

Kitty saw him glance at the bloodstained gloves lying on the side table. 'Now then, Mrs Drummond. It seems that you were first on the scene, can you tell me what happened please?'

CHAPTER NINETEEN

Lilith opened her eyes and sniffed. 'I had gone out to the back lane to meet Leo, Doctor Masters. After yesterday I was so upset that my husband had suggested a little outing might soothe my nerves. Doctor Masters had offered me a lift to the train station, he often dropped me off there so that I didn't have to walk. I intended to run into Harrogate for a few hours to do some shopping. A new hat and some more stockings, followed by lunch in one of the department stores.' Lilith paused to dab at her eyes once more. 'I got myself ready and went down to meet him. He always collected me from the end of the back garden. His car is garaged nearby, and he always picked me up from the lane,' she explained.

'I see.' Inspector Woolley scribbled busily in his notebook. 'Do please continue, Mrs Drummond.'

'I opened the gate and saw that Leo's car was already there. I was a little late. I opened the passenger door and went to get in.' Lilith's voice faltered for a moment before she continued. 'I sat down and turned to tick him off for not getting out to open the door for me and then I saw...' She swallowed and closed her eyes for a moment.

'Inspector, please.' Reverend Drummond glared at the solid figure of the policeman who remained unmoved in his seat.

'When you are ready, Mrs Drummond, please continue,' Inspector Woolley said.

'I saw... I saw... he looked odd. His eyes were open, and he was looking forwards. He didn't turn to me. Then I noticed the red on his shirt front seeping out from under his jacket.' A tear rolled down Lilith's cheek. 'There was something there, sticking out of his chest. A wooden handle. I think... I think I must have touched it. I don't remember. There was blood, so much blood. I had blood on my hand, and I got out of the car and screamed for help.'

The vicar knelt at her side once more and took her free hand in his. 'There, there, my angel.'

Lilith gave another little sob in response.

Inspector Woolley lifted his gaze from his notebook and looked at Matt. 'I presume this was when you and Mrs Bryant came across the scene?'

Matt confirmed this and gave a brief recitation of the events following their discovery of Lilith standing screaming at the side of the car.

'Thank you, sir, that was very concise and helpful.' Inspector Woolley looked around at the other occupants of the room. 'Did anyone else see or hear anything before Captain Bryant here came to raise the alarm?'

Ruth shook her head. 'I was on my way to the kitchen to speak to Mrs Copperthwaite, our cook. She's as deaf as a post so she won't have heard a thing. After the storms we had closed most of the windows on that side of the house and the back garden, as you saw, is quite long. The first I knew was when Captain Bryant appeared in the hallway and said there had been an accident. I called to Father and Frank and we all came running out.'

'I was on my way downstairs. I didn't hear or see anything until I heard Ruth shout,' Frank said.

'I was in my study, preparing notes for my sermon. It faces the front garden, so I certainly didn't notice anything. Frank opened my study door and said something had happened to Lilith, so naturally I rushed outside with the children.' The vicar looked at his wife.

'Captain Bryant, you and Mrs Bryant entered the lane behind the house from the gate at the rear of the churchyard?' Inspector Woolley asked.

'Yes, sir. The churchyard and the lane were quiet. We saw no one as we walked.' Kitty guessed the inspector was hoping they may have seen someone fleeing the scene or who could have been a witness.

The inspector switched his attention back to Lilith. 'Did you see or hear anyone as you entered the lane, Mrs Drummond?'

'No, no one at all. Just Leo in the car.' Lilith closed her eyes once more as if to shut away the memory.

'I see, and I take it, Captain Bryant, that you and Mrs Bryant didn't hear the engine of the doctor's car and he didn't drive past you?' The inspector lifted his pen from his notebook to wait for their reply.

'No, sir. The engine of the car was off when we got to Mrs Drummond and we didn't hear it, so I can only assume he had been parked for a little while waiting,' Kitty said.

'It's all my fault for being late. If I had only been on time...' Lilith broke off into another bout of sobs causing the vicar to glare furiously at the inspector.

'Now then, my dear, you must not blame yourself,' Reverend Drummond soothed.

'Thank you, Mrs Drummond.' The inspector disregarded the vicar's obvious annoyance at his questions.

Inspector Woolley returned his notebook and pen to his

pocket after checking what time Lilith had arranged to meet the doctor and what time she had actually arrived in the lane to get in the car. It seemed she had been almost fifteen minutes late.

The inspector discreetly collected Lilith's bloodstained gloves and placed them inside a large brown envelope. 'I would request that none of you leave Quixshotte village for the next few days until my enquiries are complete.'

Matt, Kitty and Bertie rose and followed the inspector as he left the room. It seemed there was little more they could do at the vicarage. They had just entered the hall when the constable appeared from the direction of the scullery.

He beckoned the inspector, and they went into a huddle. Inspector Woolley said something to the uniformed officer, and he disappeared in the direction of the back garden.

When the inspector turned back towards Kitty and Matt his expression was grave. 'It seems that Mrs Copperthwaite is missing a wooden-handled kitchen knife.'

Kitty glanced at Matt. 'The knife that was used came from here? Then that would mean that someone from this house must have killed him.'

'Or someone who frequently visited the house and was familiar with its occupants and their routines,' Matt said.

A cough sounded behind them and they turned to discover Reverend Drummond had entered the hall.

'Inspector, I assume that you have no more questions for my wife? Lilith is terribly distressed as you have seen, and I think she should retire to her room for a rest.' The vicar's high fore-head was creased with worry.

'Of course, Reverend. I shall need to speak to her again later, however.' Inspector Woolley seemed to be deep in thought. As the vicar turned to return to the drawing room the inspector asked, 'Reverend, apart from your servants, who else has access to the kitchen?'

The vicar looked bemused by the question. 'Well, myself,

Lilith, and the children use the kitchen. I suppose certain family visitors might drop in for cake.'

'Any regular visitors?' the inspector asked.

Reverend Drummond blinked and Kitty wondered how much notice he ever took of who was in his house. 'I'm not sure. Doctor Masters was very partial to Mrs Copperthwaite's apple cake. Jamie, the colonel's nephew is here quite often to see the twins. Mrs Brothers exchanges recipes with Mrs Copperthwaite and brings some of her surplus fruit for the kitchen, which is most Christian of her.'

'And have any of these visitors called in the last couple of days?' the inspector asked.

'Well, yes, I should think all of them have visited at some point. Jamie has definitely been here, and Mrs Brothers called about taking on some of Miss Crowther's tasks. Mrs Copperthwaite will know more. I am out of the house a lot of the time on parish work.' Reverend Drummond still appeared confused about the direction of the inspector's questions.

'One more thing, Reverend. Who knew that the doctor was calling to give your wife a lift to the station today?' Inspector Woolley enquired.

The lines on the vicar's forehead deepened as he tried to think. 'Myself, Lilith, the twins and Jamie Martin was here when the arrangement was made. I can't think who else, but I suppose the doctor himself could have told people. Poor Lilith, this was supposed to be a little outing to cheer her up. Shopping always lifts her spirits.'

'Thank you, sir.' The inspector turned to leave as the vicar slipped away back inside the drawing room.

Kitty was relieved to be back outside the house. She had no desire to return to the lane where no doubt the police would still be busy dealing with the doctor's car. Bertie seemed to share her misgivings and pulled her towards a path leading through the shrubbery that looked as if it led to the front of the vicarage.

'Are you all right, Mrs Bryant? Two bodies in less than a week is quite a shock for anyone. And, of course, you found Mr Choudhury, the elephant keeper after he had been attacked.' The inspector regarded her gravely.

Kitty managed a small smile. 'Goodness, it does sound bad when you say it like that. I am a little shaken, I will admit. I had not expected that Doctor Masters would be a victim.'

'You were inclined to believe he might be a suspect in Miss Crowther's death?' the inspector asked shrewdly.

Kitty blushed. 'I must admit my ideas had begun to turn that way.' She lowered her voice. 'I might be mistaken but the friendship between Mrs Drummond and the doctor, well, I thought the relationship might be more than that.'

The inspector nodded slowly. 'I think your supposition is correct, Mrs Bryant. In your opinion, do you think the vicar was aware of their affection?'

Kitty frowned. 'I would think probably not. Reverend Drummond seems dreadfully absent-minded and not terribly observant. He also idolises Lilith. She can do no wrong in his eyes, it seems.'

'I think even if someone, say Miss Crowther, had told him that Mrs Drummond was having an affair that he would not believe them,' Matt said.

The inspector sighed. 'Hmm, I see we are minded to agree on several points. I think I need to visit Quixshotte Hall to speak to Jamie Martin. Good day, Mrs Bryant, Captain Bryant.'

He tipped his hat to Kitty and strode off down the garden in the direction of the lane.

Matt placed his hand on Kitty's waist. 'The inspector was right, it has been quite a week. I think we should still go and refresh ourselves at the tea room before we go back and break the news about Doctor Masters to Aunt Effie.'

They walked together around the side of the house and out onto the broader garden path that led to the road bordering the village green. They were almost at the gate when Ruth came flying down the path behind them.

'Captain Bryant, Mrs Bryant!' The girl panted to a halt next to them.

'Are you all right, Ruth?' Kitty asked, concerned.

'I just wanted to ask. Well, Frank and I, do you think Lilith killed Miss Crowther and Doctor Masters?' Ruth's cheeks flushed crimson.

Kitty looked at Matt uncertain how to answer the girl. 'I think she will be considered a suspect, certainly. I'm afraid you, Frank and Jamie Martin, even your father probably will be asked more questions.'

The colour receded a little in Ruth's cheeks. 'I suppose so. I expect you think Frank and I are awful for suspecting Lilith, but she does seem to be the most likely candidate. Her glove was covered in blood.' The girl shuddered.

'You and your brother have a difficult relationship with your stepmother?' Kitty phrased the question delicately.

Ruth shrugged. 'We co-exist in the same house. Lilith does her thing and we, well, we do ours. It's always been like that. We don't hate her or anything. I suppose most of the time we ignore her, and she ignores us. She's never been a mother figure to us. We still have memories of our own mother, and we had excellent nannies when we were growing up. Plus, we've always had each other you see, Frank and I, being twins.'

Kitty thought it must have been quite a strange upbringing for two motherless children. 'That's very fortunate. I am an only child. My mother disappeared when I was young and my grandmother brought me up, so I understand your position.'

A smile curved the corners of Ruth's mouth. 'Thank you, Mrs Bryant, Kitty. You've been very kind.' The girl darted back in the direction of the vicarage.

. . .

Matt lifted the iron latch on the gate so Kitty could step through. 'A restorative cup of tea, I think.'

The village green was busy. Kitty and Matt were lucky to find a free table at the tea room. It seemed that everyone was agog with whatever was going on in the lane behind the vicarage. The news of the doctor's murder had already spread like wildfire through the small community.

Kitty was very conscious of the number of curious gazes in her direction as she and Matt ordered their tea and an iced bun. Bertie drank his fill from a brown ceramic dish of water under the table and waited to see if any crumbs might come his way.

'Begging your pardon, sir, miss, but have you just come from the vicarage? Only there's talk that the doctor has been killed in the lane yonder.' The tea shop proprietress set down their tea things on the table in front of them.

'Yes, I'm afraid that's true,' Matt agreed.

'Dear me. I heard as he's been murdered, stabbed.' The woman looked to Matt and Kitty for confirmation.

'Yes,' Kitty said. She wasn't quite sure how to answer. She knew that the villagers probably knew all of this already, but she didn't want word to get back to Inspector Woolley that she and Matt were responsible for spreading gossip.

The woman clicked her tongue disapprovingly. 'I don't know what the world is coming too. First poor Miss Crowther and now the doctor. 'Tis shocking, a body doesn't feel safe.'

'It is quite awful. Let's hope that the police make an arrest soon,' Matt said.

'Oh yes, my word, it's not a nice idea that there's a murderer on the loose in the village,' the woman agreed. 'Is it right as they think someone at the vicarage did it?'

Kitty focused on placing the metal strainer over her cup

ready to pour the tea. 'I really don't know. I think there are a number of suspects.'

The woman pursed her lips as she looked knowingly at Kitty. 'Humph, well I knows who I would think could have had a hand in it. That fancy piece married to the vicar is involved if you ask me. She never liked Miss Crowther and her and the doctor was always going about together, if you catch my meaning.'

Kitty made a noncommittal noise and the woman bustled away to serve some of her other tables.

'It seems Lilith is high on the list of suspects for everyone,' Kitty said as she finished adding milk to her cup.

'Yes, it would appear so,' Matt agreed.

'It looked to me though as if someone had approached the car on the driver's side. The doctor had lowered his window to speak to them and then when he had turned towards the passenger seat, whoever it was had leaned in and stabbed him through the open window,' Kitty said.

Matt took a sip of tea. 'I agree.'

'When Lilith was screaming, she was on the passenger side with the door open and her one glove was stained with blood. She said she had opened the car door herself and gone to reprimand Doctor Masters for not getting out and opening it for her.' Kitty looked at Matt.

'Yes, that's what she said. If she is telling the truth it would account for how she got blood on her glove.' Matt looked at Kitty.

'The angle of the knife and its position would argue for him being stabbed from outside the car. If it were Lilith and she attacked him from inside the car then that doesn't fit.' Kitty took a sip of her tea. She needed it after everything that had happened.

'But she could have been the person who attacked him through the window,' Matt said, 'and then staged her screams to attract attention. Probably because she realised that with the blood on her glove, she would need an excuse.' Matt looked at Kitty.

Kitty shook her head. 'Lilith said that the doctor usually opened the car door for her. He would have been looking out for her surely and the moment she opened the door onto the lane he would have got out of the car to greet her. Why would she have killed her own lover?'

'But she also said that she was late. He could have dozed off. She may have rapped on the window and he would have let it down to speak to her. And, perhaps she wished to end the affair, or he did,' Matt countered.

Kitty nibbled thoughtfully on her bun. The sugary icing was doing much to restore her spirits as she pondered the case. Matt had made some good points, but Lilith's collapse had certainly seemed real enough to her. Matt finished eating and drained his cup of tea.

'I don't know, old thing. I think Lilith could well be the killer. Unless, of course, the inspector uncovers something of interest at Quixshotte Hall.'

CHAPTER TWENTY

They finished their tea and walked back to the Dower House. On their arrival Kitty was unsurprised to discover that the news of Doctor Masters' murder had preceded them.

'Matthew, Kitty, do come and tell me what has happened. I received a telephone call from the colonel.' Aunt Effie summoned them into the drawing room where she laid aside her gardening catalogue ready to hear all about the murder.

Kitty could only assume that either Frank or Ruth must have telephoned the Hall and spoken to Jamie.

Matt swiftly informed his aunt of everything that had occurred during their outing. 'I must say, Aunt Effie, I do place some of the blame for all of this on you,' he teased.

His aunt placed a heavily bejewelled hand to her ample bosom. 'I merely suggested a pleasant walk in the village. It's hardly my fault that you will persist in stumbling upon murders.'

Kitty could see by the twinkle in her eyes that the note of indignation in her tone was merely pretence.

'What did you hope we'd discover on our walk, Aunt Effie?' Matt asked.

His aunt looked mildly affronted. 'Nothing in particular, dear boy. I merely thought that since you hoped to speak to the occupants of the vicarage that the route I suggested might enable you to encounter them.'

'Well, we certainly achieved that.' Matt laughed.

His aunt reached over to gently rap his knuckles. 'Murder is no laughing matter, as well you should know. Poor Doctor Masters, he'll be much missed. I do hope that you were not too upset by all of this, Kitty dear?'

Kitty smiled reassuringly at Matt's aunt. 'It was a shock, as you might imagine, but in our line of work one does become somewhat immune to such surprises.'

'Even so, Kitty, it is quite a change from hotelier work,' Aunt Effie said.

This was true but Kitty had encountered plenty of deaths whilst working at the hotel, even before she had met Matt. It was far from unknown for guests to be taken ill or to sadly pass away in their rooms. Something few people considered when she mentioned her former occupation.

After lunch Aunt Effie announced her intentions of visiting one of her friends for the afternoon and departed, leaving Kitty and Matt to their own devices. Kitty suspected it was to discuss the latest murder.

'I wonder how the inspector fared at Quixshotte Hall?' Kitty mused as she settled herself on the terrace with her book.

'You mean if he established that Jamie Martin or even the colonel and Mrs Brothers had an alibi for this morning?' Matt asked, smiling at her from where he had positioned himself on the lounger with the day's crossword.

'Well, yes, that too, obviously. I know everything is pointing towards Lilith but there are other people to consider,' Kitty said.

Matt chuckled. 'I agree. There seems little we can do for now at any rate so we may as well enjoy the afternoon. Our holiday is coming to an end in the next few days.'

Kitty sighed. 'This will sound most peculiar but although there has been a lot, with Miss Crowther and now Doctor Masters being killed and Jimmi being attacked, I have still had a nice time. The Yorkshire countryside is very lovely, and your aunt has been so welcoming.'

'She is very fond of you.' Matt smiled at her. 'I think she may even prefer you to me.'

Kitty laughed at his teasing and swatted his Panama hat off his head. 'Really!'

'Steady on, old girl, this is my favourite hat.' He picked it up from the floor before Bertie could pounce and placed it back on his head to shade his face.

They passed a quiet afternoon whilst the bank of clouds grew more oppressive, and the air became muggy and close again. After Aunt Effie returned and they had finished dinner they took coffee as usual in the drawing room.

The French windows had been pushed open wide in an effort to bring more air into the room. Kitty privately thought that another storm was imminent and she was certain that she had already heard the distant rumble of thunder.

'What ho! Anyone home?' Colonel Brothers' stentorian voice sounded from the terrace as he appeared in the open doorway. Bertie roused himself to give a warning bark before greeting the visitor with a wagging tail.

'Colonel, do come in. I'm surprised you have ventured abroad in this heat and with the prospect of rain.' Aunt Effie set aside the gardening catalogue she had been studying in order to welcome her guest.

Matt jumped up and went to do his duty at the drinks trolley, while Kitty tucked her bookmark inside her book. Bertie settled back at her feet.

'Yes, it does look as if it's going to throw it down.' The colonel lowered himself into a vacant leather armchair with a sigh. 'I needed to get out of the house, clear my head.'

Matt poured a whisky for himself and the colonel. 'Aunt Effie? Kitty?' He looked at the ladies.

'A cocktail, please,' Kitty replied as his aunt requested a glass of Madeira.

'We've had that Inspector Woolley at the Hall for much of the day.' Colonel Brothers took a sip of his drink as a growl of thunder rumbled around outside the house.

'He told us this morning that he intended to call. Obviously, we were not at liberty to forewarn you, sir.' Matt handed a glass to his aunt and picked up the silver cocktail shaker to make Kitty's drink.

The colonel quirked his brow. 'Yes, of course you weren't, it being a murder and all. He said you and Mrs Bryant heard Lilith screaming in the lane when she found Doctor Masters' body?' He phrased it as a question.

'That's right, Lilith was quite hysterical with shock,' Kitty said.

Matt poured Kitty's cocktail and handed it to her, before retaking his seat beside her. 'It's a bad business.'

'What? Oh yes, very bad. The doctor was a decent enough fellow and good at his job,' the colonel agreed. He lapsed into silence.

'I assume the inspector wished to establish where everyone was when the doctor was murdered?' Kitty glanced at Matt. She didn't add that he would also have been investigating who took the murder weapon from the vicarage kitchen.

'Yes, oh yes. He wanted to know if we knew if Doctor Masters was taking Lilith to the station and what the arrangements were. Jamie said that he knew as he was in the house when the matter was discussed.' The colonel stared gloomily into his whisky. 'The boy's a fool. I told him several times to keep away from the vicarage.'

'Oh dear, sir, why was that?' Matt asked in a mild tone.

The colonel sighed and blinked. 'He spends too much time

there. Always hanging around with that girl, Ruth. I told him it will give rise to expectations in a small place like Quixshotte. Then there's her brother, Frank. He always seems to be hanging around the Hall too.'

Kitty had her own thoughts on why Jamie was so often at the vicarage and she suspected that it was Frank rather than Ruth who was the draw. The discovery of the boulder with the carved initials and Frank's furtive escape from the vicarage had hinted at something more than friendship. It would also explain why Miss Crowther had threatened Jamie on the day of the fair.

Kitty suspected that the colonel was also aware of why his nephew was so often with the Drummond twins. It would certainly explain the argument she and Matt had overheard at the start of the week.

'Were you all able to satisfy the inspector's questions, sir?' she asked.

'Oh yes. I believe so. Jamie and I were with my land agent up until Inspector Woolley called at the Hall. I had insisted that Jamie pull his finger out and start learning the ropes if he was serious about managing the estate in the future.' The colonel took another meditative sip of his whisky.

'And was Mrs Brothers at home?' Kitty asked.

The colonel looked surprised at her question. 'Yes, absolutely. She was hosting a meeting of the Overseas Missionary Group. Miss Crowther had been down to look after the ladies but with what happened on Saturday Hilda offered to host them. Lilith would have been useless and young Ruth has enough on her plate really. They were all having tea in the library when the doctor was killed.'

Kitty sipped her gin cocktail thoughtfully. It sounded as if everyone at Quixshotte Hall had a cast iron alibi for when Doctor Masters was murdered. That swung the finger of suspicion firmly back towards the occupants of the vicarage.

Another rumble of thunder echoed around the house.

'Dear me, Colonel, it sounds as if the storm is moving closer.' Aunt Effie turned her head to look out at the darkening sky over the garden.

'Indeed, I may need to trespass on your hospitality for a little longer until it passes over, Effie m'dear,' the colonel said.

'Of course, you know you may stay as long as you please,' Matt's aunt replied.

As she spoke the rain started, bouncing down on the stone flags. Kitty jumped up and rushed to close the French doors to prevent the parquet floor from receiving a soaking. Within a minute the water was teeming down the outside of the window-panes to form a puddle on the terrace floor.

'A regular monsoon, reminds me of India.' The colonel drained his glass as lightning flashed and illuminated the room.

'Kitty dear, put the lamps on. It has gone quite dark in here,' Aunt Effie instructed.

'You sound as if you miss India a great deal,' Kitty said to the colonel as she obeyed Matt's aunt's instructions.

'Yes, Hilda and I were both very happy out there. Still, Hilda's sister Gertie became ill, and she was struggling with young Jamie back here in England. My retirement was due, and I contracted malaria. A case of events conspiring you might say. Saw the advertisement for the sale of the Hall in a newspaper and came here.' The colonel looked at his glass as if surprised to find it empty.

'Another drink, sir?' Matt took the hint and the glass.

'Thank you, very good of you,' the colonel accepted a refill.

All potential conversation was stopped for a few minutes by the relentless drumming of the rain and crashing of thunder as the storm appeared to pass directly over the house.

'I expect the inspector will have to question everyone at the vicarage again,' Kitty mused thoughtfully once the noise from outside started to die down.

'Bound too. I don't suppose you and your husband noticed anything untoward this morning before you came across the doctor and Lilith?' the colonel asked.

'No, nothing. It was very quiet and peaceful while we were walking. I suppose someone could have entered the lane from the other end of the village. We entered from the churchyard,' Kitty said.

'Yes, that's a possibility. They could have seen the doctor getting his car out and noticed the direction. Robbery gone wrong, perhaps?' The colonel brightened at the suggestion.

He doesn't know that the knife came from the vicarage kitchen, Kitty thought. She also seemed to recall that the doctor was still wearing a rather nice gold tie pin when she had looked at the body. So robbery was unlikely to be a motive.

'You think then it might not be connected with Miss Crowther's murder?' Matt asked.

The colonel sighed once more. 'One would prefer that it wasn't, since it means that someone we know committed both deeds.'

'I understand, sir. It's not pleasant to think that a friend or neighbour is capable of something so wicked,' Matt replied.

The drumming of the rain started to die away and the thunder following the lightning flashes grew more distant. The colonel had almost finished his second drink when Aunt Effie's butler entered the room.

'Master Martin, madam, to collect Colonel Brothers.'

Jamie Martin followed the manservant into the room. 'I thought I should run down and collect you in the car, Uncle Stanley. Aunt Hilda said you would be here, and she was getting anxious about you being caught out in the storm.'

'Do have a seat, Jamie, while your uncle finishes his drink. Can we get you something?' Aunt Effie asked.

'Why not, a whisky and soda would be most welcome,

thank you,' Jamie accepted and took one of the side chairs near the window. 'What a day! Has Uncle Stanley told you about our inquisition by the police?'

Matt poured a whisky and soda and passed it to Jamie. 'Yes, he said the inspector had been to the Hall to ask questions.'

'First Creepy Crowther and now the doc. Quixshotte is becoming quite a hotbed of crime,' Jamie remarked cheerfully.

'Jamie!' His uncle glared at him.

'Sorry, Uncle. Doctor Masters' murder is quite horrid, and unexpected, don't you think?' Jamie took a sip from his glass.

'I suppose all murders are unexpected, young man,' Aunt Effie remarked with a touch of asperity.

'That's true, but Miss Crowther wasn't terribly popular, was she? So, lots of people could have had it in for her. The doc was a decent sort of cove though,' Jamie mused.

Kitty's lips quirked slightly at Jamie's irreverent way of looking at the crimes. 'I'm afraid in our experience that being a horrid person doesn't necessarily mean you are more likely to be murdered. Sometimes you can simply be in the wrong place at the wrong time.'

Jamie raised his glass in the air in her direction. 'Very true, Mrs Bryant. I wonder, do you think that's what happened to the doctor? Wrong place, wrong time?'

'This morning you mean?' Matt asked. 'Or do you think he may have inadvertently witnessed something significant at the fair?'

The younger man appeared to consider the question. 'I suppose it could be either case. The inspector was banging on about who knew that the doctor was collecting lovely Lilith from the lane, but I suppose lots of people would have known. He did it quite often. The doc used to give Lilith lifts in his motor car all over the place. Reverend Drummond relies on his bicycle and the train to get about. Frank keeps on at him to get a car. He's jolly fit though for his age you know, the vicar. He moves at one heck of a pace on that bike.' Jamie grinned as he spoke. 'I should know, I've had a job to pass him sometimes.'

'The doctor was at the refreshment stall for quite a large part of the afternoon on Saturday,' Kitty said.

'Gosh yes. I saw him there when I was running around the place. I think they were glad of his help,' Jamie agreed. 'He was there more than the vicar. Ruth and Frank were doing most of the work though. Poor Ruth was exhausted at the end of the day. Lilith mainly just poured tea and looked decorative.'

'He could have noticed something then, and not realised it was important,' Matt suggested.

'I suppose so. I daresay Inspector Woolley will be digging around. If not, then my money has to be on Lilith as our murderess. Let's face it, she was in both places and the inspector certainly seems to have her card marked.' Jamie knocked back the last of his drink.

'Really, Jamie,' the colonel tutted at his unrepentant nephew.

Kitty suspected that Jamie was probably right. Could Lilith have killed Miss Crowther and then the doctor? She glanced at Jamie who was talking amicably now with Matt's aunt about his ideas for the estate. Or could Jamie have conspired with Frank to commit the crimes? Jamie might have an alibi for this morning, but he could still be working with someone. Or did he suspect Ruth and Frank and wished to throw everyone off the scent by framing Lilith?

'Well, come on, Uncle, or Aunt Hilda will send out a second search party. At least the rain has knocked off for now.' Jamie rose from his seat as his uncle finished his drink.

'Very well, dear boy, and thank you, Effie, my dear, for your hospitality.' The colonel stood somewhat stiffly, and he and his nephew made their goodbyes.

'Dear, dear, that young man will blurt out whatever is on his mind,' Aunt Effie tutted as she picked up her gardening catalogue once more. 'Mark my words, one of these days it will get him into serious trouble.'

CHAPTER TWENTY-ONE

The storm continued to rumble around the house for much of the night. Kitty slept poorly, disturbed by the bursts of rain, the sticky air and strange dreams about the murders. Consequently, she woke later than usual to a fresh, bright morning.

Matt had already finished eating when she went downstairs.

'You're a little late this morning, darling.' Matt folded the newspaper he had been reading and looked at her with concern.

'I didn't sleep well. It was so hot during the night, and I kept thinking about Miss Crowther and Doctor Masters.' She slid onto a seat opposite Matt and helped herself to a now cold triangle of toast from the silver rack. She wrinkled her nose as she slathered on some butter and nibbled at the corner of the toast.

Matt rang the bell for a fresh pot of tea. 'And what were your conclusions as you lay tossing and turning?'

'That's the problem. I don't think I have any. At least none that feel wholly satisfying.' Kitty smiled her thanks to the house-maid who had appeared bearing a teapot and a new rack of toast.

Matt leaned back in his seat and crossed his ankles, displacing Bertie from his prime begging spot under the table. 'Well, Jamie and the inspector both seem to have Mrs Drummond fixed as the murderess,' he said after the servant had left the room.

'Yes, I know. I can see how that would work if she and the doctor had perhaps conspired to kill Miss Crowther to prevent her from revealing their affair. The doctor could have been responsible for attacking Jimmi at the circus to stop him from revealing anything if he saw something at the fair. Lilith would then have killed Doctor Masters, but why?' Kitty looked at Matt.

Matt shrugged. 'The doctor could have developed cold feet over the whole thing. Remorse about Miss Crowther? Worry that Jimmi might be able to identify him? Lilith could have killed him to protect herself.' He warmed to his theme. 'Or she may have tired of the affair and wished to end it. The doctor could have blackmailed her into continuing.'

Kitty sighed as she poured herself a hot cup of tea. 'It just doesn't feel quite right somehow.'

Matt raised a quizzical eyebrow. 'Who else is in the frame?'

Kitty stirred her tea as she considered his question. 'Jamie Martin, I suppose.'

'Jamie? He was with the colonel and the land agent when Doctor Masters was killed,' Matt said.

'He may have an accomplice, or he could even possibly have slipped away for a few minutes. It wouldn't take long to drive that sporty car of his into the village, stab the doctor and then get back,' Kitty said.

Matt shook his head. 'Risky, he could have been missed or someone could have seen or heard his car. Who do you have in mind as his accomplice?'

'One of the twins is the most likely option,' she suggested.

'Ruth or Frank or both?' Matt smiled at her as he posed his question.

'Frank, because I am pretty certain that there is more than friendship between those two. The initials on the boulder gave me the idea and then Frank's sneaking around and constant visits to the Hall.' Kitty paused to take a sip of tea.

'Interesting. You think the colonel is aware of the possibility?' Matt asked.

'I think so and I think he is afraid of what would happen if even the suggestion of what he would see as an improper and illegal connection were to get out. It would be terrible for Jamie and Frank, but the consequences would be felt by both the family at the Hall and the one at the vicarage. I think that's why he told Jamie to stay away from there,' Kitty said.

'So, Frank or Jamie killed Miss Crowther, then Jamie attacked Jimmi and Frank killed Doctor Masters?' Matt tried her suggestion out for size. 'Possible, I suppose.'

'They would have a motive, the means and the opportunity,' Kitty said before taking a bite of her toast.

She could see the wheels turning in Matt's mind as he digested her suggestion. 'And Ruth?'

Kitty frowned. 'She is covering for her brother. They are twins after all, and twins often have an even closer bond. Frank and Jamie may have persuaded her to help them allay suspicions. After all, if everyone thinks that it's Ruth who Jamie goes to see they won't consider that it's her brother that he has feelings for.'

Matt drummed his fingers on the tabletop. 'And you think that they could have murdered Miss Crowther because she had that argument with Jamie? That she was threatening Frank and Jamie with exposure?'

Kitty nodded. 'You heard Miss Crowther when she came to the Dower House on the Thursday before the murder. It was clear then that she disliked Jamie.'

'And you also think that the twins could have acted alone?'
Matt asked.

'I think it's a possibility. They would certainly not be
concerned about making Lilith the scapegoat. Ruth could have
poisoned Miss Crowther and her brother could have killed the
doctor.' Kitty popped the last morsel of toast into her mouth.

'I can see you gave all this a lot of thought.' Matt's blue eyes
twinkled as he looked at her.

'If you are not going to take this seriously,' Kitty warned.

'I'm sorry, darling. Of course I'm taking you seriously. Yes,
you're right if what you think is true, then it does open up the
circle of possibilities a little wider,' Matt agreed.

'Well, thank you.' Her feelings mollified, Kitty finished her
tea. 'Now, what are our plans for today?'

'Sleuthing plans or holiday plans?' Matt asked.

'Both ideally. It would be nice to have a drive out to that
beauty spot Aunt Effie told us about the other day, but at the
same time I would love to have a talk to Lilith.' Kitty looked
innocently at her husband. 'It would be polite to call at the
vicarage to ask how she is.'

'While on our way to the beauty spot?' The dimple in
Matt's cheek flashed as he smiled at her.

'Two birds, one stone.' Kitty rose from her seat.

'Very well, go and fetch your hat,' Matt said with a mock
sigh.

Kitty laughed and scampered away to get herself ready for
the day's outing.

* * *

While Kitty readied herself for their trip Matt considered her
suggestions about who could have been responsible for the
murders. He supposed the one thing that had come out of
Doctor Masters' murder was that the colonel and his wife could

not have been involved. The colonel had been with Jamie and the land agent. Hilda had been with a whole group of ladies acting as their hostess.

It was highly unlikely that there were two separate murderers on the loose in pretty Quixshotte, so whoever killed Miss Crowther must be responsible for Doctor Masters' death too. The attack on the elephant keeper also had to be connected. Why else would someone target Jimmi Choudhury? He was not wealthy, and appeared to be well liked in both the circus community and elsewhere. Certainly, there had been no reports of arguments or disagreements that he knew of between Jimmi and anyone else.

He collected Bertie's leather leash from the hall table and went outside to see if Kitty had fetched her car from the large wooden garage at the side of the house. Aunt Effie was already outside dressed in her gardening attire, leaning on her cane next to Kitty's red motor.

'Your wife tells me you are off for a drive,' Aunt Effie called as he rounded the corner of the house.

'Yes, we thought we should go to that viewpoint you mentioned. The one with the standing stone.' Matt led Bertie around to the back seat of Kitty's car where he secured the dog.

'Excellent idea, make the most of your last few days here.' Aunt Effie smiled approvingly.

Kitty backed her car up carefully to turn around and waved her gloved hand cheerfully at his aunt as they set off towards the village.

'You didn't mention that we intended to call on Lilith?' Matt asked.

'I thought it best not too. She was telling me that she hoped our stay hadn't been spoiled by the murders just before you came outside. I didn't want to worry her,' Kitty said.

Matt smiled. He knew his aunt well and very little ever troubled her. She was quite a formidable lady and made of stern stuff. Kitty drove into the village and parked in the road outside the vicarage gate. The tea room across the road was already open and he gave the proprietress a friendly wave as he unhooked Bertie to let him out of the car.

He noticed that the police car was parked once more outside the Quixshotte Arms. He wondered if the inspector had returned to ask Lilith more questions after his visit to the Hall yesterday, or if he would call at the vicarage today instead.

The doorbell was answered at the first ring by Ruth. He thought she looked a little disappointed to discover them on her doorstep.

'Captain Bryant, Kitty, what a surprise.' Ruth threw a glare in the direction of the tea room where the proprietress was continuing to openly stand on the green watching the vicarage. 'Please come inside.'

'We were travelling this way, and I simply couldn't go past the house without stopping to enquire about your stepmother.' Kitty gave the girl a winning smile.

'Lilith? Oh, she's all right. Please come through, she's in the sitting room.' Ruth led the way into the large, comfortable-looking room where they had been the previous day.

Lilith, dressed in a pale-green silk floral day dress was arranged prettily on the sofa. A china cup of tea stood at her elbow on the low table where the stained gloves had been the previous day.

'My dear Mrs Drummond, I do hope we aren't intruding but I said to Matt that we really should call and see if you have recovered from yesterday. You had such a terrible experience.' Kitty took a seat on the faded chintz armchair opposite the sofa. Matt took the other vacant seat.

'It was so upsetting, I am still rather shaken up.' Lilith had a pleasant, well-modulated voice with a hint of a Northern accent. Matt noticed that she appeared to have recovered well enough to apply her make-up and style her hair.

'I can imagine. It was so awful, and especially as you and Doctor Masters were such good friends, so I'm told,' Kitty agreed.

Ruth made a sound that could have been a laugh that she turned into a cough.

'Ruth dear, perhaps Captain and Mrs Bryant might care for some tea?' Lilith fixed her gaze on her stepdaughter.

'No, thank you, nothing for us.' Kitty smiled at Ruth.

'Well, I must go and do something,' Ruth said vaguely and slipped out of the room before her stepmother could request anything else from her.

'I'm so sorry, Mrs Bryant. The twins are at that awkward age, I'm afraid. Frank is off to university in the autumn, however, and Ruth is talking about doing something.' Lilith made a helpless fluttery gesture with her hands.

'I expect it will feel strange for you and your husband to be without them in the house when they are both gone?' Kitty said.

Lilith gave a gracious if somewhat tight-lipped smile. 'Yes, they were quite young when their mother died, and my husband and I married.'

'Aunt Effie said it was a very romantic tale, how the two of you met,' Matt said.

Lilith's gaze shifted slightly. 'Yes, I suppose so. I was very young, barely twenty. I have several older sisters so I suppose I was the baby of the family. Consequently, I expect I was a little spoiled. My older sister is a seamstress so she would make me beautiful clothes. The day we met I had a new dress and a darling new hat with a feather in it.' She sighed happily and a contented smile played at the corner of her mouth.

'It can't have been easy for you then, leaving your home and taking on a ready-made family with all the parish work that tends to fall upon a vicar's wife.' Kitty looked sympathetic.

'Not at all, people don't understand. My husband is a good man but some years older than myself and it was all so overwhelming. He is a very scholarly man and somewhat detached from everyday life. Fortunately, Miss Crowther had the parish matters well in hand and the children's nanny was very good.' Lilith smiled contentedly and examined her well-manicured hands. 'My own health is delicate so I mustn't exert myself too much. As you saw yesterday, I don't cope well with sudden shocks.'

'What shall you do now, without Miss Crowther?' Matt asked. 'She was still running many of the committees and meetings, wasn't she?'

Colour crept into Lilith's face. 'Yes, she was, it's a terrible loss, but dear Mrs Brothers has said she will take on a couple of things and Ruth is at home, of course.'

'That will be very helpful to you,' Kitty said. 'Colonel Brothers called at the Dower House last night and said the inspector had been there asking questions yesterday. Did he call here again too?'

Lilith pursed her lips at this, her eyes widened in distress. 'No, although I expect he will be back. I felt so ill I was forced to take to my bed yesterday. It really is most tiresome of the inspector to keep bothering me. I have no idea what else he thinks I can tell him, about Saturday or yesterday. It makes me afraid, Mrs Bryant. It's almost as if he thinks that I did it.' Her heavily lip-sticked lips trembled.

'That you murdered Doctor Masters?' Matt asked.

Lilith looked at him and he could see the fear in her large brown eyes. 'Both of them, Captain Bryant. That I poisoned Miss Crowther and that I stabbed dear Leo. But why ever would I do such a thing? Emily could be annoying, always looking down on me and making snide remarks but that's not a reason to kill her.' Lilith tugged a lace-edged handkerchief from her pocket and dabbed delicately at her nose.

'And Doctor Masters? Forgive me if I'm speaking out of

turn, but you were more than friends I take it?' Kitty asked in a low voice.

Lilith's eyes opened even wider, and her hands shook. 'Oh, Mrs Bryant, whatever must you think of me? Please, my husband doesn't know. It was the only way I could be happy. You don't know how lonely my life is.' She bit back a sob.

Matt met Kitty's gaze.

'Please do not distress yourself, Mrs Drummond,' Kitty soothed.

Lilith hiccoughed and dried her eyes. 'I shall miss Leo so much. He was a true friend to me. I would never have harmed him, never.'

There was a tap on the door of the drawing room and Ruth entered, her face pale. Behind her stood the solid figure of Inspector Woolley and one of his uniformed constables.

'The inspector is here again to see you, Lilith.' Ruth's voice held a small tremor as she stepped aside to allow the policemen into the room.

Inspector Woolley's expression was stern. 'Lilith Elizabeth Drummond, I am here to arrest you for the murder of Miss Emily Evangeline Crowther and Doctor Leonard Victor Masters.'

CHAPTER TWENTY-TWO

Kitty watched from her armchair as the vicarage promptly erupted into chaos. Lilith screamed so loudly that the vicar came running in from his study. Bertie started to bark. Ruth started to sob and her twin rushed in to comfort her.

The police escorted Lilith from the house with the vicar still berating the inspector and the constable right up to the open door of the car. Ruth collapsed down on the sofa next to Frank who looked as pale and shaken as his sister.

Kitty was surprised when the vicar returned, not to comfort or reassure his children but to take himself off back into his study.

'I expect Father has gone to telephone a solicitor,' Frank muttered by way of an explanation. He had clearly noticed Kitty's surprised expression.

'Of course. I'm so sorry, my dears, this is a dreadful situation for you both. Is there anything Matt or I can do to assist you in any way?' Kitty asked as her husband continued to calm the overexcited Bertie who seemed to think what had happened was some sort of game.

Ruth lifted her tear-stained face from where she had been

leaning on her brother's shoulder. 'That's very kind of you, Kitty. I think we will be all right. It's just the shock of it. You know when something happens that you've been half-expecting, but it still takes you by surprise?'

Kitty nodded. She knew exactly what the girl meant. 'Of course. I expect your father will be able to contact someone to help Lilith.'

Frank licked his lips. 'Do you think she really did do it, Mrs Bryant? Poison Miss Crowther and stab the doctor?'

'I don't know, Frank. It seems impossible, doesn't it? Still the inspector must believe he has enough evidence to make a case,' Kitty said.

'I didn't sleep at all last night. It was the noise from the storm and then I kept seeing Lilith's white gloves, all covered with blood.' Ruth shivered. 'Like Lady Macbeth. I kept dreaming such horrid dreams.'

'I know you will wish to support your father but if it is too distressing for you to stay here for now, I'm sure my aunt would wish me to offer you rooms at the Dower House,' Matt suggested.

Ruth sniffed and pulled herself more upright. 'Thank you, that is very kind of you and Miss Bryant, but I think Frank and I should stay here to be with Father.'

'Of course, my dear, but the offer remains open at any time. I know this is an awful situation to be in. If there is anything at all you need then please call on us or come to see us,' Kitty said.

'We will, thank you.' Ruth gave her a small grateful smile.

Frank walked with them as they left the room. 'I'll take care of Ruth.' He opened the front door of the vicarage.

'I'm sure you will.' Kitty patted his arm. He looked very young in that moment and determined to be brave.

She glanced at the closed panelled door of the study. It seemed the vicar was still using the telephone as she could hear the murmur of conversation.

As Kitty, Matt and Bertie made their way along the path to Kitty's car she could see that the green outside the tea room was unusually busy with villagers. Many of them making no attempt to hide their curiosity as they stared at the vicarage. Matt stowed Bertie on the back seat of her motor as Kitty took her place at the wheel.

'Let us get off.' She turned the key to start the engine. The openly speculative gaze of the vicar's neighbours and the events of the past week suddenly combined to make her feel quite nauseous.

Matt gave her a concerned glance as she drove away from the village centre. 'Are you all right, old thing? That was all rather ghastly, wasn't it?'

'I feel awful for those two, Ruth and Frank. Murder is such a dreadful thing.' Kitty clashed her gears with unusual force as she pointed her car up the hill leading from the village.

'You think now then that they may be innocent?' Matt asked her.

'I really don't know, it's so confusing. I just think they are so young and Reverend Drummond is such a vague man. He'll probably forget how they are being affected in all of this. He only ever appears to think about Lilith.' Kitty slowed down so they could read the white fingerpost ahead of them at the road junction.

'Very true. I suppose though he has to find a solicitor to represent his wife and no doubt speak to the bishop. Tomorrow is Sunday and, surely, he will not take the services himself.' Matt pulled the folded map from the glovebox to check their direction.

'Oh, yes I hadn't thought of that. Of course, you're right. What a mess everything is. I wonder what your aunt will have to say about it all when she hears what's happened.' Kitty glanced at the map and took the turn.

'I daresay the news of Lilith's arrest will go around the

village like a wildfire. There certainly seemed to be a lot of activity on the green.' Matt held tight to the map to prevent it blowing about in the breeze.

Kitty had lowered the roof on the car and both the map and Bertie's ears were being tossed about. The sun was shining and the countryside around them seemed to have recovered its colour thanks to the recent downpours of rain. Cow parsley softened the grey stone walls that lined the side of the road and crimson poppies poked their heads out in the yellow corn fields.

'I noticed the tea room and post office looked very busy,' Kitty said, steering her car adeptly past a small horse-drawn wagon. 'Your aunt will no doubt be fully informed of everything by the time we return this afternoon.'

Matt grinned and directed Kitty to take the next left turn. 'Of course. You know as well as I how things work in small communities. Yorkshire is not so different from Devon in that aspect.'

'Very true,' she agreed.

Kitty was forced to put the matter from her mind while she concentrated on finding the place Matt's aunt had recommended they visit. It was off the beaten track, but she had assured them that they would like it.

'This is it.' Matt indicated a long pull in at the side of the road next to a stile with a fingerpost indicating a footpath that led upwards to the top of a hill.

Kitty parked her car just off the road and they got out. Bertie capered about happily sniffing for traces of rabbit in the hedgerow, while Matt put the roof back up on her car. There were still some clouds in the sky and despite the sun she didn't fully trust that it would not rain.

'All done.' Matt took Bertie's leash back from her. 'Now, I propose we leave all thoughts of Lilith and the murders behind and concentrate on our holiday.' He kissed the tip of Kitty's nose. 'The view from the top here is supposed to be worth the walk.'

Kitty happily agreed and tucked her hand in the crook of his arm ready to explore. Bertie trotted enthusiastically ahead of them, and they set off along the upward path at the side of the field.

By the time they returned a couple of hours later, Kitty felt much better. They paused near the stile for Bertie to drink his fill from the tiny crystal-clear spring that burbled its way down the hillside.

The village appeared back to normal when they drove through on their way to the Dower House. The police car had gone from outside the Quixshotte Arms and there was only one table occupied on the green outside the tea room.

When Kitty pulled her car to a halt outside Matt's aunt's house, another vehicle, a small dark-blue car, was already in the driveway.

'Your aunt has a visitor,' Kitty said as she helped to retrieve Bertie from the rear seat.

They followed the sound of female voices around the side and back of the house onto the terrace where Matt's aunt was entertaining an unfamiliar lady.

'Matthew, Kitty, this is Emily Crowther's cousin, Margery. She has finished emptying Miss Crowther's cottage and has come to bring me a couple of small mementos that she thought Emily wished me to have,' Aunt Effie explained.

Matt and Kitty shook hands with the visitor and took a seat, while Aunt Effie rang the bell for more refreshments.

'The talk in the village as I came away from the house was that the vicar's wife had been took away by the police. Someone said as your red motor car had been parked outside at the time,' Miss Crowther's cousin remarked looking at Matt and Kitty.

Kitty thought Margery resembled her deceased cousin. She too was tall and skinny with a prominent nose and sharp eyes.

Her hair in an untidy heap of greying blonde curls under an unbecoming dark-green Chinese-style summer hat.

'Yes, that's right. We were at the vicarage earlier when the inspector came to see Mrs Drummond,' Matt said.

Miss Crowther's cousin pursed her thin lips. 'Fancy the murderer being the vicar's wife. Who would have thought it? I always said to Emily though not to trust her. No better than she should be, that one. Breeding always tells in the end, that's what I say.'

Kitty bit her tongue at this. She was relieved when a fresh pot of tea and a plate of small cakes appeared. She and Matt had missed lunch while they were walking and had only had an apple each from Kitty's handbag when they had reached the viewpoint.

'It is all quite dreadful,' Aunt Effie agreed. 'I wonder who will take the services at church tomorrow? I suppose the churchwarden will have to do it. He is frightfully deaf though and inclined to leave bits out if he loses his place. Still, perhaps Ruth or Frank might assist him.'

'Humph, I doubt if any of the family will dare to show their face. I mean, my poor cousin was poisoned and then the doctor was stabbed in cold blood. I ask you, it would take some brass-neck, wouldn't it?' Miss Crowther's cousin glared at them all as if daring them to contradict her.

'It is terrible, I do see your point. What are your plans for the cottage, my dear?' Aunt Effie enquired in a soothing tone.

'I have asked an agent to place it for rent for the time being. It's a nice little house and happen with all of Emily's clutter gone it should fetch a good price.' Margery slurped her tea, the prospect of money seemingly serving to lift her spirits.

'I should think it will rent easily being in such a good position on the green. It always seemed a very comfortable house,' Aunt Effie agreed.

'I've arranged for the walls to be painted in what was

Kenneth's room. It hasn't been touched since he died. Naturally there was a lot to deal with there. You know how Emily was about him, proper soft. I used to say to her, he's not coming back you know, clear the place out.' Margery set her cup back on its saucer, her lips compressed in a narrow line.

'I'm sure there must have been a lot for you to do. We heard that Miss Crowther was devoted to her brother's memory,' Kitty agreed.

Margery sniffed. 'Yes, she was, God rest her soul. Still, it's done now.'

'Margery has given me some lovely things to remember Miss Crowther by.' Aunt Effie delved into a cardboard box next to the table and produced what Kitty considered to be the most hideous china statuette.

It appeared to be of a very pink, naked and ugly cupid firing an arrow from his bow. Kitty blinked, lost for words that Aunt Effie seemed to like this monstrosity.

'Gosh, that's quite stunning, Aunt Effie,' Matt managed. Kitty suspected he was trying not to laugh.

'Dear Emily said it always seemed to draw your attention when you visited. She knew how much you admired it,' Margery said.

Kitty bit her lip and averted her gaze from Aunt Effie. 'It is very eye-catching.' The cupid seemed to be watching her with a slightly cross-eyed painted gaze.

'Margery has also very kindly gifted me Emily's photograph albums of the village. She has quite a collection of interesting pictures of village events. She was something of an archivist for Quixshotte,' Aunt Effie said.

'Oh, that does sound fascinating.' Kitty was relieved that this gift at least sounded like something she could praise with sincerity.

'Emily was fond of her photographs. Well, I must be getting off. Thank you for the tea, Miss Bryant. I'm off to the Hall next as I've a potted aspidistra in the car that I thought Mrs Brothers would care for. Her being so fond of plants and everything.' Margery stood ready to leave and drew her gloves back on.

'Thank you for the gifts, my dear, it's very kind of you and do let me know about the funeral arrangements for Miss Crowther,' Aunt Effie said.

Matt stood and offered to walk Margery to her car. Something she accepted graciously.

'Oh dear, Aunt Effie, whatever shall you do with that cherub?' Kitty asked as soon as Margery was out of earshot.

The statuette stood in the middle of the table winking pinkly and malevolently at them in the afternoon sunshine.

'It is dreadfully pink and ghastly, isn't it? I don't suppose that you and Matthew...'

Kitty stepped swiftly in before she could finish her sentence. 'No, thank you very much, I couldn't possibly deprive you of such a treasure. After all you did admire it so in Miss Crowther's cottage.'

Matt arrived back to find them both roaring with laughter and his aunt dabbing at her eyes with her handkerchief. 'What have I missed that is so amusing?'

Kitty waved her hand at the cherub.

'Ha, I see. Bless me that thing is ugly.' Matt's comment set them off in a fresh paroxysm of laughter.

'It did always draw my eye whenever I visited, that is certainly true. Miss Crowther's front parlour was quite small and wherever I sat the wretched thing seemed to be in my eyeline, looking at me. She told me once that it had been a gift from a suitor when she was a girl. Her mother was alive at the time and considered the man in question to be beneath her, so she squashed the budding romance quite flat. Emily kept the cherub as a memento,' Aunt Effie explained.

'Well, I have to say I'm on Miss Crowther's mother's side on this one. Can you imagine if she had married the giver of that cherub? A whole house filled with similar knick-knacks.' Matt grinned as he shook his head. 'No, she had a lucky escape there.'

'And now I am forced to keep it.' Aunt Effie looked sadly at the cherub.

'I suggest you employ a clumsy housemaid and place it in a precarious position,' Matt suggested.

'Or explain that having it on show is distressing as it reminds you too much of poor Miss Crowther so you have it in a private room. Then stick it in the attic,' Kitty said.

Aunt Effie lifted the cherub from the table. 'Excellent suggestions both. Perhaps I may add it to my will. Your mother might care for it, Matthew?'

'I think it would hasten my father's demise if you gave that thing to Mother. He would go into apoplexy.' Matt grinned.

Aunt Effie placed the statuette carefully back inside the cardboard box. 'I am looking forward to going through the photographs, however. The early ones were taken by Kenneth before he left for India. He had a Brownie and was very keen on photography. He had a developing room in the outhouse at the back of the cottage. Emily used to complain about the smell of the chemicals and her best clothes pegs going missing.'

'They do sound interesting. You will have to show me later. I wonder if Quixshotte has changed a lot?' Kitty said. She always enjoyed seeing pictures of places and people and hearing the stories.

'Of course. I rather fancy there may be some of the vicar and his first wife, Martha, in there when the twins were small. Oh, and of course the Hall before Colonel Brothers bought it,' Aunt Effie said as Matt tucked into some of the small cakes that had been left on the stand.

Kitty helped herself to another cup of tea and thought that going through the pictures would be the perfect diversion from thinking about the murder cases and Lilith's arrest.

CHAPTER TWENTY-THREE

Kitty succumbed to the lure of one of the steamer chairs and had a pleasant nap next to Matt for the rest of the afternoon. Later that evening after they had finished a most enjoyable dinner of roast pork, followed by steamed pudding and custard, Kitty was feeling much more herself again.

Aunt Effie decided to temporarily banish Miss Crowther's cherub to the confines of the attic, safely packed away in an old hat box. Once after dinner coffee had been consumed and the dining table cleared, she fetched out the rest of the contents of the box that Margery had left.

'The light is much brighter in here and I thought we could see the images more clearly.' Aunt Effie produced two smaller cardboard boxes which appeared to contain random photographs and five substantial leather-bound albums.

Matt had wandered off to the drawing room to get himself a whisky while Kitty assisted his aunt with the pictures.

'I think she has written some dates and names on the backs of these loose photographs,' Kitty remarked, having quickly looked at a couple of pictures inside one of the smaller boxes.

'I seem to recall her saying that she had started this as a

project and had sorted everything into years. I hope she has labelled some of the pictures in the albums. She thought that they would be a good record of village life and of its inhabitants.' Aunt Effie peered at the cover of the topmost album. 'Yes, it seems I was correct. This one is from 1918 to 1920. I think these must be Kenneth's pictures as he was posted abroad in 1920.'

'The colonel said he came to Quixshotte in 1922.' Kitty could see that the dates on the other album covers were later so she assumed those must contain other photographers' images.

'That's right, my dear, the Hall was sold after Sir Bartholomew Webbings died and the family had trouble with the death duty. Now, Miss Crowther took some pictures herself using Kenneth's old camera, but she would take them into Barnsover to have them developed. So the other albums may contain her pictures and those of the photographic society,' Aunt Effie said.

'I didn't know Quixshotte had a photographic society?' Kitty was surprised, as this was the first mention of such a thing.

'Yes, my dear. The colonel belongs to it I believe, and Miss Crowther, Doctor Masters, the vicar, the postmaster, Miss Talland the school mistress. Yes, quite a few people.' Aunt Effie smiled at Kitty and opened the album marked 1918–20.

The faint sound of music drifted in from the other room and Kitty guessed that Matt had decided an evening listening to the wireless would be more interesting than Miss Crowther's photograph collection.

'This page seems to be village scenes. Look, there is the smithy. Of course, that is still there but they have expanded to sell petrol and motoring equipment.' Aunt Effie peered at the picture.

'The Quixshotte Arms looks unchanged, except the wisteria has grown larger along the front,' Kitty said.

They continued to turn the pages with Aunt Effie

exclaiming happily over each building or scene she recognised. Some of them Kitty could identify, other's required Aunt Effie's explanation.

Midway through the album the photographs changed to scenes which included people. Miss Crowther's neat, crabbed handwriting beneath each picture identified both the date, place and subject.

'That's Doctor Pardoe, the previous doctor before Leonard Masters,' Aunt Effie identified a very elderly man sporting a bushy, full white beard and a top hat.

Kitty turned the page and instantly recognised the front of the vicarage. A much younger Reverend Drummond was standing near the front door next to a very pretty woman. Ruth had a doll's perambulator and Frank was seated on a tricycle.

'That was Martha, the vicar's first wife. Such a delightful woman, very clever, cleverer even than Reverend Drummond. Such a sad loss when she passed away. She was an excellent vicar's wife and a good mother.' Aunt Effie shook her head sadly at the recollection.

She turned the page to reveal a group of people in Harlequinade costumes. 'Oh my dear, the village drama group. I had completely forgotten about this. We used to put on plays and skits in the school hall. I even appeared in a couple myself. This was from an early production. There is Miss Crowther. She used to play the piano for the musical scenes.' Aunt Effie smiled at Kitty.

'Is that the vicar and his wife?' Kitty asked as she looked at the faces behind the make-up.

'Yes, I rather think the idea of the drama group was Martha's to begin with. She and the vicar were terribly keen. Reverend Drummond was quite the star. Martha used to say he could have gone into films. It all folded of course after Martha died. The heart seemed to go out of everything.' Aunt Effie sighed.

There were more photographs of the casts of various shows. The last few pages contained more general scenes of the village, including the school and the children, the blacksmith and the landlord of the public house.

Kitty closed the book and pulled out the next one. 1921–1925. 'This one must have Miss Crowther's own photographs and those of the photographic society members in it.'

'Splendid. This is such fun. Shall we have a cocktail while we look at this one?' Aunt Effie twinkled at Kitty.

'That sounds like a good idea. I shall press Matt into service.' Kitty slipped from her seat and popped into the drawing room.

'How is it going?' Matt asked as Bertie eyed her sleepily from his position at Matt's feet.

'Actually, it's frightfully interesting.' Kitty requested their cocktails and went back to join his aunt at the dining table.

Matt carried their drinks through to them on a small silver tray a few minutes later doing his best impression of Aunt Effie's butler.

'Drinks are served.' He gave a mock bow as he set their glasses in front of them.

'Thank you, darling.' Kitty smiled happily at him and turned the next page of the photograph album.

'That must have been taken just after the colonel and Mrs Brothers came to the Hall. Dear me, even the tiger looks younger there.' Aunt Effie laughed as she looked at the photograph.

Matt took a quick peek and chuckling to himself he returned to the drawing room.

'Miss Crowther seems to have done her best to label all of these,' Kitty said as she read the neat print below various pictures of village activities. 'The football team and the cricket team. The bowls team and croquet on the lawn at the Hall.'

'The colonel and Doctor Masters fishing in the river. Doctor Masters must have just moved here then. Oh, and this must have been when the vicar remarried. How odd, I could have sworn it was later than 1925. One's memory does play tricks.' Aunt Effie happily sipped her cocktail. 'Here is a picture of Reverend Drummond marrying Lilith. No expense spared by the look of it.'

Kitty peered at the picture. Lilith in white satin with an enormous bouquet and a long lace veil. The well-dressed ladies standing behind her she assumed must be the older sisters she had mentioned. Ruth and Frank were dressed smartly, Frank in a sailor suit and Ruth in lace, staring solemnly at the camera. Lilith looked very young and pretty. The vicar, his hair already receding and his face grave behind his spectacles looked much older than his bride.

'Reverend Drummond and his bride. No mention of who took the photograph or where they married,' Kitty said.

'They married in the village church. I can't recall now quite why. I believe they were originally to marry in Leeds. They make an unlikely couple even in this picture.' Aunt Effie frowned. 'I was away when the wedding took place. Matthew's parents had invited me on a holiday to Italy.'

Kitty was thoughtful as she looked at the remaining pictures in the album, which were mainly of the village green and its surroundings.

'1926 to 1931,' Aunt Effie said as she closed the album and prepared to open the next one. 'Miss Crowther must have finished these and sorted those loose pictures ready for some more albums. She mentioned that she thought a small exhibition might be nice in the summer at the schoolhouse.'

The final album had more pictures of various village events and notable local figures. There were a couple of the twins looking about thirteen, dressed for tennis and holding racquets. The vicar sitting at his desk writing. A portrait of Lilith looking pensive next to the fountain at the Hall and one of Colonel Brothers and Hilda in a motor car.

There were other pictures of the various societies. The colonel front and centre. Doctor Masters looking confident and poised. The vicar somewhere in the background, almost unnoticed.

Kitty closed the album after they had studied the last page. 'Aunt Effie, you've known Lilith for many years now. Do you think she murdered Miss Crowther and Doctor Masters?'

Aunt Effie raised her eyebrows. 'Do I think she is capable of murder you mean? Well, I suppose most people are, my dear, if the motive is there. I do see what you mean though. I suppose if we believe that perhaps the doctor assisted her and then she stabbed him for some reason, then it's possible I suppose.'

Kitty helped Matt's aunt put the albums and the loose photographs away and they rejoined Matt in the drawing room for the rest of the evening.

Kitty dressed for church the following morning wondering who might take the service. Aunt Effie was convinced that the churchwarden would step in, but of course there would be no communion.

She pinned on her hat and hurried downstairs to meet Matt and his aunt. It had been agreed that Kitty would drive them there. The weather was a little cooler and duller but still pleasant as she fetched her car around and Matt assisted his aunt into the passenger seat. Bertie had been left in the care of the butler for the morning.

Colonel Brothers, Hilda and Jamie were in the colonel's black Rolls Royce ahead of Kitty as she pulled off the drive into the lane.

'I expect there will be a good turnout for the service this

morning. People love the opportunity to gossip,' Aunt Effie remarked as Kitty slowed up as they approached the church.

Aunt Effie's prediction appeared to be correct judging by the number of cars and horse-drawn vehicles parked around the village green. Kitty spotted a space and slid her car into it. Matt aided his aunt from the car while Kitty came to join them.

There was a buzz of speculative chatter all around them as they walked together towards the church.

'Good morning, Effie, Captain Bryant, Mrs Bryant.' The colonel raised his hat to them as they approached.

'Good morning,' Kitty joined in with the others. She noticed that Jamie Martin looked quite pale under the brim of his Panama hat as he escorted his aunt along the path.

'I don't suppose we shall see any of the Drummonds today,' Hilda murmured to Matt's aunt.

'No, most unlikely, I would have thought,' Aunt Effie agreed.

They filed inside and took their place in the pews. It seemed to Kitty that almost all the village must be there. There was no sign of the twins, however, or their father. Aunt Effie's pronouncement that the churchwarden would take the service was correct.

At the end of the service the warden read a short, prepared statement from Reverend Drummond. 'My dear friends and parishioners, I thank you for your kind and considerate behaviour towards myself and my family at this deeply troubling time. I ask that you continue to keep us in your prayers and that my beloved wife Lilith may be exonerated and returned home safely to us. God bless you all.'

A ripple of conversation ran around the church at the close of the warden's words.

Kitty followed Matt and his aunt out of the church and back into the morning sunshine. The villagers were dispersing gradually, many of them in small groups, their heads together as they talked over the recent events.

'I expect the vicar is feeling it dreadfully.' Hilda had caught them up on the path outside the church.

'Got to be. He is absolutely devoted to Lilith,' the colonel agreed.

'Well, it's the twins I feel sorry for. They lost their mother as little more than infants and now this happens,' Aunt Effie said.

Kitty glanced towards the vicarage. The windows were blank and there were no signs of life. 'Are the family still at home do you know?' Kitty addressed Jamie, drawing him a little away from where his aunt and uncle were engaged in deep discourse with Aunt Effie.

'I think so, at least for now. Frank telephoned last night to say that the warden was taking the service today while the bishop sorted out some kind of temporary arrangement.' Jamie glanced curiously at Kitty.

'Are he and Ruth all right? Matt and I were at the house when Lilith was arrested,' Kitty said.

Jamie gave a slight shrug. His normal slightly cocky air seemed to have deserted him. 'I think so. We didn't speak for long. Uncle Stanley doesn't approve of my friendship with the Drummonds.'

'Both the Drummonds? Or just Frank?' Kitty asked in a low voice after checking they could not be overheard.

Jamie's face paled. 'I don't think I understand you, Mrs Bryant.'

'I think you understand me very well and I believe your uncle also understands and is worried for you.' Kitty touched the sleeve of his jacket in a sympathetic gesture.

A rush of colour replaced the paleness in Jamie's cheeks. 'Thank you, Mrs Bryant, neither he nor you need have any concerns for me or Frank. Frank is leaving tomorrow. I doubt I shall see him again for a while.' His tone was stiff, and he moved his arm away from her.

'I'm so sorry.' She was sincere in her concern. Kitty stepped back to return to Matt's side.

'Are you all right, old thing?' Matt glanced to where Jamie had lit a cigarette and was standing smoking at the side of his uncle's car.

'Yes. I just had something confirmed but I fear I may have caused offence in doing so,' Kitty said with a sigh.

'Ah.' Matt smiled at her and placed his arm about her waist to give her a gentle reassuring squeeze.

Aunt Effie made her farewells to the colonel and Mrs Brothers and returned to Kitty's car.

'We are all invited to the Hall later this afternoon for tea if you would care to accompany me,' Aunt Effie said as Matt opened the car door for her.

'That's very kind.' Kitty took her place in the driver's seat while Matt jumped into the back of the car.

She put her car in gear and set off back to the Dower House. The conversation with Jamie had unsettled her and there was something that still niggled at her about Lilith's arrest.

CHAPTER TWENTY-FOUR

Jamie was absent from the Hall when Kitty and Matt joined Aunt Effie on her visit there for tea.

'He's taken himself off somewhere in that blooming motor,' Colonel Brothers explained when Aunt Effie asked if he would be joining them.

Aunt Effie told the colonel and Hilda about Miss Crowther's cousin's gift while they nibbled on dainty cucumber sandwiches.

'Not that hideous pink statue of Eros?' Hilda rolled her eyes. 'I always felt as if that thing was watching me. I have been blessed with a rather large aspidistra as my memento.'

'That blessed cherub is rather like it's owner keeping an eye on the village goings-on.' Aunt Effie chuckled.

'It all seems so unreal. Such ghastly events in such a short space of time. I wonder if the vicar will stay here?' the colonel asked.

'I suppose that may depend on the bishop.' Aunt Effie helped herself to a savoury tartlet.

'Do you think he would wish to stay?' Matt asked.

Kitty had wondered about that. Reverend Drummond had lived in the vicarage for a long time. It held memories of his first marriage as well as his marriage to Lilith. It was the only home the twins had known. Still, if Jamie was correct and Frank was being sent away, then perhaps he was also intending to leave with Ruth.

'He told me once that he would like to live near Oxford to pursue his studies of the classics. I suppose with Frank going there to university then this may prove the right time to relocate.' Hilda shook her head sadly. 'I still can't quite believe it. Just over a week ago we were preparing for the fair.'

'I suppose the inspector must feel he has a good case against Mrs Drummond,' Aunt Effie mused.

'I'm certain he would not have arrested Lilith otherwise,' Matt agreed.

The conversation moved on with the colonel and his wife asking Matt about their planned route back to Devon in a day or so. Kitty listened inattentively. She was looking forward to going home and they had planned a delightful journey with stops in places that Kitty had longed to visit. However, she couldn't shake the niggling feeling that something about Lilith's arrest wasn't right.

'A penny for your thoughts,' Matt asked her later when they were back at the Dower House preparing to retire for the night.

'I'm not certain they are worth a whole penny. Maybe a ha'penny.' Kitty smiled at him.

'You've been distracted ever since church this morning.' Matt eyed her curiously. 'I know you, you're up to something.'

'It's nothing. I think I probably just need a good night's sleep.' Kitty kissed his cheek.

'Hmm.' Matt gave her an amused smile. 'We'll see.'

. . .

Kitty half expected to have trouble falling asleep. Her mind was still full of unformed ideas and vague theories. She wondered if she had done the right thing by letting Jamie know that she knew the true nature of his and Frank's relationship. It had, though, confirmed her instincts on the matter.

Her head barely hit the pillow and she was asleep, waking with a start the following morning when she heard the maid clattering about outside her bedroom. As she sat herself up in bed, the feelings that had been bothering her about the case the previous evening felt even stronger.

She dressed quickly and hurried downstairs to the dining room. Matt was there before her reading his newspaper while tucking into bacon and eggs. He set the paper to one side and rose to greet her with a kiss.

'Good morning, darling. The tea has just arrived and there are kippers today if you would like some.' He resumed his seat.

'How lovely.' Kitty took her place opposite him and absent-mindedly helped herself to tea and toast.

Matt folded his paper up into small squares and tucked it into his jacket pocket. Kitty continued to apply herself to her breakfast. All the time her mind was working over everything they had discovered in the last week.

'Kitty, my love, are you all right?' Matt was observing her with a quizzical expression on his face.

'Perfectly, why?' Kitty asked.

'You've buttered that slice of toast three times now,' her husband replied with a grin.

Kitty rested the butter knife down on her side plate. 'I like butter.'

Matt laughed. 'I know, but not usually that much. What's bothering you? You may as well spill the beans.'

Kitty frowned, slightly annoyed that she was apparently so transparent. 'Lilith's arrest. There is something not right. It's been niggling away at me.'

Matt dabbed his lips with his linen napkin before setting it aside. 'What will settle your mind on the matter? Do you wish to try and speak to the inspector?'

Kitty considered his suggestion before rejecting it. 'No, that would look awfully as if I were questioning his abilities. I don't even have a sound reason yet, but I feel as if I've seen something that's important or someone has said something recently that is the key to the whole thing.'

'Perhaps a walk then, to clear your head?' Matt suggested.

'It might help me to order my thoughts,' Kitty agreed as she finished her breakfast.

Matt secured Bertie on his lead, and they headed towards the village. The weather had turned cooler, and Kitty was glad of the thin woollen cardigan she had slipped on over her cotton dress. A gentle breeze tugged at the brim of her hat and at the topknot of fur on Bertie's head.

Kitty had no particular plan in mind. She simply felt restless and needed to be out and about. Matt seemed to understand her needs and was content to walk quietly beside her as they strolled.

The village green looked less busy than it had done the day before. Kitty was somewhat surprised to see the inspector's car was parked once again outside the Quixshotte Arms. She noticed that Jamie Martin's car was also parked on the green near the tea room. Another car was parked in the road at the front gate of the vicarage.

As they drew closer to the vicarage Kitty saw that the car was being loaded with luggage. A uniformed chauffeur stood nearby assisting with the cases and boxes. Frank emerged from the house looking very young and upset as he watched the last items being safely stowed.

As he climbed into the rear seat ready to leave, Ruth came hurrying along the path to hug her twin and say goodbye. By the time Kitty, Matt and Bertie drew closer, the car was pulling away and Ruth was waving her handkerchief as a small white flag of farewell.

Once the car was out of sight the girl covered her face with her hands, her slender shoulders shaking.

'Ruth, dear, are you all right? Can we help you?' Kitty hurried forward to hug the girl.

'I'm fine, really. Thank you, Kitty. It's just that this is the first time Frank and I have ever been parted.' Ruth sniffed and scrubbed her eyes fiercely with her handkerchief. 'It's for the best. Frank will stay with some family friends in the Cotswolds and go on to university from there.'

'And what about you?' Kitty asked, stepping back to study the girl's expression.

'I will stay here with Father. At least for a little while longer while we close up the house. I believe the bishop is organising a new place for us so we shall be leaving Quixshotte soon.' Ruth dabbed at her nose.

'This has all happened very quickly. I take it then that it seems certain that Lilith will be convicted when the case goes to trial?' Matt said.

Ruth raised her shoulders in a despairing gesture. 'I don't know. Father seems unwilling to discuss it with either myself or Frank. He seems to be making all kinds of decisions quite quickly. I know he has spoken to the police inspector and to the solicitor he appointed to look after Lilith. I can only assume that the news is not good.'

'I'm so very sorry, my dear,' Kitty said. 'Where is your father now? I'm surprised he did not wish to see Frank off.' That odd sense of something being wrong was growing stronger.

Ruth shrugged again. 'I think he may have gone into the church. I'm supervising packing up the house. All of Lilith's clothes and things.' The girl's expression was bleak and Kitty could see it was taking all of her strength not to break down again.

'We shall let you get on. If you need to get away for a while, then come to the Dower House. I know that I speak for my aunt when I say that we should be glad to see you. Indeed, you are welcome to stay if you need some respite,' Matt offered for the second time.

'Thank you, Captain Bryant, and please thank your aunt too. You and Kitty have been very good.' Ruth turned away and darted back along the path into the safety of the vicarage.

'Poor girl, this must be so hard for her, and to be parted from her twin. She has lost everything that is dear and familiar to her.' Kitty slipped her hand into the crook of Matt's arm finding comfort in his solid, muscular support. Jamie's car was still parked on the far side of the green.

They meandered on in a desultory fashion for a few paces before Kitty found herself heading through the lychgate towards the church. Matt seemed unsurprised by her direction and he and Bertie accompanied her. The arched topped, double oak doors of the church were standing slightly open.

'I rather think I need to speak to Reverend Drummond.' Kitty looked thoughtfully at the open doors of the church. It was as if a missing piece of the jigsaw had suddenly clicked into place. She suddenly knew who had killed Miss Crowther and the doctor and why.

'Are you certain, Kitty? Bertie and I will be right out here. Any problem come straight out or shout for me. I won't be far away,' Matt said. She could see concern in his eyes, and she wondered if he too had realised who the murderer must be.

'I will not do anything foolish, I assure you. I think we both learned a lesson on our last case.' She kissed her husband's cheek and took a final glance at Jamie's car.

Kitty released her hold on Matt's arm and ventured into the dimly lit interior of the church. Matt remained outside in the churchyard holding on to Bertie's leash while the small dog explored the area near the path sniffing for rabbits.

At first Kitty thought the church was empty and that Reverend Drummond must have already gone. The air smelled faintly of damp and lavender polish and the decaying scent of the foliage of the lilies that were arranged in copper jugs on either side of the altar.

Light spilled onto the stone flags of the floor in a myriad of different colours from where the sun was hitting the central stained-glass window. Dust motes floated in the air and there was a sense of calm stillness.

Reverend Drummond was kneeling on a tapestry-covered cushion in the first row of the carved oak wooden pews. His gaze seemingly fixed on the window and the large brass cross that stood on a table in front of it. His face was blank, devoid of all expression and Kitty, while reluctant to disturb his devotions, was concerned that all was not well.

'Reverend?' she asked quietly when he appeared to stir in his seat.

He turned his head to peer myopically though his glasses in her direction. 'Ah, yes, Mrs Bryant, I believe? You and your husband discovered Miss Crowther and then stumbled upon my wife and Doctor Masters?'

Kitty nodded. 'Yes, sir.'

An odd chill ran along her spine at the way he appeared to almost be looking through her or past her at someone or something she could not see.

'I am not disturbing you, I hope? I just saw your son leaving and Ruth said she thought you were here.' Kitty perched on the end of the pew on the row opposite to the vicar.

'Ruth is a good girl. Every day she looks more and more like Martha, my first wife.' The vicar seemed almost to be speaking to himself rather than Kitty.

'Matt's aunt showed me some pictures. Miss Crowther's cousin gave her some albums that she thought she would like.

There were lots of photographs of the village, and of various people.' Kitty rested her cream leather handbag on her lap.

'Yes, I believe the photographic society gave her some photographs for a project she was doing,' the vicar said.

'There was one of the twins when they were small and one of your wedding to Lilith.' Kitty licked her lips nervously, unsure what his reaction might be to the mention of his second wife's name.

'Lilith, my angel. She was so beautiful, Mrs Bryant. Who could have known what wickedness lay behind that beautiful face?' The vicar's gaze drifted away from Kitty and back towards the cross standing on the altar.

Kitty blinked, a sudden understanding of what he meant flooded into her mind. 'You knew about her love affair with Doctor Masters.'

The corners of Reverend Drummonds lips curved upwards in a cruel and mirthless smile. 'Oh yes. I masterminded the whole thing. It was an arrangement that worked well for all of us. Anything for Lilith. Anything to make her happy, to keep her here with me. I knew she would never leave me. He gave her something I could not do.'

'And then Miss Crowther discovered the affair?' Kitty plucked up her courage. 'I suppose she saw them from her house and put two and two together.'

She thought she heard a faint movement behind her in the vestibule of the church but she dared not turn her head to see who was there. She assumed it must be Matt. He must have returned to wait for her with Bertie. Knowing her husband was close at hand made her feel bolder as she waited for Reverend Drummond to answer her.

'Miss Crowther came to me, the day before the fair. She was most indignant. She intended to make her feelings known to the doctor. She was furious on my behalf but when I did not react the way she expected, she said that I was encouraging immoral behaviour. She was going to go to the bishop.' Reverend Drummond sounded calm and matter of fact. His tone flat and devoid of emotion.

'I had no choice but to kill her.'

CHAPTER TWENTY-FIVE

Kitty released a long slow breath and pressed her legs together to stop her knees from shaking at the vicar's admission. 'That was when you decided to poison her?'

Reverend Drummond switched his attention back to Kitty as if seeing her in focus for the first time. 'It had to be done that day before the fair ended and Miss Crowther went around telling everyone what she knew. She told me she would write to the bishop. I couldn't allow that to happen. I knew there was the poison in the gardeners' shed at the Hall and where the key was kept. I insisted that Lilith had to assist on the refreshment stall. Lilith is lazy so I had no doubt that she would do little more than pour tea while the twins ran around. I knew the doctor would find a reason to call there to see her.'

'Jimmi saw you coming back across the field, but he didn't know who you were. He said he saw a man in dark clothing,' Kitty said.

'It occurred to me later that he may have seen me. He was the only person on the field in a position to do so. I was concerned he had seen me approach the refreshment stall. No one else remembered me being there. People never do, I'm part of the furniture,' Reverend Drummond agreed.

'That was a risk. That someone would mention seeing you there,' Kitty said as she kept her own gaze on the vicar's pale impassive face.

Reverend Drummond smiled. 'No one notices me. One of the quirks of my personality and the luck of my vocation. I'm part of the scenery, virtually invisible. I was there only for a moment. Long enough to slip the poison into a cup when Miss Crowther approached and to ensure that it was the one Lilith gave her.'

'Miss Crowther was in too much of a temper to notice you. She had already argued with Jamie, the colonel and Hilda that day. She was hot, tired and wanted the cup of tea that everyone had been too busy to take to her tent,' Kitty said.

'I see you understand perfectly, my dear.' Reverend Drummond gave her an approving nod.

'You attacked Jimmi that night at the circus.' The vicar's calm demeanour was scaring Kitty, but she was determined to understand the full story.

'As I said, I didn't know if he had recognised me returning from the gardeners' shed. Or indeed if he had noticed me at the stall. I cycled to the station and took the train to Barnsover and waited for the show to end. I heard you and your husband approaching just after I had hit him so had no time to check if he was dead. I barely managed to get away as you found him lying on the floor. Fortunately for him he does not seem to have realised it was me.' The vicar sighed. 'Hitting that man is the one part of this whole affair that I most regret.'

Kitty stared at him. 'You murdered two people. Miss Crowther and Doctor Masters and I assume were willing to see Lilith hang for your crimes. Jimmi could also have died.'

The vicar's expression changed and hardened. 'Doctor Masters betrayed me. I thought we had an unspoken arrangement. A gentleman's agreement of sorts. Then I discovered that they were planning to leave, to run away together. He was going to take my angel away. Lilith thought I didn't know but I had discovered brochures in her handbag. When Miss Crowther had told me she knew of their affair she said she had already confronted Lilith about it. She was going to leave me and the twins, start afresh in France or Spain. Wickedness.' The vicar's voice rose and trembled. 'Wickedness should always be punished, Mrs Bryant.'

Kitty thought she heard the door to the church creak.

'You stabbed Doctor Masters to stop him from eloping with Lilith and then intended her to be punished for daring to think of leaving you, culminating in her death by hanging for murders she didn't commit.' Kitty struggled to sound calm. Inside her chest her heart raced and she longed to rise from her seat and to run from the church. She hoped that Matt was listening and had heard the vicar's confession.

'She had been wicked. She had coveted another man. Broken our marriage vows and committed adultery.' Reverend Drummond looked at her.

'But you have killed two people and attacked a third. You admit that you encouraged her adultery with Doctor Masters to keep her in your marriage,' Kitty said.

'I adored Lilith. I gave her everything. A life of ease and luxury, a lover to satisfy her carnal desires. All I asked was that she was pure for me. I was mistaken to place her upon so lofty a pedestal. Her beauty and grace blinded me to her sinfulness and pride.' The vicar's eyes gleamed behind his spectacles.

'And when she wished to step down from the perch you had placed her upon you decided to exact your revenge.' Kitty clasped her hands more tightly together in order not to betray how she much she was shaking hearing the reverend's twisted logic.

'Lilith had no right to leave me. She was my angel.' The vicar's eyes bulged, and his hands formed into fists.

'Should not any punishment come from God rather than man? Isn't that what you usually preach here on Sundays?' Fear was creeping up inside Kitty like a rising tide. She felt sick listening to the vicar's deranged train of thought.

The vicar rose slowly from his knees and Kitty automatically shrank back in her seat. He stood and turned so that he was fully facing the altar. The play of multicoloured light from the stained glass played in a pattern over the black of his clothing.

The expression on his face chilled Kitty to the bone and she edged forward slightly in her seat, ready to run should he advance towards her. Her heart raced and she hoped Matt was close by now.

'I am an instrument of the Lord. I only work to carry out his bidding.' Reverend Drummond lifted his chin, his eyes fixed on the altar, a fanatical gleam in his eyes.

'How very convenient that your wishes and those of the Lord you say you serve coincide.' Inspector Woolley had entered the church.

Kitty sagged with relief at the comforting sight of the policeman's solid form standing patiently at the end of the aisle.

Reverend Drummond whirled around at the sound of the inspector's voice. 'The law of God is higher than that of man.'

Kitty could see other shadows on the stone flag floor of the church and guessed that Matt, Bertie and possibly a constable were within the vestibule.

'I thought the highest commandment was Thou shalt not kill,' the inspector sounded unmoved.

Kitty saw the vicar's eyes dart from side to side like those of a cornered animal. She stayed as still as she could, not wishing to draw any attention to herself.

'I have men waiting outside this building, Reverend Drummond. I suggest you accompany me peacefully,' the inspector continued.

The vicar moved swiftly to the side of the church where the articles for communion were placed on a silver tray covered with a white embroidered linen cloth. Kitty could only assume that the warden had been remiss in locking them away after the previous day's services when they had not been used.

Inspector Woolley took a few steps further forward into the body of the church. 'Do not attempt to do anything foolish, sir.'

Kitty couldn't see what the vicar intended. The only exit from the church was the way they had entered. She supposed there might be another exit via the vestry, but that door was closed, and the inspector had said his men were surrounding the church.

'Do not come any closer!' the vicar commanded. He held his hand aloft signalling the inspector to stop.

'Your wife has been released from our custody. She is gone to her family in Leeds. The sisters you forbade her to have contact with during your marriage.' Inspector Woolley took another couple of steps closer.

'No!' The vicar shook his head vigorously as if the motion would force the inspector's words to leave his ears.

'Your son is gone to the Cotswolds to friends. Your daughter is safe at the Hall with the colonel and his wife. Lilith is free and will never be yours again.' The inspector spoke as if he were stating facts in a court of law. 'Surrender yourself and seek peace with your God.'

The vicar was still shaking his head in denial. He lifted the cloth aside and poured some water from a glass decanter into the silver gilt communion goblet before adding something from a pocket in his cassock.

The inspector moved forward surprisingly quickly for a

man of his size, but he was not fast enough to prevent the vicar from drinking the contents of the cup. Kitty sprang to her feet as the vicar gave a triumphant smile.

'My justice will be served in a higher court.' Reverend Drummond's last words were hard to make out as he collapsed to the floor in a crumpled heap just as the inspector reached his side.

Kitty hurried across the aisle to where the inspector was now kneeling next to Reverend Drummond's lifeless body.

'He kept back some of the poison,' the inspector said as he rose slowly to his feet.

Kitty swallowed and was forced to sit down again on a nearby pew. Her legs suddenly too weak to take her weight.

Inspector Woolley called to his constable as Matt rushed inside the church straight to Kitty's side.

'Darling, are you all right?' Matt glanced at the vicar's body.

She nodded slowly. 'I think so. Did you... could you hear everything?' she asked.

Matt placed a tender arm around her. 'Everything. So did the inspector. It seemed that he too was not entirely satisfied with the case against Lilith. He thought she might even be in some physical danger, so he arrested her for her own safety.'

Kitty glanced to where the police constables were now gathered about Reverend Drummond's body. 'I think he was right. Who knows what the vicar would have been capable of where Lilith was concerned.'

'I've left Bertie tied to the gate. Do you feel able to stand yet, my love?' Matt asked.

Kitty rose and accepted Matt's arm for support. She was anxious now to get outside into the fresh air, away from the cloying scent of the lilies and almonds.

Bertie greeted them with a short volley of woofs, his plumed tail wagging like a flag at their approach. Inspector Woolley caught up with them as they were unfastening Bertie from the gate.

'Mrs Bryant, I hope you are not unduly distressed by the scenes you have just witnessed?' His dark-brown eyes scanned her face as if to reassure himself of her composure.

'It was upsetting, Inspector, and tragic but I am thankful at least that Lilith and the twins are safe.' Kitty was anxious to be reassured that Ruth had indeed gone to Quixshotte Hall.

'One of my officers has accompanied Miss Drummond and an officer from the Oxford constabulary will meet Mr Drummond on his arrival. Mrs Brothers has assured me that she will take good care of Miss Drummond, although I suspect she will join her brother as soon as she is able,' the inspector said.

'I'm glad. It has been the most awful ordeal for them all.' Kitty could only feel relief that it was all over.

'Captain Bryant told me that he thought you had reached the same conclusion as myself which was why you had entered the church. A brave, if somewhat slightly foolhardy, move.' The inspector's tone, however, held no hint of condemnation or censure at her decision.

'Matt was nearby, and I didn't feel as if I would personally be in any danger. I suspected that the vicar had entered the church almost as if seeking approval for his actions or needing to confess his sins,' Kitty explained. 'I know there was a case to be made against Lilith but it didn't fit with her character or that of Doctor Masters.'

The inspector nodded. 'What led you to Reverend Drummond? There was evidence that could have taken you to young Jamie Martin or even the twins?'

'I agree, they all could have been implicated in some way. It seemed at one point as if almost everyone in this village had a secret.' Kitty looked at the inspector and he gave her an understanding smile.

'I think you may be correct. May I buy you both a tea before you return to the Dower House? I am sure you are not yet ready to walk home, and I can take a few notes for your statement,' the inspector suggested.

Kitty and Matt accompanied the inspector across the green to the tea room. The crowd that had begun to gather and loiter outside the post office melted away as they approached, and Kitty noticed that Jamie's car had now gone.

The tea room proprietress who had served them in the past bustled over swiftly to take their order, her face alive with avid curiosity. The inspector selected a quiet table inside the tea room rather than out on the green and ordered a pot of tea for three.

Once the tea things had been delivered and the owner of the tea rooms had retreated to a safe distance, the inspector discreetly drew out his notebook.

'Now, Mrs Bryant, you were telling me what made you put the pieces together?' the inspector said.

Kitty sighed as she spooned a little sugar into her tea. 'I think it was the photographs that Miss Crowther's cousin gave to Matt's aunt. There were all kinds of pictures in there. There was one of Reverend Drummond and the twins with his first wife and some of him acting in various productions and plays. Then there was one of his wedding to Lilith. I kept thinking how it felt as if he were playing a part. All his solicitude was for Lilith, but then he ignored the twins, and had been doing so for years. He was a very detached man as a parent. It didn't add up. Then I noticed that although he was in lots of the pictures, he was hard to see, invisible almost. I remembered someone, Jamie, I think, said Reverend Drummond had been at the refreshment stall, yet no one seemed to have noticed him.'

Kitty took a sip of her tea and shuddered. She didn't really

care much for sweet tea but since it was supposed to be benefi-
cial for shock and she doubted that Matt had his hip flask to
hand, so it would have to do.

'Reverend Drummond explained too that his marriage was
unusual. It was more of a business arrangement, in fact. Her
husband simply required her to look beautiful and to accompany him whenever he wished. There was no affection or
indeed any congress between them. In effect he had
purchased her, placed her on a pedestal and admired her from
afar.'

Inspector Woolley added generous spoons of sugar to his
own cup of tea and sent a warning glance in the direction of the
tea room proprietress who had edged closer while they had
been talking.

'That was more or less what he said in the church. He knew
of her affair with Doctor Masters. In fact, he had almost tacitly
encouraged it thinking it would make her happy.' Kitty set her
cup down on its saucer. 'He was right though when he said his
nature and vocation rendered him almost invisible. The day of
the fair no one was sure if they had seen him attend or not. He
was in the background all the while but never really seen. It was
the same in the photographs.'

'Then Miss Crowther, with her penchant for knowing
everyone's business, came along and rocked the boat,' Matt said.

'Yes, poor Miss Crowther. She had been in love with
Reverend Drummond for years and he went off and married
Lilith. Then she had a crush on Doctor Masters who also made
it plain that he was not interested in her,' Kitty said with a sigh.

'I fear she went to the vicar assuming that he would cast
Lilith aside and she might even possibly stand a chance with
him once again. She was a woman who liked the moral high
ground too. It also served her purpose to spite the doctor and
Mrs Drummond.' Inspector Woolley topped up his teacup with
more tea.

'There was no love lost between Lilith and Miss Crowther so she would have relished discovering the affair,' Matt agreed.

They finished their tea while the inspector concluded his notes. He had heard the majority of the reverend's confession from the vestibule. Once he had concluded the discussion, he tucked his notebook back inside his pocket and paid the bill.

'Your husband tells me that you are due to begin your return journey to Devon in the next couple of days, Mrs Bryant?' the inspector said as Kitty drew her gloves back on ready to go.

'Yes, we are planning on taking in more of the countryside with a few stops along the way,' Kitty said.

The inspector smiled and extended his hand to her. 'It has been a pleasure to meet you both and I trust that the reputation of our police force in Yorkshire has been restored a little in your eyes?'

Kitty shook his hand and noticed the twinkle in his eye. 'Most definitely, Inspector.'

'I am very pleased to hear it. Do give my regards to Inspector Lewis on your return to Torquay.' The inspector's smile widened.

'It will be our pleasure, sir,' Matt assured him.

Kitty took her husband's arm once more as they started back to the Dower House. 'Well, it has been a most extraordinary holiday,' she remarked.

Matt grinned at her, the dimple flashing in his cheek. 'I don't know. A new place, a dead body. Sounds like a typical Kitty kind of vacation to me.'

Kitty joined in with his laughter as they left the village. 'I have to say that I would prefer our next outing to be for pleasure only. A girl can only take so much excitement, and I dread to think what Grams and Alice will have to say about all this when we get home.'

Matt's smile widened even further. 'They may not let us leave Devon again. Let's hope our next case is something less deadly.'

Bertie gave a woof of agreement, and they headed back to the Dower House to tell Aunt Effie all about their morning.

A LETTER FROM HELENA

Dear reader,

I want to say a huge thank you for choosing to read *Murder at the Village Fair*. If you did enjoy it and would like to keep up-to-date with all my latest releases, just sign up at the following link. Your email address will never be shared, and you can unsubscribe at any time. You also get a free short story!

www.bookouture.com/helena-dixon

Kitty and Matt are settling into married life, and I hope that you've enjoyed this new adventure in Yorkshire. There are lots more stories to come with new characters to meet.

I do hope you loved *Murder at the Village Fair* and if you did, I would be very grateful if you could write a review. I'd love to hear what you think, and it makes such a difference helping new readers to discover one of my books for the first time.

I love hearing from my readers – you can get in touch on my Facebook page, through Twitter or my website.

Thanks,

Helena

KEEP IN TOUCH WITH HELENA

www.nelldixon.com

 facebook.com/nelldixonauthor
twitter.com/NellDixon

ACKNOWLEDGEMENTS

Many thanks to my Yorkshire readers who provided me with such lovely background information.

Thank you to the Tuesday zoom gang for writerly support and, of course, the Coffee Crew for sage wisdom and much laughter.

This book brought back many happy memories of time spent with friends and family attending various country fairs very similar to the one described in this book – minus the bodies, of course!

Thank you to my lovely agent Kate Nash who gives me so much support and wise advice. Lots of love and thanks to everyone at Bookouture for all their help and hard work. Producing a book is very much a team effort and I'm so lucky that you are my team. Thank you.